THE FALL

BOOK ONE OF
THE LAST DRUID TRILOGY

GLEN L. HALL

G22 PUBLISHING

Published in 2017 by G22 Publishing

Copyright © Glen L. Hall 2017

Glen L. Hall has asserted his right to be identified as the
author of this Work in accordance with
the Copyright, Designs and Patents Act 1988

ISBN: 978-0-9957985-0-2

A CIP catalogue copy of this book can be found in the British Library.

Published with the help of Indie Authors World

IndieAuthors
World

To Mum

Acknowledgements

Many people have played a part in helping me write *The Last Druid* and I am grateful for and humbled by each and every one of them.

I must begin by thanking Lizzie Henry, my editor, who has worked with me to make the book the very best it can be. In fact, when I really think about it, she has transformed (almost) every aspect of the story, and for that I am eternally grateful.

To Jill Davidson from Purdy Lodge (they do the best breakfast in the whole of Northumberland), thank you for putting up with my writing schedule. I couldn't have done it without your love and understanding. The view of Bamburgh Castle is simply amazing.

I approached Niki Jupp, my illustrator, with one paragraph, and over the next few months she brought the text to life. She captured the images in my mind perfectly and I couldn't be happier. Thank you, Niki. Thanks also to Will Welsh for becoming Sam for a day.

My love affair with books started with my primary school teacher, Mrs Flather, who gave me a copy of *Prince Caspian* when I was seven years old and sparked a lifelong love affair with fantasy. I wrote to her in 1997 and received a reply which I will keep forever.

Thanks also to Adam Cooke, who put together the web-site and made it work. He understood exactly what I wanted. I suppose that's what comes from a seventeen years business relationship.

The book would not have seen the light of day without David Hamilton, author of *The Five Side-Effects of Kindness*. When the path to publishing got a little tricky, he threw light into the darkness.

A big thank you to Kim and Sinclair Macleod from Indie Authors World, who made everything seem so easy and who managed my 'attention to detail' (some would say 'obsessiveness') with a firm but honest guiding hand.

My publicist, Camilla Leask from Willow Publicity, who kept sweeping away my self-doubt and telling me to believe in myself and in what I had written. For that, I will be eternally grateful.

Thanks also to the talented people at Everything Different. Ben Quigley, their CEO, brought together an exceptional group of people, who between them took the book from my imagination and made it real. Special thanks to Mike Roberts, a very patient client partner, Marcus de' Jesus, who created the book's overall style, Frazer Barrington, who blew my socks off more than once with the book's trailer, Mell Black, who came up with a very smart social media plan, and Emma Clark and Claire Knight, who made sure everything ran smoothly.

Last but not least, thanks to Philip Stuckey, who read extracts from the book each morning. He was even brave enough to tell me the first three chapters didn't work. I went back to the beginning and the rest is history.

'Tell the professors, Samuel, that the Circle is broken and a Shadow moves through the Otherland. Tell them that the Dead Water is lost and the Fall is dying. Tell them that they must seek the help of the Three. You must be wondering whether these words are those of the wise or the mad. On the road ahead you will find out...'

CONTENTS

MAP OF NORTHUMBERLAND

Bamburgh

Dunstanburgh

Craster

Howick

Alnmouth

Alnwick

Birling
Woods

Warkworth

THE FALL

It came without warning, rising from the cold black waters, a dark resonance of lightless silk.

To the north the giant ridged spine of the borderland broke in great waves against the threatening Cheviot night, whilst to the south the ancient lands of Northumberland gave way to wild woods and fast-flowing rivers moving east to the sea.

Surfacing from the Dead Water, the darkness coalesced into a solitary wave, the last light of the Fall still dancing around its pitch-black form.

Across the vast barren waters, a tortuous wail bled its anguish into the dark night and out through the fells and burns of the wilderness. The murmuring voices of the dead called its name, but quickly faded as the light turned to darkness and the Shadow was amongst the living.

It moved through the chilling waters, where even the grasping fingers of the fallen could not touch it, towards an unseen shore.

A man, bent with age, looked out across the waters. He could feel the malevolence growing with every second as the wave spread out across the vast lake. He knew it meant to crush him.

He had heard another voice amongst those of the fallen, but there was no time to ponder its meaning. Already the air around him was cold and the waters were beginning to glimmer with the arrival of a deadly chill, a white sheen creeping across the waters.

He could feel the horror of what he was about to face, a nameless servant of a primeval enemy. It had freshly come through the Fall and he knew it was still gathering itself. They had not been vigilant. They had become like the dead and they would pay a heavy price for ignoring the warnings of the living.

The waters gently brushing his naked feet were turning to ice and a dark mist was hanging above and beyond the water. The air was freezing and the ice began to cut into his legs as it thickened. As the blood flowed, a deathly silence hung over the dark water. Black despair was arriving at the shores of the living. Something was rising up – a suffocating mist that was swirling, twisting, drawing long shards of ice into its pulsing heart as it span faster and faster, forming a giant tempest in the darkness.

The silence was broken by a wordless sound that spoke directly to the old man now locked into the frozen water. It was a cruel resonance that could have once been a voice of rattling bones, heartless and inhuman, reminding him of centuries of pain and loss.

There was blood around his feet, but defiantly he swept his arms down and the ice broke around him as he turned to face the whirling darkness. His voice spiralled out in a flash of frozen air, strong despite his feeble frame.

'I am the Ruad Roshessa and you cannot pass.'

His voice thundered above the roaring wind.

'I am Fer Benn. Go back – you cannot pass.'

The tempest rose before him like a black mountain. Dark winds blew down to meet him, answering his words with primordial power that sent the swirling tempest and its long cutting ice to rupture both body and soul. It hit the old man with such force that he shattered into pieces that fell down through the ice. It flared crimson and he was gone.

A shadow appeared on the shore, in the world of the living.

But where the old man had fallen, subtle cracks were appearing. The ice was whispering his name. Soon it was echoing across the valley and through its secret ways. Droplets of light flickered through the water and the old man stepped again into the world of the living and again faced the Shadow.

* * * * * *

As they fought, the crack of thunder fell in the deepest places of the Earth. In the darkness, eyes opened. Still they were blind, but the power that had kept them asleep had been broken. Down in the Underland, a murmur arose in the caverns and halls as those long imprisoned stretched and found themselves free.

There was one amongst them without wings or giant maw, one whose hate for those who had imprisoned her people flowed like molten lava, one who knew the meaning of this awakening.

The murmur in the depths slowly swelled. Angry calls rang out. Soon the darkness was alive with sound, a chorus of cawing and screeching.

* * * * * *

They came through the waters gasping for breath, memories of the flowing waters of the dead still clinging to their hearts. They were like ghosts themselves, colourless skin and silver hair contrasting sharply with grey eyes.

They were a strange company dressed in shifting colours. Each carried a finely woven bow with a single string that appeared to be cut from glass. On the shores of the Dead Water they didn't stop to consider where they had come from or where they were going. They had come this way before, and their forefathers before them. In the dying night they, too, passed into the world of the living.

As they vanished into the trees, their coming signalled the end of the beginning.

* * * * * *

Two thousand years of history lay crumbling into the Northumberland night, and she had endured each one. She stood motionless on the high wall, her attention fixed on the north. The night was still, yet there was a disquiet moving unseen. She felt the babble trickling through her thoughts and it brought back memories long forgotten. Memories that she would rather keep locked away.

There beside the Knag Burn Gate, a twisted and broken relic of ancient enemies and fallen heroes, the ripple caught her by surprise and she found herself reaching for the reassuring presence of the gate. She could feel her father's thunder and see his light echoing through the Otherland, but there was something else there too. In the vast Northumberland night, atop Hadrian's Wall, stretching eighty miles from east to west, she knew that peril had come to the Mid-land.

CHERWELL COLLEGE

Cherwell College was a real oddity. It was set in the grounds of Magdalen College, Oxford, tucked away in a corner of the Fellows' Garden. According to those in the know, it had been the last Oxford college to receive a royal charter, shortly after the Second World War. It had supposedly been founded by C.S. Lewis, J.R.R. Tolkien, Charles Williams and others of the literary group known as the Inklings. No one really knew the reason why they had set it up and over the course of several decades facts had mingled with urban myth. What was certain was that its emblem was a circle with an unknown tree at the centre.

With the last of the Inklings now fading to memory, the college was mainly home to visiting professors and a small group of post-graduates, though the odd undergraduate would also be admitted to its small gatherings, blinking in the light of quantum metaphysics or the philosophy of coincidence or some other arcane subject matter. It offered a collection of disciplines that had fallen through the cracks of more conventional universities, and its strangeness was mirrored by its students and professors.

One of these students, a big-framed red-headed young man, was sitting in one of his favourite places, his very own room looking out over the Fellows' Garden. Sam Wood had spent the final term of his first year gracing the curious buildings of Cherwell, and felt lucky to have gained a place there. He'd never heard of it before coming to Oxford. There was no prospectus for it and you couldn't apply to it either. He had initially been studying physics at Magdalen and had been invited to a private meeting one evening at the Eagle and Child pub. His own tutors, professors Stuckley and Whitehart, had been there, along with a handful of undergraduates who had subsequently debated the nature of light until the early hours. He had eventually stumbled back to his lodgings exhausted and a little bewildered. Then a week later, a letter from a 'Jack' had appeared in his pigeonhole, inviting him to spend a term at Cherwell College.

He had moved with Angus, the only other undergraduate chosen, to a grand Georgian house known as the Fellows' House. His room was simple – there was a bed that was rarely made, a wardrobe on the far wall and a large writing desk that sat neatly in the bay window that made for a remarkable centrepiece.

From this vantage point, he could see the neatly trimmed shrubs, green lawns and ancient trees of the Fellows' Garden below. He had seen the seasons pass through that window – the unfurling of the spring leaves, the ancient oaks' giant canopies offering quiet shelter from the summer sun and now the creeping curl of autumn leaves heralding a carpet of the finest conkers anywhere in England. A touch of Rivendell, one friend had called it, and it did remind him of the haven in *The Lord of the Rings*.

He had even spent many evenings walking with friends along the tree-lined Addison's Walk, where Tolkien himself had strolled. The river Cherwell would meander quietly alongside and now and then the silence would be broken by some far-off merriment from the fine lawns of Christ Church Meadow or the splash of a pole as a punt sent ripples across the still water.

Back in his room, he would often stop his studies and watch several of his professors making their way towards the pond in the

Fellows' Garden, which was hidden by a circle of trees. They would always appear on the first Sunday of the month, their long walking sticks like the staffs of sorcerers, and he would wonder what secret society they were part of.

It was late August now, and he was planning on going home for a short while. He had stayed in Oxford over the summer to resit his end-of-year exams and then been asked to wait to receive his results in person. He had been surprised and horrified to have fallen short. He had failed on the electromagnetic flow and its relationship with time. Amazingly, it had been the very subject he had debated at the Eagle and Child the night that had given him entry to Cherwell. So that in itself had been a great shock.

Over the summer he had seen the city slowly empty of students and the tourists arrive in droves. Angus had gone back to his parents in Edinburgh's New Town, and right now Sam was writing him a letter. But as the afternoon sun shone through the open window and fell across the page, his eyes were drawn to the view before him.

Over the past few weeks he had watched the gentle colours of early autumn spread from the flowerbeds to the hedges until finally even the trees couldn't deny the inevitable rusting of their leaves. Now the sun and the rhythmic purring of the Cherwell were making him feel sleepy. He stretched his back against the leather chair and looked west across Addison's Walk towards Angel Meadow and the spires of Magdalen College. There were very few places that gave him such feelings of blissful contentment.

He'd wanted to go to Oxford for a long time. His eyes came back to the book that had started his journey down from Newcastle. With a smile, he reached for it and placed it on his knee. He had numerous copies of *The Hobbit*, but this was his most treasured. Tolkien had illustrated this edition himself. How beautiful it was, with its green-leaved trees stretching into the forest and the Lonely Mountain rising ominously in the distance.

For a second he was eleven years old again, remembering the incident that had set him on the path. He had been taking a short cut through the school library when a tattered old book had fallen from the shelf, just missing him. It was as if someone had nudged it as he was passing, but the library was empty. He picked it up and read, 'In a hole in the ground there lived a hobbit…' and, just like Tolkien, who had, by all accounts, written this on the back of an undergraduate's exam book in 1935, he wanted to understand what a hobbit was and where it lived.

He took the book home and read it in a week. *The Lord of the Rings* took him to Middle Earth and he would eventually stumble on the Inklings. Eight years later he would be in Oxford, retracing Tolkien's footsteps to the Eagle and Child pub.

Sam didn't want to spoil this moment, with Magdalen's spires sending their shadows peacefully down to the walk and the meadow before him. This was the Oxford he had dreamed about, and it was perfect.

But, as he tried to refocus on his letter to Angus, the sound of the gently flowing river brought other memories to his mind. He tried to push them back, but it was like trying to hold back the tide.

He'd finished his first term at Oxford and, buzzing with the knowledge he had acquired, had returned home to a hero's welcome from his mum. Later that Christmas holiday, Angus had come to stay and he'd taken him to Warkworth to stay overnight with his friend Emily's uncle and aunt, who lived in an old school house on the banks of the river Coquet.

It had started off well. He and Angus had had a perfectly good breakfast and spent a pleasant afternoon in Bamburgh, trawling through the rock pools and sipping a delightful cup of tea in Sam's favourite tearoom. They'd arrived in Warkworth as the winter sun was fading and a cold silence was enveloping the Northumberland village, and had spent an enjoyable evening with Emily and her uncle and aunt. But then Sam had been woken in the middle of the night by what could have been a noise, although he still wasn't sure whether it had been a noise or a feeling.

Leaving the others sleeping, Sam had found himself going down to the old school house library, standing at Emily's uncle's desk and looking out into the blackness of the winter's night. Then he'd gone out, right down to the water's edge, where the Coquet was in full flow…

The thought ran an icy-cold finger down the length of his spine and he again turned to the letter he was writing. But the memories would not be denied. Second by second, they crept into his mind and there was nothing he could do to stop them. One by one they came, creeping and slithering, until the brooding Shadow was standing once again on the bank of the Coquet…

Sam was brought back to the present by two of Magdalen's gardeners appearing suddenly in their green dungarees, pushing wheelbarrows full of hedge clippings. The garden was now empty of tourists and he guessed Magdalen had closed its gates to visitors.

The letter to Angus would have to wait. He'd arranged to meet Professor Stuckley in his tutorial room at 5 p.m. to receive his results. He couldn't be late.

* * * * * *

As he left his study bedroom and went out into the afternoon sun, apprehension flickered butterfly wings through his stomach. What would he tell his mother if he'd failed again? And he certainly didn't want his life here to end. This was a special place, with every cobbled street leading to its own sanctuary. And there was nowhere quite like the Fellows' Garden.

Closing the circular oak door to the walled garden, he walked off down the narrow footpath that skirted Bat Willow Meadow and would lead him to Addison's Walk and eventually the gates of Magdalen.

Half an hour later he was passing through the imposing gates of the college and could see the cloisters just ahead. In them, he knew Professor Stuckley would be waiting.

He quickly crossed the short walk and entered the building through its arched doorway. One or two visitors were still milling about, but the cloisters were quiet now compared to the busyness of term time. The tutorial rooms of both Magdalen and Cherwell College faced out onto a square lawn, surrounded by the most dazzling white hydrangeas to be found in the whole of Oxford.

Sam stood at the bottom of a small stone staircase, his hands clammy and his stomach beginning to churn. This could be an embarrassing meeting.

Taking a deep breath, he walked tentatively up the stairs to a wooden door. There he paused, a little out of breath, holding his clenched fist inches from the door and gathering the courage to knock.

'Come in.'

Sam stepped back, surprised. Before he had the chance to carry out the instruction, the door opened with a vigorous creak and he was face to face with an unmistakable figure.

'Professor Stuckley,' he stumbled, feeling his cheeks begin to go red with both excitement and trepidation.

Before he could utter another word, the grey-bearded professor, dressed in an immaculate purple blazer and open sandals, took him by the arm and led him into the room.

'Good to see you, Samuel.'

The professor plonked himself down on a rickety chair whilst Sam sat in one of the many leather chairs, his heart thudding. All around him were bookcases stuffed full of hardbacks and paperbacks of all shapes and sizes. It was clear that at some point the professor had stopped trying to cram any more books on the creaking shelves and instead had built precarious-looking piles randomly across the floor.

He was one of the more animated academics in the Department of Quantum Metaphysics, a person of quite unconventional thinking. He would often throw his book down in his cramped tutorial room, shoot across the stone floor on his rickety chair and march students outside into the fresh air. Whether it was raining or not, he would take them into the very heart of Holywell Ford on a journey of scientific and artistic discovery and would make connections where perhaps there should have been none.

'What a glorious day,' he began now, reaching into his top pocket for a rather fanciful handkerchief and dabbing his brow.

Sam couldn't help but smile. Despite his nerves, he was glad to see the professor. He knew that behind his sometimes eccentric manner lay a sharp intellect and a wealth of knowledge on a wide range of subjects. As well as lecture on quantum mechanics, the professor could write prose and poetry and without a moment's hesitation lend his rich voice to Magdalen's choir.

There were rumours of other activities too. Sam had once overheard a group of academics from All Souls talking about the fact that the professor was working for one of the intelligence services and had even ended up in hospital after one of his many 'adventures' had gone wrong. Apparently all that had been verified from his past was that he had spent time at Durham University in the School of English, which seemed a far cry from physics and the nature of light.

But it was physics that intrigued Sam the most. Through the professor's teachings he had fallen in love with Einstein's theories. The physics of quantum mechanics would take him on strange journeys through entanglement and probability, and he pondered long and hard on how these facets could be connected. Could they be unified? Would there ever be a theory of everything? Could the physics of the big be reconciled with that of the very small?

He even noticed that the more he learned about how strange reality was, the more his own reality sprung its surprises. It wasn't long before these surprises were coming thick and fast – subtle coincidences, such as friends he hadn't seen for a while turning up the day after he'd thought about them. He wanted to figure it all out, to find out what—

'Light, Sam.'

Professor Stuckley brought him sharply back to the present, to the murmuring Cherwell, the warmth of early evening and the light from the window highlighting the long streams of dust that were settling on the professor's desk.

'Light cannot be easily tied down.'

The professor looked across at Sam with a mischievous grin, then leaned forward in his chair and rested his elbows on the tea-stained table.

'Er, no,' said Sam, smiling back. 'You told me that. Do you know, I think your lecture on light was one of the first I attended here? Angus said he felt as though you were sharpening your metaphysical sword.'

The professor let out a chuckle, whilst simultaneously shaking his head. 'Metaphysical sword? No, no, no! I was making the case that light should not exist! It is massless, it is not affected by time, and yet I'm not the least bit surprised it was there at the beginning, for there is a chance that it will be there at the end too.'

Sam had grown used to the professor's random outbursts and he had to smile. Part of him simply wanted to know whether he would be coming back next year or whether he should be packing for good, but he realised he would have to wait, for the professor was on a roll.

'"In the beginning was the Word",' he declaimed. 'What they *should* have been saying was "In the beginning was the *light*, and when time slows and comes to a shuddering stop, at the very last moment, at the very last second, at the very end of the universe, only light can be left." To be more exact, Sam, what they should have said was "In the beginning was the light and at the end there will be light. And when both the beginning and the end are the same, there will be light." You see, Sam, there is something very elegant about light. If it were not for light, there would be no beginning, only the end, and that is my point. Light is the great entangler – it exists everywhere and nowhere at the same time.'

Sam found himself nodding, appreciating the professor's tantalising display of intellect whilst simultaneously wondering whether this was a roundabout way of telling him he'd failed.

'Professor Whitehart sings your praises from the rooftops,' Professor Stuckley remarked. 'Tells me you believe that knowledge has an inevitable evolutionary flow. You may want to tell me what that means one day, but at first draft it sounds good to me.'

His saggy face was broken by a half smile.

'The greatest minds,' he continued, oblivious to Sam's surprised look, 'across the disciplines, believe that it's not just light that's entangled, but the very language used to describe it. They believe that all knowledge is entwined. You know that physicists believe the universe at the quantum level is entangled through vibrating strings?'

The professor's unkempt grey hair nodded vigorously as if trying to persuade Sam to nod along in agreement.

'Then there are biologists who believe that knowledge is caught up in some blind evolutionary play.'

The professor's smile broadened a little further.

'Then there are philosophers – ha, yes, those who dare suggest that we should bridge the hidden chasm between art and science, between the physical and the metaphysical, and between that which can be seen and that which cannot!'

He sat back in his chair, as if satisfied, and reached for his silver pipe.

'By now, Sam, you should have realised that Cherwell College is much more than meets the eye. It is trying to teach the unteachable, to get students to think the unthinkable. You should come away from your time at Cherwell with the understanding that you can never quite trust reality, that you should certainly not trust your senses and that you should not believe everything that people tell you.'

The professor gave a half-chuckle and stuck the pipe between his lips.

'You will see the truth soon enough.'

Sam was beginning to feel a little frustrated. What truth did the professor mean?

'Do you know who taught in this very room?'

The question caught him off-guard. 'Erm…' He racked his brains, feeling embarrassed by his ignorance.

'C.S. Lewis.' The professor answered his own question. 'This is a room that has been witness to many a theological battle. It has heard the tortured conversations of many restless souls who have passed this way.'

He smiled again, fixing his eyes on Sam.

'You, Angus and the others have been very privileged to have studied here.'

'This is it,' thought Sam, his mouth feeling a little drier.

But the professor was back in the past. 'The foundations of Cherwell were laid more than forty years ago by a group calling themselves the Inklings. They wanted to protect their heritage, protect the notion that their work spoke of a truth. What do you know about the Inklings, Sam?'

'The Inklings were a literary group who met to discuss their work,' said Sam eagerly. 'They would meet in the Eagle and Child, or the

Bird and Baby, as it became known. C.S. Lewis would read snippets from *The Chronicles of Narnia* and Tolkien would read excerpts from *The Hobbit*.'

The professor was gently shaking his head.

'That's true, but there's a lot more to it than that. I had an old colleague who knew Tolkien. I remember him telling me that he thought there was something about his works that went far deeper than a flair for words and a knowledge of Norse mythology. He had learned much more than forgotten languages and their histories.'

Sam was becoming slightly perplexed. All he really wanted was his results. Was he staying or going?

'When the moment takes you, study them keenly.'

The professor's words hung in the air.

'Er, yes, of course,' Sam muttered.

Professor Stuckley lowered his voice and leaned forward. Sam watched as the professor's fingers began strumming some forgotten tune on the table's now peeling antiquity. 'Whatever curious words have been said about them fall short.'

Then he stood, walked a short distance to the open window and looked out. He appeared to be lighting his pipe, but it was almost, thought Sam, as if he was making sure the coast was clear.

Seemingly satisfied, the professor turned and walked back to stand in front of him.

'Truth speaks deeply in those works. Revisit them with vigour. Understand that truth and how it speaks to you.'

Sam nodded, trying to look as though he really did understand how important it was.

'Now close your eyes,' the professor continued, 'and tell me what you see and feel.'

Sam sighed. The professor was really turning his results day into some kind of dramatic performance. Dutifully, he closed his eyes.

'Don't be fooled by your senses,' the professor warned. 'Keep your eyes closed and go beyond the earthly smells that conspire against you, go past the warmth and the comfort. What do you see?'

With his eyes closed, Sam was more aware of the earthy scents of the old books. From the window there came a hint of lavender on the breeze, mingled with the danker scent of the Cherwell. And then far off, the sweet sound of voices as the Magdalen choir sprang into life, their soothing harmonies seeming to mingle with the light from the window dancing on the inside of his eyelids. Out in the middle of the light, a slender figure dressed in white was dancing and swirling, perhaps to the music of the choir. And then a single black slither opened up behind the dancing figure and he was standing, shouting out a warning, but no words were coming from his mouth.

When he opened his eyes, he was struggling for breath, as if he'd been through an ordeal. He was still in the chair, gripping its arms, his knuckles white. He unclenched his hands, feeling rather foolish and wondering what had just happened.

Professor Stuckley was watching him, his pipe hanging precariously from his mouth and his eyes wide with alarm.

'What shadow?'

'I'm not sure.'

Sam leaned back in his chair, feeling his breathing returning to normal.

'Come now – you said you saw a shadow.'

Sam felt himself blushing under the professor's gaze. 'Did I? I was daydreaming perhaps, but … well, now you mention shadows, I did see one a while ago.'

The professor leaned forward again.

'When?'

'December.'

'Where?'

'Birling Wood. That's just above Warkworth, in Northumberland.'

The professor turned away. Almost under his breath, he muttered, 'Then it is moving.'

'*Moving*?'

Ignoring the question, the professor learned forward again, balancing on the edge of his chair.

'Describe it to me.'

Sam sat back for a moment. That was the last thing he wanted. But, as a breeze blew through the open window, lifting the exam papers on the professor's desk, he was suddenly unable to lock his thoughts away a moment longer.

'I woke one night with a terrible foreboding. At first I thought it must have been in my head, a voice or something similar calling to me. I was staying with some friends in Warkworth. I don't know why I didn't wake them. Instead I felt compelled to go outside. I just stood there in the darkness, looking out across the river Coquet to the edge of Birling Wood. And I can't really say what happened next, but it scares me even now. I've only told two other people, and neither of them believed me.'

Sam looked up anxiously and met the professor's steady gaze. Suddenly he was glad of his company.

'I was rooted to the spot, unable to move. At first I couldn't see anything. It was dark and cold. And icy. I know it was winter, but I'd never seen ice on the river before. But the weirdest thing was that I knew that I was being watched. Out across the water, at the edge of the wood, something was waiting for me. All I could see was a shadow. Then it moved.'

Even in the comfort of the professor's room, Sam felt cold.

'It began to cross the river – silently, without breaking the surface of the water. I was terrified. I don't think I've ever been so frightened. I knew it meant to do me great harm. But I couldn't run away.'

He stopped. To his embarrassment, tears were welling up.

'Then I come to you with not a moment to lose,' the professor said quickly. 'But first tell me, how did you stop it from reaching you?'

'How can you be certain that I did?'

The professor held him with a serious look.

'It can't have reached you, for you wouldn't be sitting here if it had. And for that, I am most grateful.'

'What? What do you mean? What would have happened?'

The professor shook his head. 'Just be glad you are here, Sam.'

Sam sat there for a second, wondering whether he was in a tutorial room or some kind of dream.

'Well, anyway, it wasn't me who stopped it, but the river.'

Emily and Angus hadn't believed him and, as he said it out loud, he could hardly believe it either.

'The river?' repeated the professor, his face remaining impassive.

'One minute the waters were high and fast-flowing, the next they dropped, and then a second later a giant wave came down. It took the Shadow away with it and almost everything else. It practically swept my friend's rowing boat out to sea.'

'Hmm.'

The professor sat back in his chair and looked out through the window, idly tapping the table with his left hand whilst drawing on his pipe.

'It know it all sounds crazy,' Sam muttered, blushing and looking down.

'*I* believe you.'

Sam jerked his head back up. 'What? I mean—'

The professor interrupted quickly, 'There is much to tell you, but not now. I'm not certain what this Shadow is, or why it came to you in Warkworth, but there are those whose counsel I respect and I shall pay them a visit.'

He stood up and leaned forward to close the window. When he turned back to Sam, purpose blazed from his grey eyes.

'I must go. Meet me tomorrow evening at the Eagle and Child and we will have a bite to eat. There are a number of people I would like you to meet.'

Picking up his long walking stick, he ushered Sam out of the small room, down the steps and into the corridor.

As he stood there watching the professor stride off through the cloisters, Sam suddenly realised he still didn't know whether he had passed his exams.

THE FELLOWS' GARDEN

Sam left the cloisters wondering what had just happened. Having prepared himself all day for the moment of truth, here he was, no further forward.

He went out through Magdalen gates, crossed the arched bridge linking the college with Addison's Walk and the meadows beyond and settled himself on his favourite bench beneath a giant oak. It stood at a small crossroads. One road led to the Grove, Magdalen's deer park, and the other wound its way through the grasslands surrounding the college. In this place, with the early evening sun falling on him and the gentle hum of the river in his ears, he tried to piece together what was happening to him.

It had all started with the night in Warkworth. Then in the new year he'd begun to feel that everywhere he went in Oxford he was being followed. He'd tried to convince himself he was just being paranoid, but it had gone on for a while and had even continued when he'd been admitted to Cherwell College and had moved to the Fellows' House.

There was something about Cherwell College, he thought. Unusual events were happening to Angus too, even in Edinburgh. His letters had described how the crows in the New Town were becoming a real nuisance and he'd been attacked by several in the garden of his family house. He'd been rescued by Professor Lawrence, who'd said he'd been passing on his way to the Edinburgh Festival.

'The problem with this,' wrote Angus, 'is that you'd have to make a significant detour to pass my house – we're miles from the Festival. And I've no idea how Professor Lawrence circumnavigated the locked garden gate. What is it with these people – don't they know it's the holidays?'

Sam knew what Angus meant. Even though college had broken for summer, almost every day he'd bumped into Professor Stuckley or Professor Whitehart. No matter where he went in Oxford, he was almost guaranteed to find them there. It was almost as if they didn't want to let him out of their sight. And even now Professor Stuckley had managed to avoid giving him his results.

He threw his head back in frustration and looked up into the dense foliage of the oak. But as he gazed at the autumn rust beginning to creep across the leaves, he felt the weight of the professor's conversation begin to fall away. That was typical Stuckley, leaping from place to place in a whirl of ideas, making you think on your feet, never sure whether he was trying to fire your imagination or just following his own train of thought, or whether there was any real science behind it all! The professor was quirky, but Sam knew he was also generous with his time, in love with his subject matter and kind to those who cared to listen.

Taking one last look at the inner landscape of his favourite tree, Sam stood and stretched, arching his back before emerging from under the shadowy canopy and setting off back to the Fellows' House.

Addison's Walk welcomed him as it had done many times before, its trees and flowers merging into a profusion of soft colours. Evening was descending, but Sam didn't quicken his pace; instead he slowed and watched the last of the visitors drifting away. Soon he was alone with only his thoughts for company.

The lights were coming on over Magdalen and he had now reached the point on the walk where it bent sharply right. Ahead, just over a small bridge, were the grand gates to the deer park. He looked back over his shoulder at the long empty walk behind him. How beautiful it seemed in the fading light.

As he turned into the home stretch, the sunlight was sending its last rays across Angel Meadow, flushing it crimson. With sunset, robins and song thrushes joined together in lamenting the fading light, and Sam reached a place on the walk where the roots of the trees seemed to emerge like tentacles from beneath the rusty earth. It was here, so the story went, that J.R.R. Tolkien had sat with C.S. Lewis and had the conversation that led to Lewis's conversion to Christianity. Sam found himself stopping, breathing in the scents of the river and meadow, and, for just a moment, imagining the two authors sitting together with pipes in hands and rich conversation flowing between them.

As he reached the end of Holywell Ford, with the Fellows' Garden clearly visible ahead of him, the professor's words came back to him. One minute the physics of light, the next the Inklings – and what about the Shadow in Warkworth?

Approaching the small bridge that connected Addison's Walk to the Fellows' Garden, he noticed several crows sitting motionless in the gathering twilight. Or were they crows? They seemed bigger than crows and rather edgy. Perhaps they were ravens?

Suddenly recalling the crow attack on Angus, Sam came to a complete stop and waved his arms to scare the birds off. They took to the air suddenly, making him jump, and as they flew higher, they let out a series of angry caws before heading off into the gathering gloom.

'Keeping strange company this evening, Sam?'

Sam jumped. 'Professor Whitehart! I didn't see you there. Where have you come from?'

This was a good question, but one the professor didn't bother answering.

'I'm just on my way to Evensong,' he said casually. 'Come with me, if you like. We can grab early supper.'

Professor Whitehart was a small man, slightly built, with thick dark curly hair and the most piercing blue eyes Sam had ever seen. Apart from his academic work on the mind–matter conundrum, he was well known for finishing his lectures with card tricks. And just on cue, a pack of white faceless cards appeared in his hands, moving seamlessly through his fingers, glimmering with a ghostly light.

Somewhere far above, angry caws broke out.

'Thanks, professor, but I have to pack this evening. I'm supposed to be going home in a couple of days. Well, if I ever get my results, that is.'

'Then let me bid you good evening,' Professor Whitehart said, ignoring the results hint. 'But let's have breakfast tomorrow.'

He made as if to go, then stopped and turned back to Sam, his pack of cards turning in his hands like a Catherine wheel.

'Should the crows come back this evening, you have my number in your top pocket.'

With that, he turned and left.

Reaching into his pocket, Sam withdrew a plain card with a phone number scribbled across it. He turned back to watch the professor disappear down the path with just a little awe. How could he have got the card into his top pocket without touching him? Could it have taken place when he'd been watching the cards flying high into the air?

He was still reflecting on the sleight of hand when he reached the round oak door to the Fellows' Garden. It had the emblem of Cherwell College, the circle with an unknown tree in the middle, carved with beautiful symmetry into its now dark and stained wood.

Sam reached for the large brass key in his pocket and entered the secret garden in the heart of Oxford. It was now empty and the evening sun was throwing long shadows across Sam's path. Around him were trees dating back to when Magdalen itself had been built in the fifteenth century. In the gathering darkness they looked like aged giants, twisted and misshapen. One group formed the circle around the Fellows' Pond, where koi, sarasa and golden orfes sent their colours rippling through the water, whilst elsewhere flower-beds of erysimum, foxgloves and verbenas created pools of blue as deep as the pond itself.

Instead of going to the Fellows' House, Sam decided to pay a visit to the pond. He took one final look down the length of the garden, past the Fellows' House, half concealed by a copse of trees, to the Cherwell winding its way casually towards the meadows beyond the garden wall, and then sat down on one of the benches around the pond. There were twenty-two of these, all set back from the water's edge. It was here that academics would seek solitude, a moment's respite from the hustle and bustle of college life. Sam himself had spent many hours dipping his toes into the cold waters and watching the fish swarm curiously around them.

Now, in the dying light, he was suddenly aware of the silence. The birdsong had faded away and even the cawing of the crows had ceased. The pond before him was still, like a mirror. He felt his eyes growing heavy and his head beginning to nod until one final yawn sent him to sleep.

* * * * * *

He woke with the garden in near darkness. The hair on the back of his neck sprang into life and he knew he was being observed. Slowly he raised his head.

Sitting on the bench to his left was a man he had never seen before. Shadowy lines criss-crossed his face, he had a straggly grey beard and wild grey hair, and his jacket and trousers looked tattered and worn. Though obviously tired, he looked strongly built. Could he be a tramp?

Even in the half-light Sam could tell he was looking straight at him, and it sent a shiver down his spine.

'Who are you?' he asked shakily.

'My name is Oscar.'

'What are you doing here? I mean, only Fellows are allowed here, or people from the Fellows' House.'

'I think chance brought me here,' Oscar said slowly. 'Of course, if chance you call it. Now tell me – where are we?'

'In the Fellows' Garden, but—'

Sam froze. Just behind Oscar stood a tall figure dressed in shadow.

'Culluhin, wait for me at the tree.'

Sam wasn't sure if the figure had moved or not, but when he blinked, it had gone.

'Don't be afraid,' Oscar said softly. 'Tell me your name and come and sit next to me.'

'It's Sam.'

Without quite knowing why, Sam stood, crossed the short distance between them and sat down next to Oscar.

He now realised the man had been in some kind of accident. His hair was untidy, his face seemed painted with soot and one of his eyes was slightly closed. His arms seemed to have been burned – even in the poor light Sam could see blackened skin.

'What's happened to you?' he asked, horrified.

'I have no time to tell you why I look the way I do, or what my story may be, or why I am here,' Oscar replied enigmatically. 'But I am seeking Professor Stuckley and Professor Whitehart. Do you know them? Ah yes, I see you do.'

Sam's face had betrayed him.

'Then let me leave a message with you, for I cannot delay my departure.'

'I don't understand…' Sam began.

'That doesn't matter! In seven days' time it will all make sense. I simply ask that you deliver my message before the night is over. Tell the professors the girl is safe, but much darkness comes this way.'

Oscar stopped talking and sighed as if a great burden had come to rest upon him. He took hold of his left hand as if it pained him, and his head sank against his chest.

'Should I get help?' Sam asked, reaching out to touch him.

Oscar turned sharply, his blue eyes blazing into Sam's. 'I've felt that touch before! Yes, as if it was only a moment ago! Most unexpected. Yes, most unexpected.'

'You said it,' Sam thought. He began to wonder whether he was dreaming. But somehow he couldn't dismiss it. Whoever this man was and whatever message he had to deliver, there was a sadness about him as if he had suffered a great loss.

'Tell me your name again,' Oscar said eagerly.

'Samuel Wood.'

'Of course it is! That's the name you gave me a moment ago.'

'Well, I didn't give you my full name then. But what do you mean?'

Sam was curious now. Somehow he had to get a grip on this strange situation.

But Oscar was looking away from him at the great trees in the garden, and when he spoke, it seemed as though he was talking to himself.

'So very little time, so very little.'

'Are you injured?' Sam persisted.

The question seemed to bring calmness to the man's tired face. He turned back to Sam with a flicker of a smile.

'Only in spirit, Samuel. I wish I had a day to tell you my tale. I would like to understand who you are, perhaps tell you who I am, but to stay too long would bring danger to this place, if danger isn't already here.'

'*Already* here?'

'Tell the professors, Samuel, that the Circle is broken and a Shadow moves through the Otherland. Tell them that the Dead Water is lost and the Fall is dying. Tell them that they must seek the help of the Three. You must be wondering whether these words are those of the wise or the mad. On the road ahead you will find out...'

'*Oscar.*'

The chilling voice came from behind Sam. He knew without looking that the tall figure had returned.

'Is it time already, Culluhin? Please, give me a moment.'

Once more Culluhin withdrew.

'I still don't understand,' Sam said anxiously.

'You will understand my words when the time is right,' Oscar replied. 'One day you will understand my words only too well.'

He leaned a little closer to Sam, and when he spoke, his voice was lower, sadder, almost breaking with the weight of the words.

'Tell them also that there is a traitor who has already done great mischief. Tell them that the Underland is awake and moving through the Otherland in ever-greater numbers. And now, Sam, I must go and I can offer you nothing in return for delivering my message.'

Oscar was standing, holding out his hand. Sam found himself recoiling as he saw the full extent of his injuries.

'We will meet again, sooner that you think,' Oscar said, 'for chance brought us together and it has its own purpose.'

He reached into his jacket pocket and withdrew two envelopes that were torn and discoloured by age.

'Once you have met the Keepers, it will be time to open these.'

And with that, Oscar turned and ran, with surprising speed and nimbleness, around the pond and out through the ancient ring of trees.

* * * * * *

Sam sat still for a moment, blinking back his amazement. What had just happened there? Then he found himself getting to his feet and taking the same path Oscar had taken. Emerging from the trees, he looked around him and then turned a full circle. There was no one there. It was as if Oscar and his terrifying bodyguard had never existed.

Puzzled, Sam stood there, wondering whether his studies had at last taken their toll. There was only one way out of the garden – no one could just simply disappear. Unless Oscar had doubled back at the far end of the garden, he and – who was it? Culluhin? – had simply melted away. But he knew that was impossible.

He made his way back through the trees, heading in what he thought was the direction of the pond. But somehow he couldn't find his way back through the trees. How odd. He turned and tried to go back the way he'd come, but everything looked different.

Static electricity was humming around his head and cobwebs seemed to be brushing against his face, but when he brushed them away, nothing was there. He was beginning to feel a little panicky by the time he at last broke through the trees. Then he stood still.

In front of him, the pond had been replaced by an unfamiliar tree. Not quite as broad as an English oak, nor as thrusting as a hornbeam, it had the look of a yew, but its trunk looked especially gnarled. Sam could not put a name to it or understand how it had come to be there. He felt disorientated. He whirled round to look back behind him, down the hill, and realised he could no longer see the lights of Magdalen. Where was he? He'd walked in the garden many times since coming to Oxford, had walked it from one end to the other. How could it be that he'd never seen this tree and – what were those?

An electric shock of fear ran through his body as he saw the figures facing inwards towards the tree. They were all shapes and sizes, but what *were* they?

As his eyes adjusted to the dim light, he realised they were statues – statues carved out of stone. The question should have been *who* were they? He was sure there were subtle features carved on their stony faces. They looked ancient, as if they'd been standing on this spot for eternity, but how could that be? How could all this have somehow lain hidden in the Fellows' Garden?

Intrigued, Sam moved forward through the stone statues to the tree. In the silence he could hear the sound of his own breathing and it seemed to him that each footstep was a clash of cymbals trying to wake the tree from its sleep. Its shape was even shifting as though it was about to stir, as if it wasn't even a tree... An urge to reach out to it took hold of him. He placed his hands against the rough bark and found it oddly warm.

His mind was racing. Who was Oscar? And the man acting like his shadow? Where had they gone? What was going to happen in seven days' time?

All the questions jostling for position in his mind were making him feel a little dizzy, and his hands were beginning to grow warmer – or was it the bark?

Then he heard his name – a ripple in the quiet night, a gentle vibration that scattered through his mind. Or was it his imagination? His mind playing tricks in the darkness?

There it came again – a voice calling out his name, and there was a new word not far behind. Was that 'danger'?

His fingers were now hot and the heat was travelling to his wrists and up his arms. Perhaps he should let go, perhaps the tree was dangerous, but the warmth was soothing, comforting him, lulling him... He relaxed and drank it in, as though he'd found a cold river in the middle of a vast desert.

There it was again – a voice calling his name and then the word 'danger' caught on the evening breeze. But the voice was distant, far beyond the garden wall, or hidden within his mind. And here was the silent warmth, compelling him to drift, to lean into the tree just a little more. After all, this was his favourite place. No harm could come to him here, not in the Fellows' Garden…

For a second, a ripple, a hint, a babbling doubt lapped against the warmth like an unwelcome chill, suggesting this was not quite the place it had been a moment earlier. There was still a voice, now perhaps a little less distant, saying new words that eddied round in his head: 'Shadow' and 'run'. Was that Oscar's voice? What was this chill punctuating the warmth? What was this cold water all around him? Why was Oscar shouting?

'The Otherland is no longer safe, Sam! The Shadow is here. Run! Run!'

Shaken from his stupor, Sam let go of the tree. Instantly, an icy chill took his breath away. A suffocating fear reached out and enveloped him, drowning out all his senses. He would have turned and fled if his legs hadn't buckled underneath him. As he fell, everything was slowing, he was almost senseless and time's arrow was trickling past him.

Someone was lifting him from cold waters as blackness took him.

OXFORD SHADOWS

He awoke with a start and was surprised to find himself in the library room of the Fellows' House, sitting just in front of its large bay window, his face laced with sweat and his palms wet. He rubbed a hand across his face, guessing that it must be the middle of the night. Oscar, his shadow guard, the tree – what a strange dream that had been! But how had he fallen asleep at the Fellows' Pond, only to wake up here?

'I found you floating face down in the pond. I'm just glad I was passing.'

Sam froze. Professor Stuckley was sitting quietly in a leather chair, his trusty pipe in his hand.

'Face down in the pond? That's impossible!'

'Is it?' exclaimed the professor, his eyebrows arching. 'Really? But tell me about Oscar, Samuel, for you've been mumbling his name these past few hours.'

'Oscar? Yes … um, I did meet a man called Oscar. Or I thought I did.'

Sam felt quite embarrassed. Falling into the pond had been bad enough. Now it seemed as though he'd been delirious as well. He felt his face reddening.

'I fell asleep at the pond and I must have started dreaming. That's all, professor. Although I have to say it felt very real at the time.'

'Tell me about it, and start from the beginning. Leave no stone unturned.'

'I'm sorry?' Sam felt just a little perturbed. Why was the professor so insistent?

'Forgive me, this is important. You will have answers to your questions soon enough.'

'But professor, it didn't make any sort of sense. It was just a weird dream. I really think I just need to go to bed and forget about it.'

'You can't run away from this so easily!'

The professor had got to his feet more quickly than Sam had thought possible for a man his age.

'Tell me about Oscar!' The professor's voice had raised a notch.

'Look, I've *told* you. I'm sorry, professor, but there's nothing *to* tell – it was just a dream.'

'You don't dream about people you don't know – real people. *I'm* sorry, Sam, but Oscar visited you, and he wouldn't have come without a good reason. What did he want?'

'He wanted to deliver a message to you,' Sam said slowly. This was getting really strange.

The professor sank back into his chair, whilst all around the tall bookcases watched silently. 'What was it?' he murmured.

'The Circle is broken and a Shadow moves through the Otherland.'

Sam jumped as the professor's silver pipe clattered to the wooden floor.

'How can that be possible?!'

'He mentioned something about the Dead Water being lost.'

The professor turned his face away from Sam, rested his chin on his outstretched hand and closed his eyes.

'Professor?' Sam started to rise from his chair, but stopped as the professor raised a hand.

'I feel his grief, Sam, that's all.' He paused, then added quietly, 'That was no dream, for Oscar is an old friend from a life I had before taking my seat at Cherwell.'

Taking a deep breath, he fixed his eyes on Sam.

'Tomorrow we will visit the Eagle and Child as planned. Then you will take the train back home. It will do you no good staying around here when your peers have all left.'

'Oh – so does that mean I've passed? But wait—' Sam broke off. 'What is the Dead Water? What is the Otherland?'

As he spoke, the library seemed to fall quiet and the oak bookshelves to tower around him.

The professor was silent.

'Can't you tell me what's going on, professor? Things have been really weird lately – not just Oscar, but our conversation this afternoon. What was all that about? And then I met Professor Whitehart, and he was definitely acting oddly. And while we're at it, why are Angus and I the only undergraduates to be housed here?'

'I hear what you say, Sam,' the professor said wearily. 'I suppose you can have too many riddles in one day. I will try and answer some of them, but let me make us both a brew first.'

* * * * * *

When they were both holding a hot cup and the professor was sitting in his favourite chair, his silver pipe once again pressed against his pursed lips, he seemed to have recovered his composure.

'I suppose the Dead Water and the Otherland are places that are more metaphysical than physical,' he began. 'They represent how the past, present and future come together as one.'

'So how can they be lost?'

The professor seemed slightly irked by Sam's blunt question. He took a sip of his tea before answering, 'They are the between places, the corridor between one room and another.'

He took another sip of his tea.

'These places can be lost if you lose faith in them. I think that's what Oscar meant.'

'But who has lost faith? And how can they act like a corridor when they don't exist?'

Sam felt his face burning. Perhaps he was pushing his luck, but he felt he had a right to know what was going on. He watched the professor shift a little uneasily in his chair, passing his intricate pipe from hand to hand.

'These places *do* exist,' the professor said quietly. 'They are representations of those uncertainties.'

There was a pause. The room was eerily quiet.

'There are those who know how to listen to those uncertainties,' the professor continued, his gaze falling on Sam, 'those who can feel their resonance in this world. There are very few left now who can do this, but Oscar is one of them. It worries me that he chose to come here, for the resonances are not only felt by the good.'

Sam felt the hair on the back of his neck stand up. He shivered despite the warmth of the room.

'Oscar mentioned the Underland was awake and moving through the Otherland in ever-greater numbers – is that what you mean when you say there are others who can feel these vibrations?'

The professor lowered his gaze as if a new weight had settled upon him.

'I have already told you too much and the night grows late. I am tired. You should go.'

'In the dream,' continued Sam doggedly, 'Oscar mentioned the Three. He said you must seek their help.'

The professor visibly sagged beneath the impact of the words. 'I'm sorry, Sam,' he muttered, 'but it has been a long day and my bed calls. Let us meet for breakfast in Magdalen and we can discuss this in the light of day.'

'But if it *wasn't* a dream, professor, then surely I deserve to understand what is going on!' Sam's cheeks were burning with anger. 'Your explanation is just a physicist's puzzle! Oscar looked haggard, as if he'd been travelling for days, and he'd been battered and burned, and he came to deliver that message to you. Who is he, professor? How did he get into the garden when there's only one way in? How did he vanish into thin air?'

'Samuel,' said the professor firmly, 'it would seem that Oscar has given us both a lot to think about. I will say that I know him through my travels around Northumberland and that the Dead Water and the Otherland are as real as the atoms that go into creating them – but we both know how elusive atoms can be. After all, if the very small can be in two places at once, then why not something much bigger?'

He smiled enquiringly at Sam. But Sam looked away, into the dark landscape beyond the great bay window.

'It just feels as though you are being evasive,' he said bitterly.

For a moment, there was silence between them, broken only by the distant cawing of many birds circling high above.

Then Sam remembered something. He pulled Oscar's letters from his coat pocket.

'Look, he gave me two letters.'

He read the envelopes, then frowned as he held one out to the professor.

Professor Stuckley slowly closed his hands over the tattered envelope. 'What about the other one?' he asked.

Sam was looking at it with a puzzled expression. 'It's addressed to me. But how can that be? He'd only just met me. What's going on?'

'Well,' the professor muttered, 'whatever it is, I don't think we should venture back out this evening and find out.'

'What are you afraid of, professor?'

Sam knew very well he was now pushing his luck. But he had to know.

The professor sighed and drew thoughtfully on his pipe. 'Frankly, I'm no longer sure, Sam, and that in itself worries me. You have every right to be perplexed, and believe me, you're not the only one. You have become caught up in this in a way that I can no longer comprehend. The last person I expected to see in Oxford was Oscar.'

'Caught up in what?'

This time the professor raised his eyes to meet Sam's gaze.

'I am afraid that even if I had the answer, I might not be able to tell you.'

'And you expect me to just keep on ignoring things and not have a say in what's happening?' Sam was outraged. 'I'm persuaded to move to a college I've never applied to, I'm one of only two undergraduates housed here, I bump into either you or Professor Whitehart no matter where I go, and then today Oscar appears out of thin air and brings a message about circles and shadows, and you say you can't tell me why!'

He paused for breath. In the silence the sound of crows could be heard again, calling to one another over the rooftops.

'You know I deserve some answers, professor. I think you know what that Shadow is. And you know who Oscar is. So why was he here?'

The professor pulled out his fanciful handkerchief and wiped his brow.

'Sam,' he said wearily, 'I might not be in a position to give you all the answers, but I can take you to someone who can help you understand a little of what's going on.'

Seeing his hurt look, Sam couldn't help but feel slightly guilty. 'Thank you,' he said more quietly. 'Actually, there's more to the story too. There's a tree in the middle of the garden, one that I've never seen before.'

'A tree,' repeated the professor, looking even more uncomfortable.

'Right in the middle of a circle of stone statues.'

The professor leaned his head on his hand.

'Professor…?'

With a sigh, the professor shook himself and said, 'It's time to get some rest, Sam. In the morning we can talk some more over breakfast, then in the early evening we can catch up with Professor Whitehart at the Eagle and Child.'

They both rose and stood awkwardly in the dim light of the study, listening to the far-off squawking.

'There were crows sitting on the bridge today,' Sam remarked. 'Do you know about Angus's encounter with them in Edinburgh?'

Ignoring the question, the professor walked towards the door. 'Get some sleep, Sam. We're both tired. I'm only down the corridor, so if you need anything, don't be afraid to wake me.'

As he reached the door, he turned back.

'By the way, you passed – well done.'

And with that he was gone.

* * * * * *

'What an evening,' thought Sam, as he sat once again in front of the large bay window in his study bedroom. Whatever was happening, the professor knew more than he was saying – that much was certain. He'd been taken aback by the appearance of Oscar, not to mention his message. And there had even been fear in his eyes at the mention of the Shadow.

Sam shuddered at the memory of the thing he'd glimpsed across the Coquet. He'd only truly seen it when it had moved. Before then he'd just been aware that something was there, watching and waiting. But if it hadn't been for the freak wave, it would have reached his side of the river and then he'd have come face to face with it.

He looked back out into the garden. In the darkness it appeared like a vast sea moving in a gentle wind. He glanced over towards the pond. Was the tree still there? What about Oscar? But all he could really see was his own reflection.

Suddenly he had an urge to move from the window. Then a caterwaul split the silence from the darkness below.

Sam fell back into the chair as a chill dread surged over him. He heard his door open and then the light was switched off.

The next moment, Professor Stuckley was grabbing him and throwing him against the wall before positioning himself on the opposite side of the window and pressing a finger to his lips, silencing Sam before he had the chance to say a word.

They stood there in the darkness waiting. Then, as Sam's eyes adjusted to the gloom, he noticed someone standing beside them. He tried to shout, but his voice cracked with terror. Only the flashing white cards brought him to his senses.

Professor Stuckley whispered, 'Drust, lock the door quickly.'

Without replying, Professor Whitehart shot towards the door, locked it and slid the top and bottom bolts into place. Then, in response to a nod from Professor Stuckley, he threw his weight against Sam's heavy oak wardrobe and pushed it firmly against the door.

'What's going on?' he asked, quickly glancing at Sam.

'Oscar was here,' Professor Stuckley replied.

'Oscar! How can that be?'

Professor Stuckley continued in whispered tones, 'He gave a message to Sam. There is a Shadow moving through the Otherland.'

'It's here!' Sam cried.

Yet again hideous fear was swamping his senses and he knew without a moment's hesitation that the Shadow from Warkworth had found its way to the Fellows' Garden.

'Drust, take Sam to my room, collect what he needs and then meet me at the Eagle and Child. If I am gone more than an hour, don't come back here, but tell Professor Lawrence to meet us there and—'

The professor's words were drowned out as the window shattered and all hell broke loose. In the madness, Professor Whitehart's voice could be heard booming out as the cards in his hands flew towards the window. Then a flash of light burst across Sam's vision and for a moment he was blinded.

Professor Stuckley was grabbing him by the arm, propelling him towards the bookcases. With the light still dazzling him and Professor Whitehart's voice roaring in his ears, one minute he was standing upright against the wall and the next he was thrown upside down. His head was hitting wood and he was sliding down into darkness.

Then he landed with a thud and for a moment he lay there stunned, unable to see.

How far he had slid he couldn't tell. But from somewhere above there were grinding noises, thuds and raised voices, and every now and then he could tell furniture was being dislodged and turned over.

The fear was still thick around him, so he knew the Shadow was close by. He scrambled to his feet, feeling a hot pain shooting through his ankle.

Disorientated, he looked around. He seemed to be in a narrow tunnel. For a moment all he could hear was his own breathing and it dawned on him that the noises from above had stopped.

He didn't want to be caught with nowhere to run. He moved tentatively into the murk, hobbling along with his arms outstretched.

There were other noises coming from above now. Shouts were punctuating the silence, becoming fainter as he shuffled down the passage. He blocked them from his mind. He had no idea who had the upper hand.

The passage was going down and the walls seemed to be closing in. Sam stopped for a moment, trying to get his breath. Should he go back? Was this an escape route or a trap? For a second he turned, but was stopped in his tracks by a hissing noise starting up in his ears. Or was it in his head? Or behind him? What was it?

The sense of dread that swelled through the darkness told him he was no longer alone. Something had found the secret tunnel. There was no choice but to go forward.

Panic swirling now like an angry tide around him, Sam kept on moving, biting his lip to overcome the burning pain in his ankle. The darkness seemed thicker, heavier, and as the corridor grew even smaller, he half expected a shadowy hand to reach out and smother him. He started to run.

Then a sound spiked through his body, making him reel with nausea. It was a single word, delivered by an inhuman voice: 'Druidae.'

A sense of dread was rushing down the tunnel to snuff out his existence. In despair Sam threw himself forwards, then fell, letting out a fearful howl as he flailed into empty air.

Then he was in icy water. There was no up and no down, only water and darkness and the sudden realisation that his lungs were bursting.

Thrashing with all his strength, he burst above the waterline. Gasping and sobbing with relief, he grabbed hold of something solid.

As he shook the water from his eyes, a new fear quickly took hold, as he realised that he was holding onto the reeds along the banks of the Cherwell and the tug of the river was already trying to dislodge his grip. Teeth chattering, he pulled himself further into the reed bed.

He had surfaced just across from the Fellows' Garden in Bat Willow Meadow. He drove deeper into the reeds, gasping and floundering until he was clinging to the riverbank itself. There he paused for a moment before dragging himself out of the water and collapsing on the grass verge.

He knew he had to go on. Whatever had been in the tunnel could have found its way into the river. And if he hadn't been safe in the

Fellows' House, he wouldn't be safe in the open. As it was, he could see flickers of light like sharp, snapping lightning emanating from behind the Fellows' Garden, accompanied by the raucous jeers of a murder of crows circling high above the garden walls. He scrambled to his feet. All he could think of was to try and make Magdalen College and hope the gates weren't shut.

The sky was clear but moonless. As Sam started to run, the pain in his ankle shot through him and his wet clothes felt icy cold against his skin, but he found Addison's Walk and took comfort in its familiarity. He was a mile away from the college gates, and he wasn't certain that he would be safe there, but he couldn't see an alternative.

Then out of the night a tree root caught him, sending him sprawling from the top of Addison's Walk down the short hill into the tall grass of the Water Meadow. He came to rest lying on his back. As he looked up, something moved atop the walk, something darker than the starlit night. His shadowy stalker was hunting him down.

Sam picked himself up and started running through the tall grass of the meadow. He was big and strong, but he could feel his lungs burning, his ankle searing with pain and a ghastly sickness surging through him. Behind him an icy threat was rising, a frightful horror gaining speed, hurtling through the meadow, ready to sweep down and engulf him.

Still he kept running. Breathless, stumbling, beyond crying for help, he was suddenly across the meadow and scrambling and clawing his way up the short bank by the oak tree he had sat beneath only hours earlier. This time it offered no shelter.

The small wooden bridge that spanned the Cherwell appeared like a beacon of hope. Staggering across it, Sam fell exhausted against the huge iron gates of Magdalen. They were locked.

* * * * * *

The sky was a giant black canvas hanging over the spires of Oxford. Sam lay looking up at it. Numb, cold and hurt, all he could do was wait for his pursuer to strike. Tears slid down his cheeks. On the opposite side of the arched bridge, a dark cloud was gathering and he could feel it reaching out to strip him of his senses. Even at this distance, it was smothering him with hatred. He was sure the moment it touched him he would be dead. And he didn't even know why.

He didn't have to wait long. Already it was moving, rising up, black and shapeless, a ghostly Shadow that filled the night with dread. Shrinking back with fear, Sam closed his eyes.

He expected darkness, but light was dancing on the inside of his eyelids just as it had in the professor's study. At first it was white, then one by one the colours of the rainbow emerged, swirling together as if caught in clear water. Voices were rising from a faraway place and the colours were coming together, and for an instant Sam thought they were dancing in the form of a single silhouette.

The sweeping voices were swelling and rising through his mind. 'The choir of Magdalen,' he thought dimly, 'singing evensong.'

The sea of voices washed over him, seeming to lift him and take him higher. Then he heard a commanding voice.

'It cannot hurt you here.'

He had heard this before, a long time ago, in a half-forgotten dream. As he heard it now, he noticed a strange mellifluous haze moving through his mind's eye. It seemed to envelop him in a warmth that drove the fear from his body. He saw a light flowing, drawn by a hidden current, gently pushing the long strands of darkness from his mind. Whether a form took shape in the light he couldn't tell, but when he opened his eyes there was a figure standing beside him, a woman of sublime beauty, with colours radiating from her like a newly formed rainbow after a storm.

'My dear Sam, I am here for you, but you need to listen.'

He felt a tender hand touch his face.

'Even in this place, time cannot be denied. I cannot keep the Shadow at bay, for it hunts you even here. When I take you back, it will be waiting, so run and do not look back. I have called those who will give you time.'

'Who are you?' he whispered.

'I am the Fall.'

In the distance, thunder rumbled and the light began to fade. Then Sam was back by the gates, with tears on his face and terror all around him and the sound of a distant wail in his ears.

The gates of Magdalen were opening and the nightmare was fading into a soft glow of college lights and familiar voices. He was being hauled to his feet.

'Close the gates,' growled someone off to his right.

Sam was half carried through the ancient walls whilst all around him voices were calling to each other. He was ushered quickly towards an open door and lifted up a number of steps, his arm now wrapped around the unmistakable shoulders of Professor Lawrence, with his thick beard, dark ponytail and fierce brown eyes.

With their feet echoing loudly on the stone floor, they made their way through the cloisters and away from the turmoil.

Professor Lawrence eventually slowed down as they came to a large door. Sam recognised it as the entrance to the Founder's tower.

The professor withdrew a large key-ring with keys of different lengths hanging from it. Finding the one he needed, he put it in the keyhole, then looked back over his shoulder at Sam.

'Are you injured in any way?'

'Just my ankle – what's happening?'

'We're going out through St John's Quad to the front gate. If I have to leave you or we're separated, make your way to the Eagle and Child. Once we're outside the college, you'll have no protection against the thing you saw tonight. Do you understand?'

Sam could hear and almost feel the professor's nervousness. This made him more anxious than ever.

'Do you understand?'

Sam wasn't sure he did. His mind was still numb from the last hour. He couldn't comprehend what he'd witnessed.

'What happened? Are the professors safe?'

Professor Lawrence seemed not to have heard. He was looking back down the long and beautiful archways of the cloisters. Then he was stepping back from the door and turning. Though his face was expressionless, his eyes betrayed fear and determination.

'I'm pleased you're okay. Listen, Sam, if you get to see Angus on your travels, tell him I send my regards. You must go on alone now, but we will give you the time you need. I hope to see you again soon.'

Then the professor was running back the way they had come. He passed through the archway and was gone.

Sam stood alone once more, his ankle reminding him that he could barely run, his clothes damp and exhaustion making his head swim. He reached for the key in the door and began to turn it.

Then something in the back of his befuddled mind made him stop. Hadn't the professor told him to go out into St John's Quad and through the front gate…? But if the Shadow could find him in the Fellows' House, then surely it was intelligent enough to know this was the way he would try to escape?

He let go of the key and staggered backwards. What if there was more than one of them? What if the one at the gate had been flushing him out?

The key was still in the door and footsteps were now approaching from the other side. Sam watched in mute horror as something moved the handle from the opposite side. He reached for the key with a leaden hand, turned it and heard the lock snap into place. Then the door shuddered as someone pushed on it. The handle rattled.

'Sam!' came a voice, but Sam didn't answer, for although it had sounded familiar, a chill had come over him.

Taking the key-ring from the door, he turned and fled. He would make for the deer park and then the Eagle and Child, and hope Professor Stuckley would meet him there.

* * * * * *

Approaching the doorway that led out onto the lawns of the New Buildings, Sam knew he would be vulnerable to attack. He could be seen from Addison's Walk and there was no knowing who or what had called his name and where it was now.

The door was locked and he had to try several different keys before the lock clicked back. Taking a deep breath, he pushed the door open. Just two steps and he was out from the cover of Magdalen's age-worn stones, shivering in his soaking clothes, his teeth chattering and his senses alert.

The best he could do was head diagonally across the open space, with the cloisters behind him and the New Buildings to his right. There was a chance he could be seen from St John's Quad through the gap between the President's lodgings and the Grammar Hall, but he knew that he couldn't wait to be caught.

Back towards Addison's Walk, vague cries were echoing around the lawns of the New Buildings. Ahead were the trees of the Grove, the beautiful green expanse of the deer park.

With one desperate burst of speed, Sam was through its borders and coming to rest against a tall elm tree. In the darkness he could no longer see the gap between the President's lodgings and the Grammar Hall and he knew an attack could come from there at any moment, but even with such a threat at hand, he felt his legs buckling beneath him. It was foolish not to push on, but his breathing was shallow, his eyes were heavy and his head felt as though it was made of iron. Then he felt the creeping fear begin again in the pit of his stomach. He couldn't wait until he was caught helpless beneath the tree.

Stumbling further into the Grove, Sam tried to run, but it was taking all his strength to stay upright. Exhausted, cold, almost tearful, he promised himself he would make one final effort.

As he dragged himself forward, he became aware of startled movements in the night and eyes pricking the blackness with their reflected light. Now and then a noise would break the air and something would leap from his path. The deer were skittish, but then it seemed their fear was replaced by curiosity and they started coming right up to Sam before turning and fading into the darkness. It almost felt as if they were shepherding him.

There must have been a hundred milling around, he thought. Thankfully, whatever was pursuing him would find it difficult to follow him now, for the deer were jumping around in front of him and behind him before leaping off to his left and right.

He could no longer feel the chill of his stalker, only that of his damp clothes. Was he really going to evade his pursuer? What of Professor Stuckley and Professor Whitehart. Had they escaped?

Then suddenly there was a stone wall in front of him. He was across!

He turned to thank the deer for their safe passage. He could feel their energy willing him on, their calls now almost words, telling him not to linger, that his pursuer was merely lost, not defeated.

He turned and clambered up the wall with nothing more than their encouragement for strength.

Sitting on the top, he turned to thank them again, but there was only empty space where they had been. They had vanished so quickly, he wondered whether they had been real.

Then it hit him. 'There are no deer here in summer, Sam,' he said as he half-fell over the wall and collapsed onto the pavement of Longwall Street.

Sitting against the long wall that had given the street its name, he laughed and then found himself crying, all in one breath.

THE EAGLE AND CHILD

The hard stone wall dug into his back, keeping him from drifting off. He was tired beyond anything he'd ever known, but he knew that he had to move on. He dragged himself to his feet.

Just for a second, the street swam and he had to steady himself against the unforgiving wall. It took several deep breaths before he finally got his bearings. If he went down Holywell Street, the Eagle and Child would be about a two-mile walk away. That seemed a very long way. He felt dizzy and just a little sick, his ankle hurt and his clothes were still damp, but there was nothing for it. He set off again, stumbling through the darkness.

It was now the early hours of the morning and there was just the faintest trace of dawn in the eastern sky. The streets were quiet, but behind him the high walls of Magdalen reminded him that whatever had come for him in the Fellows' House could still be searching for him. The thought sent a shudder through his weary body, but the feeling of dread did not return. Though his legs were shaking with the effort to walk, he could feel his fear seeping out of him. Whatever had been stalking him was fading away. Still, as he reached the red-bricked building that bridged Longwall Street and Holywell Street, he found himself turning to make sure nothing was following him.

Holywell Street was a favourite street of his, full of exquisite architecture. He was now passing New College, its grand Headington stone giving the darkness a yellowish hue. As he walked, he remembered that Tolkien had lived at number 99 Holywell Street back in the early 1950s.

He passed the famous Tuck Shop and eventually arrived at the end of the street. Standing between the old Indian Institute and the King's Arms, he paused for a moment to consider his options. What he would give to be inside the pub now with a warm fire at his back! Thinking of it reminded him just how cold he was. He had to keep moving.

Broad Street was the most direct way to the Eagle and Child, but Sam decided to turn left up Parks Road and cut through St John's College instead. If his stalker did realise where he was heading, he hoped that wouldn't be the way it was expecting him to go.

But, as the high walls of St John's rose up on his left, he realised the folly of his plan. It was futile to try and climb them when he could barely put one foot in front of the other. He would have to keep on going until he could turn left down Museum Road and work his way through the Lamb and Flag Passage to St Giles, where the Eagle and Child stood.

With his head almost dipping onto his chest, he trudged on. He didn't see the crow fly out of the grounds of St John's and sweep above him, wheeling sharply before flying swiftly off into the night.

He came to Museum Road without stopping, ignoring the fork in the road and taking the Lamb and Flag Passage, the hope of seeing the Eagle and Child driving him on.

As he emerged from the passage into dawn's first light, he felt as if he was waking from a bad dream. Across the road, warm and welcoming like the arms of a favourite aunt, was the Eagle and Child.

Sam stood for a long moment remembering his excitement at entering the pub for the first time. That seemed so long ago now.

Then he crossed the wide roads of St Giles and headed for the Eagle's black front door.

The realisation that he had reached safety was making him feel sick and his remaining strength was draining away. The last few steps to the Eagle's door seemed to take a lifetime. A blue haze was spreading across the dark sky as he finally reached it.

He slumped against it and starting thumping on the thick wood, closing his eyes as the ground fell out from under him and he fell into untroubled darkness.

* * * * * *

When he finally woke he found himself in a large bed covered with an equally large quilt. A thick curtain across a dormer window was keeping the room in a hazy light. The only furniture was a bedside table and an ornate wardrobe next to an equally ornate door. He could hear talking and realised there was a little radio perched beside him to keep him company, tuned to Radio 4. He was warm and dry and dressed in pyjamas that he did not recognise.

The night before already seemed like a dream. How long had he been asleep? He stretched and at once felt an ache arch through his body. When he swung his legs out of bed, he was met with the sight of an ugly bruise spreading across his right ankle and foot.

He sat there for a moment. It hadn't been a dream. It had all been real.

He didn't know what to think. He lay back and let the voices on the radio soothe his mind.

Then there was a knock at the door and a very cheery voice asked for admission. The door opened, revealing a smiling Professor Stuckley with a tray of soup and a hot drink.

'Sam, you're awake at last! I brought this just in case. Have it now – you must be hungry. Then I'm sure we both have a story to tell.'

As the professor crossed the room and turned to face him, Sam saw that his eye was swollen and half closed and there was a small cut on the bridge of his nose.

'Yes, a trophy from the night before last, Sam, but it could have been much worse. Now come, please have your soup and then we shall go and eat properly downstairs and you can tell me your tale.'

'I'm guessing I'm still at the Eagle and Child?'

'Yes, you were found slumped against the door. You were exhausted and I don't wonder at it. You've slept for a whole day and night, so I'm sure you're feeling better now. I'm glad you came here. In fact I am very pleased you did. Now, I've had your clothes washed and ironed and they are in the wardrobe, so when you're ready, get dressed and I'll see you downstairs.'

With that, walking perhaps a little more stiffly than usual, the professor disappeared through the door as quickly as he had entered it.

Sam took a sip from the cup, then stood gingerly and drew back the curtain. He realised he was at the very top of the building, looking down on an avenue full of cyclists and students going about their business.

Sunlight washed through the small room and he took a deep breath and closed his eyes, letting the warm rays still his whirling thoughts.

The Shadow had been here, in Oxford. The sudden chill and the creeping fear in the pit of his stomach, the cold reach of something quite unknown that he'd felt in the passageway beneath the Fellows' House had been the same as on that winter's night by the Coquet. Why had it followed him from Warkworth? Why was it hunting him down? And how did Oscar and his enigmatic message fit into it all?

It was time to meet the professor and get some answers.

Leaving his soup untouched, he dressed quickly and opened the door. He'd never been on the top floor of the Eagle and Child before, and walking out into a narrow corridor felt just a little peculiar. But when he finally reached the ground floor, he was back in the friendly heart of one of his favourite places.

* * * * * *

The Eagle and Child was a welcoming pub. Long ago it had been the meeting-place of the Inklings. Now it was animated by some of the most enthusiastic bar staff Sam had ever met. It had a single corridor that ran the full length of the building and the smell of wholesome food would drift through the whole pub. Sam suddenly felt hungry as he moved quickly through the throng of drinkers.

He found Professor Stuckley in one of the porches at the front of the building, sitting directly in front of a large window that looked out towards St John's.

The professor was already halfway down a pint of Broughton Elderpower. 'I've ordered you sausage and mash,' he said with a benevolent smile.

Even though the early afternoon sun wasn't coming directly through the window, the professor's injuries were now in full view. His left eye was almost closed, the bruise was spreading to his cheek and his cut nose looked slightly more crooked than before. Despite this, he seemed in surprisingly high spirits. He stopped a staff member and asked whether he would be kind enough to bring him two more pints of Elderpower.

'So what happened to you at the Fellows' House?' Sam asked cautiously. 'And where is Professor Whitehart?'

The professor took a large swig from his pint. Setting it down firmly, he gave Sam a serious look from his good eye.

'We were attacked, Sam. They came through the window *and* the door. It was most unexpected. Professor Whitehart took a worse battering than me. He's resting with a friend.'

Sam kept his voice low, not wanting to be overheard. 'I nearly drowned in the river after going down that tunnel behind the bookcase, not to mention being pursued all the way from the house to the gates of Magdalen. Whatever broke into my room knew I was there and I am convinced...'

He stopped speaking as two full pints were placed on the table.

'I think you know what the Shadow is and why it follows me from place to place, and I think it would have done me great harm if it had caught me.'

The professor took another long drink from his glass. 'Sam,' he said, 'it wasn't the Shadow that attacked the Fellows' House. We don't know what they were, not for sure, but yes, it's clear they were coming for you.'

He kept his gaze on Sam, knowing that with every answer there would be further questions.

'I am worried,' he continued slowly, 'because of Oscar's message. He is the very last person I would have expected to turn up in the middle of Oxford. I thought that impossible. So tell me more about what you saw last night.'

He leaned forward, his good eye fixed expectantly on Sam.

Sam hesitated. 'I don't think I can,' he said awkwardly. 'I don't think I ever really got a good look at it. I glimpsed it at the gates of Magdalen, but this is the problem – it was only when it moved in front of solid objects that I could see anything at all. It was as if the night itself was coming together to form something, but I don't really know what. I always knew it was there, though – I could feel its hate and emptiness...'

Remembering, he trailed off and took a long drink of his ale.

'Especially in the house,' he added. 'In that tunnel.'

He paused, and it felt for a moment as if they were alone and the world had drifted away. Then the hum of the Eagle and Child broke the silence and they were both glad of it.

The professor sat back on his wooden seat, tapping the rim of his glass, a little flushed from the alcohol.

'Why didn't it strike when it had you then?'

Sam shrugged. 'It did chase me. It was at the gates of Magdalen that it came closest.'

'Hmmm…' the professor scowled and looked out of the window.

'At the gates, professor, I thought I heard the Magdalen choir.'

'It can't have been the choir – they aren't around during the summer months.'

'But that's not possible – I heard them that afternoon as well, when I was with you.'

The professor turned back to Sam and put his pint down on the table. 'The choir breaks for summer. There are literally only me, you, Professor Whitehart and Professor Lawrence left now in the whole of Magdalen.'

'Then what did I hear?'

'I don't know, Sam, I really don't. You might think I'm just trying to avoid answering your questions, but yesterday changed everything. That attack on the house was a stark warning that things have got out of hand. I am perturbed by what is unfolding, to be perfectly honest with you, and I don't think you can go back to the Fellows' House or anywhere near Magdalen. I think you should go back to your home in Newcastle until I understand what we are up against.'

'I think you do understand what we are up against,' said Sam quietly.

The professor sighed. 'Look, just put that to one side for now. I'd like you to come with me later to meet a few old friends. I've known them many long years and they may have the answers you're looking for.'

Sam looked down into his pint. He was sure the professor knew more than he was letting on, but he didn't have strength to keep confronting him.

The gloom was punctuated by the arrival of two plates, each with two large Oxford sausages poking out of a mountain of creamy mash, surrounded by a stream of thick onion gravy.

Sam felt his mouth begin to water as he smeared English mustard across the whole of his lunch. 'Come on, Sam,' he thought, 'cheer up.' Here he was in his beloved Eagle and Child, eating his favourite food and looking out on the captivating view of St John's bathed in crisp afternoon sunshine, and across from him was one of the most mesmerising academics he'd ever met. And they'd both survived the attack on the Fellows' House.

They ate in silence whilst all around the Eagle and Child ebbed and flowed like a fine kaleidoscopic symphony. But the mingled smells of a hundred dinners and the comforting clinks of raised glasses couldn't dispel the clouds that were gathering in their minds.

When they had at last finished, it was Sam who spoke first, his cheeks just a little flushed.

'So, who are these friends you would like me to meet?'

The professor pushed away his empty plate. Looking up, he said, 'I think you'll enjoy meeting them. I think it is safe for you to expect the unexpected.'

He drained the last of his ale and surprised Sam by standing up.

'I'm going to visit Professor Whitehart and make sure he's on the mend. I don't need to tell you to stay close to this place. Why don't you retire to your room and relax?'

Sam wasn't so sure he liked the idea of being alone with his thoughts. 'Is Oxford really that dangerous, professor? There *is* protection here. Someone came to me last night before the gates – a woman calling herself the Fall.'

The sound of the professor's glass shattering against the stone floor brought a momentary hush to the Eagle's throng.

'Does that mean something to you?'

But Professor Stuckley was on his feet, busy demanding the bar staff give him a dustpan and brush so that he could help clean up the shards of glass.

When finally the commotion had subsided and they were again by themselves at the table, he said solemnly, 'I would suggest, Sam, that you remember a little of what has happened over the last couple of days. Then you will answer your own question. I don't think it's safe to go out much past early afternoon. I will return later this evening and then we can both seek some answers.'

Gathering his jacket from the back of his chair, he popped his pipe in his mouth, picked up his long walking stick and clasped Sam's hand before leaving through the front entrance.

* * * * * *

The Eagle and Child was still busy when Sam retired to his room. The hum of Radio 4 slowed his thoughts, lulling him to a place just on the edge of sleep, a place where time quickens and in the blink of an eye several hours have passed.

When Sam raised his head from the pillow, the light from the window had dimmed, and when he looked down on St Giles, he guessed it was early evening. The room gave him a great vantage point, and although the street in general was a little less busy, across the many lanes he saw a group of people milling outside the Lamb and Flag pub opposite. There, right in the middle of them, his grey hair bobbing, framed against the crimson placard of yet another favourite drinking hole, was Professor Stuckley.

Sam watched as the group slowly broke up. One person walked north, a second turned south and a third turned east and took the path Sam had used, through the passage from Museum Road. Others crossed the road to the Eagle and Child and then turned left and right, disappearing from Sam's view.

Gathering at the university's watering holes was a well-known pastime for the older generation of Oxford academics and on an ordinary day seeing the professor with a group of people wouldn't have surprised Sam, but now he couldn't help but feel uneasy. This was no ordinary day. His ankle hurt and his body felt as though he'd spent a week doing back-to-back boot camps. It wasn't just how he felt physically either – his emotions were running wild. He had an unnerving sense of his own vulnerability, along with the growing certainty that he was being kept far too much in the dark.

He waited until the light from the window had faded, and still the professor was absent. By now his thoughts were dancing like burning candles in the darkness. What would happen tonight? Would there be another attack? Who knew he was in the pub? Was he safe?

He woke again to Radio 4 doing a retrospective on the 1950s. Someone had taken the cold soup from his table. Just as he was wondering how much time had passed this time, a knock at the door made him freeze.

This time the door was opened straightaway and the professor came in without an invitation.

'Quickly, Sam, we don't have much time. I have asked Professor Whitehart to meet us in the reading room. We only have a short window of opportunity to ask our questions.'

The professor seemed out of breath and excitement was written across his bruised face.

They went quickly down to the main part of the pub, where Sam was a little surprised to find the Eagle and Child preparing to close. One or two stragglers were bent over their pints, but the last of the light was quickly draining from the sky and the large windows now reflected the almost empty interior.

One of the bar staff was blowing smoke rings at a man who was trying to enjoy a last pint.

'Sam, don't look, keep going,' called Professor Stuckley. He hurried Sam past the bar and into the back of the pub.

Sam found himself in a long corridor with bare brick walls. For a moment he was puzzled – hadn't the décor changed since lunchtime? But then he broke into a huge smile. There, at the far end of the corridor, was the unmistakable figure of Professor Whitehart, the flash of his playing cards cutting through the smoky air.

When they reached him, Sam winced at the sight of the cut on his forehead. It had been freshly stitched. But Professor Whitehart was beaming. Surprisingly, he even gave Sam a hug.

'It's really good to see you, Sam. We thought we'd lost you for a time.'

'That's quite enough, professor,' growled Professor Stuckley. 'Have they called for us yet?'

'Not yet,' answered Professor Whitehart, 'but as you can see from the smoke, they have answered your call.'

Both professors looked tense. Who were they waiting for? Sam quickly glanced back the way they'd come. The Eagle and Child was in darkness, the bar staff and stragglers gone. But they'd been there only seconds earlier.

'Don't look back, Sam,' said Professor Stuckley.

He placed a hand on Sam's shoulder and guided him into the back room of the pub.

Sam could hardly see where he was at first. The room seemed to be filled with thick smoke and there were flickers and movements and faraway voices growing closer by the second. Then the haze dissolved into smoke rings hanging thickly in the air, accompanied by a distinctive cigar smell.

The room was larger than Sam remembered and the coiling waves of smoke were diminishing, revealing figures sitting around a large open fire. Although they were no more than ten feet away, somehow they seemed more distant. They all turned to greet their visitors and Sam thought he recognised them, but a strange flicker, like shimmering heat, stopped him from focusing on them. He strained to see clearly.

There was something else going on that made little sense. The fire had been piled high with wood and yet Sam could feel no heat from it. And what was that sound, like the wings of a hummingbird flitting around his ears? Was it static electricity?

Professor Stuckley moved forward into the firelight and the humming grew louder. Now Sam could taste electricity in his mouth and feel his hair beginning to stand on end.

'Thank you for coming.'

He couldn't tell whether the professor had spoken or whether the words had sprung from the air.

One of the figures was standing now. He seemed to be a stout man with a receding hairline, but Sam couldn't be quite sure.

'Professor, it's Jack. I trust you are well. We are trying to adjust to this new way of communicating. I'm not sure whether you can see us all, but we have Ronald and Charles here, both on good form.'

Sam watched as the other two men waved. One was dressed in a tweed suit with a fine waistcoat, the second was taller and possibly wearing wired spectacles.

Sam's eyes were beginning to water with the strain of trying to bring the men into focus. There was something about their names, too, that was unsettling. He tried to speak, but he was frozen to the spot.

At his side, Professor Whitehart was also motionless, his gaze focused on the men sitting on the opposite side of the reading room.

Professor Stuckley spoke again. 'I'm sorry about using the Way-curves, gentlemen. I am seeking answers to a riddle that has brought a new danger to Oxford. It appears the Underland is on the move.'

Sam felt his stomach tighten as he remembered Oscar's message from the night before.

'That is grave news, professor.'

It was the first man who had spoken.

'A Shadow has passed through the Otherland, Jack. And into the Mid-land. It entered Magdalen the night before last.'

The men were silent for a long moment.

'Is the boy safe?'

Sam felt his face burn and his heart beat faster.

'Yes. I have brought him with me. He sees and hears you.'

Professor Stuckley turned his swollen face to Sam and beckoned him forward.

He moved forward to stand next to Professor Stuckley, but when he looked at the men he was no closer to them. The room seemed split between darkness and light.

The first man spoke again. 'We have looked forward to meeting you, Sam. We knew the day would come, though we hoped it would be under different circumstances and in a different place.'

His voice seemed to form from the hum and electricity that were flitting from place to place like angry hornets.

Sam felt confused. 'Who are you?' he said bluntly.

As he spoke, he could have sworn his words were repeated with a crackle of electric charge. The men were now no more than a few feet away and still he couldn't focus on their faces. The more he tried, the more the picture broke and bled into a million vibrating pieces.

'That is a good question, a very good question.'

Sam realised the voices really did come from the thrum of electricity that he could now feel running the full length of his skin.

'We are the Keepers of the Druids, or the flow of souls, as Ronald once put it. I think, Sam, you know who we are, and that is all that matters.'

There was something uplifting and pure about the words. Sam was no longer hearing them but seeing their resonance dancing in the electromagnetic flow. It seemed to him that they really were far away, not in space but in time. And yet they were here now.

'We have been called to understand the nature of this Shadow,' the man was saying, 'for we always had an inkling about such things. Tell us what you know and in turn we will leave nothing unsaid. You deserve the truth. That is why we are here.'

Taking a deep breath, Sam began. 'I met a man called Oscar.' He stopped and closed his eyes so he could focus on what he was saying. 'I met a man called Oscar who brought a message that frightened me, even though I didn't fully understand it.'

He could feel the alarm in the buzz of electricity that for a second swarmed around his head like angry bees.

'He said the Circle was broken and the Shadow was moving through the Otherland.'

Again there were murmurs fizzing like light bulbs ready to pop.

'He said the Dead Water was lost and the Fall was dying.'

The electricity surged and for an instant Sam thought he could feel the heat of the fire. He opened his eyes. Professor Stuckley was looking at him and the figures seemed to be too, even though he couldn't see their eyes.

'He said the professors had to seek the help of the Three.'

'The Three!'

The words whistled like a kettle brought to the boil.

'He said there was a traitor who had done much mischief.'

Suddenly Sam could no longer swallow. It felt as though his mouth was full of sand. He looked down at the floor.

'Sam.'

He looked up. One of the figures seemed closer.

'I am Ronald. I knew your father. He would often visit the Eagle and Child.'

He paused, and Sam guessed he was smoking a pipe, as smoke rings were floating up to the ceiling, only to evaporate into thin air.

'We are mightily surprised to hear that Oscar has visited you here in Oxford. We haven't seen him for nearly a decade. It seems that he has been led to you somehow and we are guessing that our time to meet him again has come. So, tell us more about this Shadow.'

'You knew my father?' Sam was intrigued. He had never known much about him.

The question sent a hundred pulsating dragonflies spinning and the static electricity humming with greater intensity.

'If time weren't against us, Sam, we would tell you his tale. But your story must come first. Please, tell us about the Shadow.'

'All right. The first time I saw it was three hundred miles away in Northumberland, in a place called Warkworth. It tried to cross the river Coquet to get to me and it didn't manage to reach the shore.'

Sam took a breath. He still couldn't get a sense of distance between himself and the man called Ronald, and it was making him feel tired. Talking about the Shadow was also making him anxious. Where was it now?

'Then last night,' he continued, 'just after Oscar left, I was with Professor Stuckley when we were attacked. I escaped through a passageway and in the darkness I felt something menacing following me, but I didn't see anything.'

He stopped again. His throat was parched and his eyes stinging from the constant buzzing.

'Keep going, Sam,' the professor urged. 'Tell them everything you know.'

Sam could see the professor's swollen eyes willing him on.

'I heard the choir, though Professor Stuckley tells me they have broken for summer.' Again Sam had to stop. His voice was quivering. He took a breath. 'A woman came to me. She called herself the Fall. She probably saved my life. I don't know what to make of it. Perhaps I'm just going mad.'

As he had been speaking, the figures beyond his sight had been standing. Now Ronald spoke again, and this time his voice was slow and deliberate.

'Sam, we know how difficult this must be. Please do not question your sanity, for we know the Shadow to be real. It is a servant of the unspeakable horror the Druids named the Ruin. And we know of the Fall.'

'*We know the Shadow to be real...*' The words scattered across Sam's mind and seemed to bring their own despair. Blackness engulfed him for a second, then he felt the professor's arms around him, shielding him from a fear that seemed to fill the room like suffocating fog.

'I *knew* it must be real,' he whispered. 'It spoke to me beneath the Fellows' House. It said a single word.'

'What did it say?'

He could not tell who was asking the question, for the static hum was growing louder. Across the room he thought the fire was beginning to dim.

'*Druidae.*'

Sam heard an intake of breath from both his left and right. He felt Professor Whitehart move closer. By the fire, the three men became fragile forms in the flickering fabric of the room. Then they gathered together, almost as if on the other side of an unseen wall.

'I do not think it is prudent to stay much longer,' one of them said. 'Professor, where is the Shadow now?'

'We believe it is trapped behind the walls of Magdalen, but we cannot be sure. I have people watching every known path night and day.'

'You must avoid using the secret ways, for they are no longer safe. You cannot be sure that even this is without danger. Sam, we must leave now, but will consider what you have told us. Wait for our message.'

Sam watched as their colours began draining to black and white. Soon they were no more than shadows themselves, fading like smoke rings in the cold and dark reading room of the Eagle and Child.

The three of them stared and could not take their eyes of the wavering shadows until they too faded like smoke rings. They stood there for long moments, their eyes growing accustomed to the emptiness of the room.

Then Professor Stuckley took a deep breath. "We will stay here this evening. Tomorrow we will travel to Newcastle together and wait for the message.'

* * * * * *

The three of them walked back through the now deserted Eagle and Child, each with their own thoughts. In the quiet corridor outside Sam's room they wished each other good night.

Sam knew it must be late, as the shipping forecast was being read. Sitting on the edge of his bed, with the small lamp just doing enough to keep the darkness at bay, he rubbed his face and thought about the remarkable meeting.

How strange that conversation had been. Had the professor's friends actually been in the room or could they have been images of some kind? There had been a jitteriness about the scene, almost as if it was a newly painted picture, its colours still liquid, still moving... Then there had been Jack and Ronald's voices – he had seen and felt them rather than heard them. It was as if they hadn't existed as sound waves but as light waves, as if their thoughts had been carried on the electromagnetic flow. Was that how they had made the connection? And Jack and Ronald – could they really be who he thought they were?

He found himself shaking his head. If he was right then the world had just gone crazy. Or perhaps it was him.

He reached out to switch the lamp off and realised the letter that Oscar had given him was lying beside it. It was tattered, had been ripped in several places and was held together with Sellotape that was now discoloured and broken.Sam shivered in the warm room and immediately locked the door.

As he slowly opened the envelope, a piece of stained paper fell into his outstretched hand, giving off a strong smell of age and stale smoke. He turned it over carefully, revealing graceful handwriting long faded.

Dearest Sam,

It was such a pleasure speaking to you. It took us back to the first time we met your father all those years ago. We miss him very much. He would have been very proud of you.

Following our chat, I spoke with Jack for long hours over several days and we remain worried about your plight. We called a meeting with the rest of the Keepers only yesterday and we are certain that you are no longer safe in Oxford.

We took it upon ourselves to make a journey north to a place little known in these times, near the mouth of the river Aln in a place called Birling Wood. Our friend there is known to you as Oscar, but he is also known by many other names in many other places. We took it upon ourselves to mention your meeting with him and he was greatly troubled by your words.

He is convinced that chance brought you to him and that your own words were always meant to be brought back to you, for if they had not been then you may not have survived the night. We are deeply concerned about the paradox that has now been created.

As of the writing of this letter, we believe the Circle to be the famed Circle of Druidae. We know of the Dead Water and we have sent a separate letter to Professor Stuckley to tell him our thoughts about what lies there and what needs to be done. Our suggestion would be to leave in the morning at first light. Do not delay your journey or deviate from your path, for the Shadow will come again.

If there is a traitor in your midst, then beware of false prophets and wise men who are counselled by their fears. Seek your own counsel and do not listen to wisdom built on sand. In the days ahead the enemy will become your friend and your friend the enemy. The way ahead will sometimes appear to be the way back, but it will be the only way.

Remember, Sam, 'in the end it's only a passing thing, this shadow; even darkness must pass'.

We know that help will meet you on the way, perhaps through chance, if chance you call it.

With warm wishes,

Ronald

Sam read the letter several times, wondering how a letter that must have been written before he was born could offer him counsel.

Finally, he lay on his bed, his thoughts turning like a merry-go-round until sleep finally came for him, soundless and unannounced.

* * * * * *

In the next room Professor Stuckley was lying awake. His injuries were more serious than he had admitted to Sam and were painful. He was restless, too – the last few days had disturbed him in a way he had not thought possible.

He remembered the creatures that had tried to come through the window of the Fellows' House – their glittering eyes and beaked faces. Then they had been flung aside. He remembered lying half-conscious, blood stinging his eyes. The heavy oak shelves and furniture had been cast aside like the toys of children. What had entered had filled the room with such enmity that even now he could still feel its suffocating presence. He was alive only because it had not come for him – he and Professor Whitehart were irritants, nothing more. How Sam had survived the tunnel he could only imagine. Why had the Shadow not struck him then – when he was alone and without help? Or when it had found him before Magdalen gates? How had he been saved by the Fall?

He turned back to his own letter. He hadn't yet opened it. He'd been too busy ensuring Sam was safe and that the Shadow hadn't left Magdalen. He was also all too aware that he wasn't going to like some of the answers it would reveal.

He toyed with the envelope for several moments, knowing the long years it had waited to be opened. Then, with great trepidation, he pulled out the letter and read:

Our dear friend,

We cannot believe after losing James this year that we are once again facing a dying of the Fall.

We write this letter with the understanding that when it reaches you we will be gone from this world and the Fellowship of Druidae will be lost to you. We do not know what this Shadow is, other than it is a servant of the Ruin. It is significant that it is hunting Samuel.

If the Underland is moving, you should seek to keep ahead of the enemy, for there is a chance that it has already infiltrated your numbers. You can no longer travel through the Otherland, for the Shadow will be waiting for you. You must disappear for a while. Show your hand only when you understand the odds of winning.

Oscar speaks of a power that still dwells in the Dead Water. Our suggestion is to send your swiftest there to seek counsel.

*Great care should be taken, of course. You must move
quickly and become like the Shadow, silent and unseen.*

'Not all who wander are lost.'

Warmest regards,

Jack

Professor Stuckley laid the letter down and felt the weight of its words heavy upon his soul. If the Fall was dying and the Fellowship lost to them, what hope did they have of protecting the boy? He felt the sting of the Shadow's touch closing his left eye and knew that Professor Whitehart, in the next room, had been deeply affected. He had yet to speak about what had happened.

Professor Stuckley's mind burned with unanswered questions until he drifted into broken dreams where the Shadow was always just one step behind him.

* * * * * *

The Eagle and Child welcomed the sunshine coursing through its dark interior the following morning, though it couldn't lift the dark moods of the three people sipping their tea in silence. Professor Stuckley's bruised eye was now closed. Professor Whitehart was distractedly flicking his cards from hand to hand. Sam was staring out of the window, watching the flow of traffic along St Giles.

'Where do we go from here?' It was Professor Whitehart who broke the silence.

'We have breakfast and depart for the north and keep our heads down.'

'I was thinking once we've arrived in the north – what's the plan?'

Sam sensed tension between the two professors, but was too deep in his own worries to take much notice.

'I spoke with Professor Lawrence first thing this morning and our path to the train station is open. We accompany Sam to Gosforth and I'm afraid that's as far as my plans run for now.'

They ate breakfast in the company of their own thoughts until it was time to go. Professor Stuckley paid for their accommodation and they left the Eagle and Child to the babble of Oxford folk and literary tourists seeking breakfast at the meeting-place of the Inklings.

The walk to the station lifted their spirits and for a while their worries faded like green autumn leaves. Sam noticed they were being trailed, though – at one point he thought he saw Professor Lawrence duck beneath an archway, but when he looked again he was gone.

It wasn't long before they were boarding the 10.05 train with a five-hour journey ahead of them. Professor Stuckley had chosen first class and the carriage was quiet. Sam was travelling with only the clothes he had escaped in and was already wondering how he was going to explain this to his mother. As the sun's radiance burst through the carriage window, he reached over, closed the small curtains and closed his eyes. For a moment, he just wanted to shut out the world. As the train juddered and pulled out of the station, he wondered whether he would ever see Oxford again.

* * * * * *

The journey became a blur of swiftly changing landscapes that reflected the travellers' swirling thoughts. Professor Stuckley was pondering on who had really brought the Shadow to them and why. Had Sam brought it down on himself with his message to the Keepers, who had then relayed it back to Oscar? Or was he himself to blame? It was, after all, he who had called the meeting. But, he reminded himself, only to seek answers to the questions posed by the Shadow's appearance. He could see a paradox in time looming, and there was no logic to unlock the web of questions and answers in this vicious circularity.

Still his thoughts went round. Was the Shadow conscious? Was it using intelligence to track the boy down or was it like a spider weaving its web and trapping whatever came into it? Did that mean they were blindly walking into a trap? Oxford wasn't safe, but Gosforth could be even less safe, and it would bring Sam within striking distance of the Dead Water.

Jack's suggestion was to seek counsel at the Dead Water, but who would travel there? He'd been there with the Forest Reivers, but that was a decade ago, and if he went, who would be Sam's protector? If there was a traitor amongst them, who could be trusted? And who would come to their aid? The Dagda and his three daughters had been their allies in the past, but one was dying and it was said that the others now served only themselves.

* * * * * *

It was long hours before Durham cathedral appeared, sending its shadows across the city's cobbled causeways and crumbling chimneys. The hustle and bustle of travellers drained from the platform, the whistle brought the train alive and it jerked and began to move again. Newcastle was now only a few minutes away and Sam was looking forward to getting home.

Ahead the shimmering Newcastle bridgescape came into view, spanning the wide-flowing Tyne as it neared the end of its journey to Tynemouth, ten miles east. This industrial intricacy criss-crossing the Tyne was of Sam's favourite spectacles.

The train slowed to a crawl as it entered the arched span of the city's central station. Sam's relief was now audible – he let out a long sigh as the train jerked awkwardly, then came to a complete stop.

He and the professors merged with the hundreds of travellers hurrying out of the station in the afternoon sun. Both professors were walking more quickly than normal, clearly on edge.

It was late afternoon when they all alighted from a taxi in the rustic avenues that surrounded Sam's home in Gosforth. The professors stood on the pavement, looking just a little out of place with their Oxford jackets and bruised faces.

'Sam,' Professor Stuckley said, placing a hand firmly on his shoulder, 'I intend to seek further counsel. Try and remain safe. If the Shadow can catch you in Oxford, it can catch you here too. Let's meet tomorrow evening at the Seven Stories – say around eight, after it has closed.'

Then with a smile and a wave, the professors were gone.

* * * * * *

Sam stood for a few moments looking at the double gates of the magnificent Georgian house set back from Elmfield Road. They were shut and locked, for this was a closed world of high brick walls and long paths to ornamental doors. He found his key and smiled as the lock turned with a familiar clank. Then he slipped through the gates. The creak of hinges heavy with rust flooded the silence for a second and then he was turning the key behind him. This was a place to hide from the real world, a secret sanctum where he had spent many happy days with only his thoughts for company. He had described it to Angus as the last homely house on the edge of the Northumberland wilderness.

He walked quickly up to the large door and turned his house key. To his surprise, the door didn't budge.

Puzzled, he raised the ornate knocker.

From within, he could hear his mother's footsteps making their way down the long hallway and a second later her round face and glowing cheeks appeared from behind the door.

'Oh, Sam,' she half shouted as she reached up and gave him a bear hug. She dragged him through the door before bolting it firmly behind them.

'Why all the bolts?'

Sam had never set eyes on the bolts now anchoring the door firmly to the oak frame.

'Oh, burglars are about, Sam. Now, never mind that, let me make you a cup of tea and get some proper food into you.'

Sam didn't mind being smothered – it was all he'd known for the past nineteen years.

'Come along!'

His mum gave him no time for further questions as she turned and disappeared down the hallway towards the kitchen.

As tea, dinner and then pudding were served, Sam allowed himself to relax. His home was a large house with five bedrooms, two sitting rooms and what had to be his favourite room – a wonderfully ornate bathroom. He had spent many hours wondering about space and time whilst soaking in the large bath. What would happen if the world didn't have time? And if time didn't have space – then what?

Now, as the evening progressed, he felt himself sinking ever deeper into his favourite armchair. His old headmaster had told him that the Old English *Gosaford* meant 'a ford where the geese dwell'. To Sam, Gosforth was simply home.

Eventually his mother wished him goodnight, hugged him and retired to her bedroom. The warmth of her welcome, dinner and perfect brew had worked their magic. At long last Sam felt the dangers of the past few days recede and was ready for his bed.

Climbing up to the third floor, he found that his mum had prepared his bed and turned his battered old bedside lamp on for him.

His bedroom ran the full length of the house and had two dormer windows on either side. The ones at the back of the house overlooked a beautifully mature and well-tended garden, with a hundred-foot lawn ending at an imposing old red-bricked wall. A large oak tree stood in front of it, and hidden in its branches was Sam's old tree house. Normally, he loved to gaze out at the place where he'd spent so many happy hours, but tonight he pulled the curtains and shut out the view.

This had been another strange day, but he was safe now. He got into bed and fell asleep.

5

THE SEVEN STORIES

The Seven Stories bookshop was on seven floors of an old building nestling amongst the Victorian terraces behind the quaint Gosforth High Street. It had been in Emily's family for several generations. It was a mesmerising place of wooden floors, leather chairs and tall shelves packed with books both old and new. The same people would come in each week and sit hidden from the world behind its high-arching shelves. There was a constant flow of colour as books came and went, and in winter the fire's glow would be reflected in spine and jacket.

It had always been Emily's sanctuary and had become more so over the last twelve months, as her parents were heading for divorce. She sat back now in her favourite chair, enveloped in rows of books, whilst her Uncle Jarl's large frame could be seen bent over his little desk with its battered old till, his grey hair, as usual, standing up in all directions.

Emily was going into the final year of sixth form when the holidays were over. The past few weeks she'd felt rather disappointed that Sam hadn't come home and had distracted herself by throwing herself into helping her uncle manage the bookshop.

She'd been surprised to see how many strange folk had started appearing there and how many meetings had taken place on the seventh floor, in what her uncle called the reading room.

Way back in the spring she'd found Brennus and Drust Hood skulking around the back of the shop. When the Hoods turned up, trouble wasn't far behind. The last time it had happened, her uncle had disappeared for six months and come back with a limp.

Though her immediate family didn't mind the comings and goings of the Hoods, in her extended family there was a general mistrust of them. Emily herself had regarded them as swashbuckling heroes when she was little, but as she'd grown up she'd come to see them more as annoying uncles. She thought she had the knack of reading people, but Drust in particular was a closed book to her, and a hardback at that. He was the strangest of all the folks who had been visiting the bookshop over the years.

She'd arrived at the bookshop early today in the hope of seeing one particular visitor. She didn't quite know when Sam was coming back from Oxford, but she wanted to make sure she was there when he did. She required a serious explanation from him. He wasn't going to get out of this one so easily.

The ornate doorbell gave a shrill tinkle and she felt her cheeks redden as her eyes settled on the big-framed red-headed young man standing in the doorwaywith bright red cheeks as if he'd come out of a winter walk rather than last throes of summer.

'Good morning, Sam,' she said.

Sam smiled at her. Just for a second he felt a little giddy.

'Hello, Emily.'

Emily's dark brown eyes sparkled with mischief and Sam knew she had something to tell him that couldn't wait.

'Well, this is a surprise and a half,' said a voice from the till. Jarl Reign had stood. Despite the limp, he was soon across the short distance and giving Sam a hug.

'Come along, tea for our guest, Emily, and make your poor uncle a spare pot too.'

You couldn't help but like Emily's uncle. Sam had heard rumours, of course. His mother and her friends were convinced he was a spy – always travelling to foreign lands without a word and always coming back with a trunk full of strange artefacts and a scar to boot.

'Yes, uncle,' said Emily dutifully, but when she left it was with a little indignant skip and a flick of her long brown hair.

Jarl turned back to Sam and, to his surprise, his smile had been replaced by a grim look.

'I don't want harm coming to Emily,' he said abruptly, with an edge to his voice that stopped Sam in his tracks. Leaning a little closer, he added, 'These times are not for games. Whatever you have planned, keep her out of it. She is to stay here for the rest of the holidays.'

Stunned, Sam opened his mouth to speak and then closed it again. Emily was on her way back.

'Everything all right?' If she had noticed Jarl's uneasiness, she didn't show it. 'Come along, Sam, this way.'

Taking him by the arm, she ushered him past her uncle. Sam felt the big man's gaze still on him as he walked off through the antique bookshelves.

The bookshop was quiet save for the gentle shuffling of feet. The large leather chairs were empty. Emily led Sam back to her special place, surrounded by a decade of books that had delighted her. Flinging herself down on a leather settee in front of the fireplace, she told him to sit next to her. Instead he chose an armchair – though he had known Emily a long time, the closer he got to her nowadays, the more uncomfortable he felt. Emily Pauperhaugh was beautiful and intelligent, and Sam found her confidence a touch scary, especially when her intensity was focused on him, as it was now.

'What's happened to you, Sam?'

She was sitting on the edge of her seat like a coiled spring about to pop, but her voice was quiet. It was clear that she did not want anyone overhearing.

Watching her from over his teacup, Sam could feel his face beginning to redden.

'Erm...'

'Come on, Sam. I've read your letters to Angus.'

'What?' Sam felt a flush of annoyance pass through him. 'Those letters happen to be private!'

Emily ignored this.

'Listen, Sam, we need to get a few things straight. First, the thing you think you saw in Warkworth doesn't exist.'

'Wait a moment, Emily,' Sam put his teacup down, wondering how he was going to begin to describe the last few days. 'The Shadow is real. It followed me to Oxford. It found me at Magdalen!'

Emily scowled. 'I'm sorry,' she said firmly, 'I'm not going to let you continue with this. Not a moment longer.'

'I can't explain it fully,' Sam admitted, 'but Professor Stuckley and Professor Whitehart have seen it too.'

'Oh yes, Professor Stuckley and Professor Whitehart – your guardians from Cherwell College!'

'It's not just them,' said Sam defensively, wondering why Emily was being quite so scathing. 'I've met a group of academics who know about the Shadow. They knew my father too.'

He paused. If she didn't believe the Shadow existed, how was she ever going to believe what had happened over the past few days?

'They wrote a letter to me,' he continued carefully, 'explaining that I was no longer safe in Oxford, that I must head north. They said that things were beginning to move and that I must not believe all I heard, that I must not listen to wisdom built on sand.'

'Built on sand?!'

Sam continued, ignoring his friend's worried look. 'Emily, I know it sounds crazy, but the professors came with me and they only left when I was outside my home. Listen, last Tuesday I met a man called Oscar, who came with a message about a broken Circle. That night, the Shadow hunted me across the whole of Magdalen and I was rescued by a woman—'

'Stop! Sam, you're scaring me. You're losing your mind! You forget I was with you that night in Warkworth, it was me who found you in the garden, soaking wet, as if you had been for midnight swim, *and* I had to put up with you going on about a wave ten foot high in the Coquet – impossible!'

Sam sighed. It did sound impossible, he knew. He needed to find Professor Stuckley. If he explained the situation to Emily, she'd have to believe him. But he and the professors might be moving on again soon.

'Emily, I'm not sure how long I can stay in Gosforth. The academics I met in Oxford think the Shadow will come again.'

'Which academics?'

Sam was silent. How was he going to explain that he'd spoken to people from the past? He'd already said too much. All he was doing was alienating Emily.

'And where do you intend to go?' she snapped. 'This is ridiculous! Aren't you just taking some fantasy to extremes?'

'No, no. I have a letter that makes it real. I know it sounds a bit far-fetched, but, well, are you telling me reality doesn't stretch the truth from time to time? You can't always rely on logic, and you certainly can't trust reality.'

Emily frowned. 'You always come out with your physics nonsense when you're losing an argument.'

'And *you* never let me speak when *you're* losing one!'

Emily slumped back in her chair with a scowl.

'Whether you believe me or not,' Sam continued, 'the Shadow is real. Those academics knew about it, and maybe my father did too. I definitely felt it, *and* saw it, a second time. In Oxford. And I'm sure it intends to do me great harm.'

'Okay, Sam,' Emily drew a long breath, 'so if it *is* real, what is it? Where has it come from? Who sent it? What's its purpose? Why are you so important to it? Just think it through!'

She couldn't help feeling satisfied as she watched Sam squirm just a fraction.

'I can't say for certain, but according to Oscar, the Shadow is moving through the Otherland and the Dead Water is lost…'

Sam stopped again. He knew he wasn't doing himself any favours. Not with Emily already wearing a cynical hat.

'And where is this Otherland?'

She was starting to press home her advantage.

Frustrated, Sam said, 'We're only beginning to put the pieces together, but I can show you the letter.'

He pulled it from his pocket and held it out to her. She looked at it with distaste, but took it from him.

'The academics who wrote it were at Cherwell College,' he explained.

'Oh yes, the infamous Cherwell College! That's what I wanted to talk to you about. I'm your friend, or so you say– don't I deserve to know where you've been for the past term?'

Sam nearly choked on his cooling tea. 'Where I've been? Emily, what are you talking about?'

Emily shoved the letter in her pocket and took a gulp of her own tea.

'No one has heard of Cherwell College,' she said flatly. 'I rang the university three days ago when—' her eyes suddenly softened, 'well, that doesn't matter. But where have you been, Sam? Where did you go when you left Magdalen?'

'You know where I've been. I've been at Cherwell, studying under professors Stuckley and Whitehart.'

'But no one has ever heard of them, Sam! There *is* no Cherwell College and there *are* no professors Stuckley and Whitehart.'

Sam stared at Emily. If he hadn't known her so well, he would have thought this was a joke.

'Look, I don't know what this is about, or what they told you at the university, but Cherwell College is part of Magdalen. Professor Stuckley is a distinguished quantum metaphysicist. If he doesn't exist, then whose lectures have I been going to? I've been living at the Fellows' House with Angus. If this is about my letters to him, then let's talk about them. How did you come to read them anyway?'

Sam paused for breath and gave Emily a meaningful look, but she just scowled at him.

'Whatever you think,' he went on, feeling his face beginning to burn, 'two days ago I was pursued across Magdalen by – well, a wraith, a shadow, a thing! I felt it, and so did the professors, *and* it I heard it speak. If you think it's my imagination, then think again.'

He stopped, suddenly conscious that he was speaking loudly and the area around them was no longer empty.

'Look,' he continued more quietly, 'Professor Stuckley said he would meet me here tonight. If he doesn't exist, then we have nothing to worry about. If he does turn up then you can ask him why the Oxford University switchboard doesn't think he exists.'

'Coming *here*, Sam? Did you tell him about this place?'

'Er, no, I don't think I did mention it actually...'

'So let me get this right – you're meeting a professor who potentially doesn't exist in a place he couldn't possibly know about. Great.'

When Emily was mad, she would start stroking her hair and looking at her feet. Sam knew the signs only too well.

'All you have to do,' he said in what he hoped was a reassuring manner, 'is meet him here with me. He can answer any questions you may have.'

'Mmm. Well, we'll see, won't we?'

Emily wasn't satisfied, but as she looked back up at Sam, the warmth was back in her eyes. They sat for a while amongst the books, watching the odd customer arrive and depart, each lost in their thoughts.

Then Emily said, 'There's something I've been meaning to show you. Uncle Jarl's moved the reading room from the second floor to the seventh floor.'

'The reading room?'

'Yes.' Emily allowed herself a little smile. She'd known Sam would be intrigued. 'You know he's been part of a group who've been writing travel books. They've mapped out the whole of Northumberland and the borderlands now, from Warkworth in the south to Holy Island in the north. He says it's taken nearly a decade. Impressive, isn't it?'

Sam nodded. Looking down the full length of the bookshop, he could see Emily's uncle bent over a book, oblivious to their conversation.

'I don't really know why he's done it, to be honest,' Emily added. 'Perhaps it's to do with you, Sam, and your Shadow!'

Sam shook his head, but relaxed when he saw Emily's smile. She reached across and took his hand.

'Come on – let me show you.'

She led him through the baroque bookshelves with their carved insignias and profusion of multi-coloured spines, the softness of her hand making Sam's heart beat a little quicker. Then she dropped his hand and went ahead of him up the steep spiral staircase to the distant heights of the bookshop.

* * * * * *

Arriving on the last and most unfamiliar of the seven floors, Sam wiped a droplet of sweat from his face.

'I thought the seventh floor was unsafe. Won't we get into trouble? Your uncle can be quite a scary bloke.'

Emily turned and pressed a finger to her lips. In the half-light Sam thought she looked even more beautiful.

'Yes. He says the seventh floor is dangerous. He'll be annoyed if he realises I've shown you the reading room.'

Her eyes met Sam's. She was so close to him he could feel the heat from her body.

'Shhh.' She pressed her finger gently against his lips. Then, with a mischievous smile, she turned and walked down the corridor.

Sam followed her. The corridor twisted and turned and door-ways on each side revealed thousands of books piled high. He was intrigued by the smell and the soft glowing colours of this quiet place. It had an atmosphere all its own. For a moment he wasn't even sure how long they had been walking, or whether they had in fact walked at all. Looking back over his shoulder, he could no longer see the spiral stairway, only the long half-lit hallway.

Then Emily stopped so suddenly that he only just avoided knocking her over. She had brought him to a door.

Stepping forward to stand beside her, Sam looked at the door more closely. It was round and made of a wood he didn't recognise. It was knotty, with a maze-like pattern.

'What's this?'

Without answering, Emily drew a key from her trouser pocket. It was made of a dark metal unlike anything Sam had ever seen before.

'Wait!' Sam found himself reaching for her arm and pulling her back behind him. 'I think the door is changing – or is it the light?'

He stepped back and there it was again, a subtle flicker, perhaps a trick of the light, but certainly movement. With a gentle ripple, the pattern of the wood seemed to be on the move.

Sam was fascinated. 'I think it's a circle,' he said. 'Yes, that's it!'

Emily peered at the door, but to her, the wood was still and unmoving.

'I've seen this before!'

In the silence of the corridor Emily could hear the excitement in Sam's voice.

'You won't believe this, but it's the circle with the unknown tree – the emblem of Cherwell College!'

'Here we go again.'

'I know you don't want to hear this, Emily, but it's the truth. This emblem is on the door leading to the Fellows' Garden.'

'Yeah, right.' Emily had lost patience. 'Forget all that, I've something to show you.'

Before Sam had time to stop her, she had turned the key.

The door opened soundlessly onto a long room that seemed to run the full length of the bookshop. Four steps led down to a wooden floor in the centre, and high above, a glass dome sent a cascade of light arching across the interior. Under the dome, a circle of wooden chairs stood around an ornate round table. At the far end of the room, hanging from the wall, was what Sam initially thought was a blank tapestry, but then realised was an intricate map, a map whose colours were coming alive in the flickering sunlight.

He took in the grand view in silence, breathing in the smell of newly polished wood and marvelling at the resplendent fall of colour.

'My uncle doesn't like people coming up to the seventh floor,' Emily said quietly, 'but a couple of weeks ago he had guests over and brought them up here. I followed them and this is where they came.'

As she spoke, Jarl's warning came back to Sam and he felt his stomach lurch. 'I suppose you don't have permission to be here, Emily?'

'Of course not.'

Without waiting for a response, she skipped down the steps into the room.

'I've brought you here because there's a new map.'

Nervous but intrigued, Sam followed her. He had no sooner stepped off the last step than he felt a warm wind brush past his face. He stopped in his tracks.

Emily had stopped too, near the circle of chairs. She pointed to a giant parchment covering the table.

'Seeing as you've spent a year in Oxford, Sam, or so you say, you might be able to throw a little light on this.'

Sam stepped through the ring of chairs and stood beside her, his eyes settling on the parchment.

'Oxenaforda!' He felt himself taking a deep breath. 'It's a map of Oxford. It used to be called Oxenaforda, the "ford where the oxen cross".'

His eyes darted from name to name, whilst his hands moved over familiar places.

'Look, there's Magdalen College, Addison's Walk, Angel Meadow…'

The names were handwritten on the map in a beautiful flow of calligraphy crossing river and hill.

'This is everywhere I've ever been in Oxford,' Sam said wonderingly. 'In fact, it places Magdalen at its centre.'

Then recognition turned to unease. Someone had marked the map with a red line. It ran from the Fellows' House to the Cherwell and Bat Willow Meadow before continuing down Addison's Walk and through the Water Meadow to Magdalen College, across the Grove, up through Longwall Street and then along Holywell Street, cutting through the Lamb and Flag Passage and crossing St Giles before stopping at the Eagle and Child. Sam felt sick.

'It's not only a map of Oxford, Emily, but a map of my flight from the Shadow. Only the professors know the exact route. What's your uncle doing with it?'

Emily turned to him, her face a mixture of exasperation and concern. '*I* don't know, Sam.'

Suddenly there were tears in her eyes. She looked down quickly and turned the key over in her hand.

'What did you mean by the circle with the unknown tree?'

'It's the emblem of Cherwell College. Representing both the beginning and the end.'

'But there is no Cherwell College, Sam.'

'Then explain why there *is* a map of Oxford, right here, a map of the route I took to escape the Shadow.'

Emily sighed. 'I just don't know. Anyway, you've seen it now. Let's go – I don't think we should stay here too long, not with my uncle downstairs and people coming and going.'

* * * * * *

As Emily turned the key in the lock and headed for the lower floors, she felt bewildered. She couldn't help feeling upset by what Sam had said. He was becoming delusional, that much was obvious. Was he having some kind of breakdown?

But as she walked back down the corridor, she found herself wondering about the map. If Cherwell College didn't exist, why was it marked on it? And why was the map there, anyway? What was the connection to Sam?

As she reached the stairwell, a sudden thought made her stop in her tracks. She'd seen the emblem of Cherwell College before. But where?

She was still puzzling over it when she finally made it to the ground floor and saw a group of people mingling near the entrance of the bookshop and talking in hushed tones. She knew at once where they were going.

'Phew – that was lucky, Sam.'

Her uncle was already waving her over to say hello to a slightly built man with silver-grey hair and a neatly cut beard who looked as though he'd been in a ring with a bull.

'Hello, Emily. It's been a while.'

'Yes, I know. Rumour has it, Brennus, that you've been travelling with the Forest Reivers,' Emily replied smoothly. She hadn't seen Brennus since he and Drust had turned up in the spring, and then it had been just a fleeting glance. Now he looked as though he hadn't slept for a week, she thought, and how did he get that bruised cheek and black eye?

'Don't pay too much attention to those rumours,' he replied calmly. 'My brother and I have travelled with the Reivers in the past, but many seasons have passed since then.'

He was looking at her with eyes ringed by age, but there was an intelligence behind them. Her mouth suddenly felt very dry, her mischief ill-placed and childish.

Awkwardly she said, 'Oh, Brennus, I'd like to introduce—' but when she turned, Sam was missing.

Luckily Brennus had been distracted by a man who had just joined him. As Emily turned her head away, she realised her uncle was watching her, a slightly bemused look on his face.

'Emily, we're holding a meeting in the reading room,' he said. 'Could you do me a big favour and provide tea for five?'

Grateful for the chance to escape, she slipped from the ground floor into a side room used as a small kitchen.

Once she had delivered the tea to the reading room, she went to look for Sam. She found him on the first floor, hidden amongst the travel books.

'Where on earth did you go? I wanted to introduce you to Brennus Hood.'

'Brennus Hood? That man is Professor Stuckley.'

Emily groaned. 'Come on, Sam, let's talk outside.'

She led him down the spiral staircase to the back door. All she could think of was to get him out in the open and shake him from his delusions.

* * * * * *

As they walked out into the sunlight, Sam's mind was reeling. Why was Professor Stuckley using an alias? If he really was a spy, who was he spying for? Had *he* made the map of Oxford? How did he know Jarl? And Emily? Could he be the traitor? Were they safe here? There were too many questions. He was glad to be out in the fresh air.

Emily was leading him down quiet cobbled alleyways back to Elmfield Road.

'Let's get a cup of tea, Sam, and you can tell me all about it.'

She was sounding like his mother, she thought grimly.

As they approached his house, she watched him fumble for his key. He was pale and looking around him with troubled glances. 'How do you treat paranoia?' she wondered, as he locked the large iron gates behind them.

He walked towards the front door in a daze, then stopped. Something had caught his eye. He turned back.

In the tall ash trees directly across from his home, several crows were perching. The moment Sam looked at them, they became restless, hopping about. The hairs on the back of his neck prickled as they started cawing.

'What is it, Sam?'

'The crows. Emily, I saw them in Oxford not long before the Shadow attacked the Fellows' House.'

'Okay, Sam. Can we just get in the house and have a cup of tea?'

'Wait a minute.'

Sam was watching a crow flying up into the air. It circled once and flew directly towards the house, then wheeled sharply as it approached the high walls and alighted back where it had come from.

'Those crows look bigger than usual,' thought Emily uneasily, just as a second crow mirrored the first and turned sharply a hundred feet above their heads. 'And they *are* acting a bit oddly. Feels like they are watching.'

'Spying on us,' muttered Sam.

Emily jumped. 'Sam! Can we just forget about the crows…?!'

Then she jumped again, as a face was pressed against the iron bars of the gates.

Emily and Sam wheeled round to face the pale skin and bald head of Morcant Pauperhaugh, Emily's cousin.

'There you are, Emily,' he said. 'Your uncle has sent me to find you. He needs you back at the bookshop.'

He pushed at the gates, trying to open them. As he realised they were locked, a look of anger flashed across his face. For a split-second, he looked so malevolent that Emily and Sam both took a step backwards.

'It's okay, Morcant,' Emily said, trying to keep her voice steady. 'You can tell my uncle I'll be back later.'

Morcant tried to smile. 'Come on, Emily. Why don't you and Sam accompany me to the shop?'

As he spoke, a third crow took off, squawking as it flew straight over the house. Morcant stepped back, watching the path the crow took. When he looked back down, Sam detected a smirk. Or was it all in his head?

Morcant pressed himself up against the gates, his eyes darting from Emily to Sam.

'What's the matter with you? Open the gates!'

His hands tightened around the iron bars and Emily could see him testing their strength.

'No. My uncle can wait. I'm joining friends for tea.'

Across the road the crows were becoming raucous.

'Very well, very well, have it your way,' Morcant hissed, 'but I'll remember your hospitality when you need my help. And mark my words, there *will* be a day when you need my help.'

Then he was gone.

Sam quickly unlocked the door, ushered Emily through it, closed it with a thud and shot the bolts home.

* * * * * *

'I didn't like that confrontation one bit, Sam.' Emily was sitting at the kitchen table with her head in her hands.

'No,' Sam agreed, as he placed a mug of tea in front of her. 'I know he's your cousin, Emily, but I don't like that Morcant chap. I don't trust him either. He's definitely up to something.'

He sat down next to her with a mug of his own and gazed thoughtfully out of the large French windows and down the long lawn.

'And so's Professor Stuckley. Tell me what you know about him. And the man who was with him. The small one with dark curly hair and blue eyes.'

'Brennus and Drust?' Emily raised her head. 'They are brothers from Bamburgh. They are musicians.'

'No, Emily, they are the professors from Cherwell College who helped me escape from the Shadow.'

Emily laid her head back in her hands.

Sam stood up and went to the French windows, opening them so he could feel the sun on his face. For a moment there was silence.

'Okay, Sam.' Emily ran her hands through her hair and raised her face. 'I admit that the map of Oxford is a bit peculiar, but no one has seen the Shadow but you. No one knows anything about it but you. Are you sure—'

'Yes, they do. I know they do.' Sam spoke without taking his eyes from the garden. 'Listen, your uncle doesn't want you travelling with me this summer. He warned me off it as soon as he saw me. Why was that? I just don't know what to think. But when I meet the professor tonight, I swear I'm going to get to the bottom of it all.'

Emily looked down at the table.

'Look, I don't *want* this to be happening,' Sam went on. 'I'm scared, and I know it sounds crazy, but you have to believe me.'

'I *can't*, Sam!' Emily wailed. 'It's all so irrational. Colleges and shadows that don't exist and the only proof you say you have is a letter. Well, that could have been written by anyone.'

Sam didn't reply.

Emily took a sip of tea, trying to restore a sense of normality to the proceedings. She'd sat and drunk tea so often in this homely kitchen and Sam had been rational, intelligent, full of fun. He'd been a good friend for so long, someone she'd looked up to…

'You need to look at this.'

'What?'

Sam turned and banged his hand down on the table. 'You need to see this *now*!'

Jumping to her feet, Emily went over to the French windows and followed Sam's gaze out across the lawn, beyond the tall Victorian wall and into the trees beyond. Dozens of crows were perched there. One by one, they flew up, circled the green behind the house, headed for the garden, then wheeled sharply away and returned to the trees, some landing awkwardly.

'They're doing the same thing as the ones at the front,' she said thoughtfully. 'What is it?'

'Spying.'

Emily shook her head. 'No, please don't get paranoid, Sam, I'm sure it is some kind of normal crow behaviour.'

Even as she spoke, though, she felt uncomfortable.

Sam turned to her. 'Look, you should come with me to meet Professor Stuckley this evening. Then you can hear it from him that he's been with me in Oxford and that the Shadow is real, and perhaps he can explain how your uncle is involved in all this. Come on, Emily, you *know* something's happening. You saw the map of Oxford for yourself. And look at these crows!'

'It just sounds so irrational,' Emily said slowly, her eyes still on the crows. They kept heading towards the garden wall and then wheeling sharply to the left and right, almost, she thought, as if they had come up against an invisible wall.

'Exactly, so let's go and meet the professor and get to the bottom of this once and for all. If it's all in my mind, well, I apologise. I'll go and seek medical attention or something.'

'But if you're right, Sam, and this Shadow is real, then what?'

Then what? The question jolted Sam. He had momentarily forgotten the wider issue.

'You can't answer me, can you?' Emily was silent for a moment. Then she sighed. 'All right. I'll come with you to meet the professor. It's all I can do, isn't it?'

But Sam had stopped listening. He was watching the crows and their acrobatic performance at the end of the garden. There were now several in flight at once, rising and then quickly arcing towards the garden wall before pivoting left and right over and over again.

* * * * * *

It was early evening before the crows gave up their strange dance. Sam's mother had returned and cooked tea, and for a while normality had returned.

Still, Sam kept thinking about the map of Oxford – how could it have got there? How could Emily's uncle have known the route he had taken? And what about Professor Stuckley and Professor Whitehart calling themselves Brennus and Drust?

He still hadn't come up with any answers when he and Emily left his mother drying the plates and cutlery and set off for the Seven Stories.

'What is it, Sam? You look like you've been stung by a wasp.'

'I don't know, Emily. I feel like a caged animal – I just can't see the wire mesh.'

Emily was watching him closely. 'I don't like you talking in riddles. It usually precedes you losing the plot.'

Perhaps he *was* losing the plot, Sam thought. As the iron gates clanked behind them, he looked anxiously up and down the leafy road for any sign of the crows. The evening sun had turned Elmfield Road orange and red, and the first leaves of autumn were falling onto the cobbled pavement. Giant trees were leaning over red-bricked walls and blackbirds were darting from one secret garden to another, but, to his relief, the crows had gone.

The walk from Sam's house to the heart of Gosforth had always been a favourite of his. It was full of hidden service alleys and passageways, and each house was different from the next. This evening felt different – he no longer felt safe. As he walked, he was sneaking glances down the alleys, half expecting something sinister to rush out and accost him.

Beside him, Emily was still puzzling over the events of the day. She couldn't deny the map of Oxford in the reading room was just a little bit odd. And the crows. But no, she wasn't going to be drawn into Sam's world. Somehow she and her uncle were going to convince him that he must seek help. Obviously he was keeping his true mental state from his mother. That wasn't surprising – she'd been so glad he'd got to Oxford, it would be embarrassing to admit the pressures of life there had caused him to blow a gasket.

Emily admitted she hadn't expected that of Sam. He'd always been such a steady character. Certainly, she'd never known him lie to her. Could what he was saying now be the truth? The thought flitted briefly through her mind before being pushed into a dark corner. Walking beside him as dusk fell, she didn't want to entertain such a thought. As they took a short cut along a narrow path, she too began to watch out for crows. She was glad when they finally reached the bookshop.

In the darkness, the bookcases stood like sentinels. Emily stood in the foyer and listened, making sure they were alone. Then she turned and headed for the spiral staircase.

'Professor Stuckley doesn't seem to be here yet, does he? Let's go to the reading room. I want to take another look at that map of Oxford.'

Sam had rarely been to the bookshop when it was closed. Every noise was amplified sevenfold. It sounded as though he and Emily were wearing clogs as they walked up the spiral staircase. The metal handrail was cold to the touch. He wondered why she hadn't put on the light, then decided she was actually afraid of getting into trouble if they were found out. It was so unlike her, he almost laughed.

As they finally reached the seventh floor, they stole a quick glance at each other. The corridor looked a little sinister as they passed down it for the second time that day. Sam felt the edginess in Emily even though she remained silent. As she produced the key to the reading room, she turned to look at him and in the dim light her eyes were wide with fear. Then there was a click and the door was opening.

A cold stale wind stroked their faces. As Sam entered the room, he noticed that Cherwell's emblem was no longer etched on the door.

The reading room had changed –there was no longer a map there, or a tapestry, only piles of dusty books and chairs arranged in a circle.

'Are we in the right room?' Sam knew the answer, but needed to hear himself ask the question.

'Of course,' Emily replied, 'but they've moved the tapestry and the map. Why would they do that?'

'Do they know we've been up here?'

'I hope not – my uncle's already warned me against letting my curiosity get the better of me.'

'Just remember what it did to the cat.'

For the first time in days, Sam found himself actually laughing out loud.

'Shh!' Emily was afraid of them being heard, but she couldn't help smiling too.

Sam was shaking with laughter, then, without knowing why, he started to sob.

'Sam?'

He turned away from Emily and wiped the tears from his face.

'It's just been a bit much.' His voice quivered. 'There's just too much of this weird stuff going on. I don't blame you for not believing me. If I were you, I wouldn't believe myself either.'

Emily found herself swallowing a feeling of guilt. Unsure how she could comfort her friend, she reached out and gave him a hug.

Voices from outside the reading room made them spring apart. Both of them looked around wildly. There was nowhere to hide. The best they could do was to throw themselves down between an upturned table and a wall of unloved books. They lay there, hearts thumping, as people entered the room.

THE TAPESTRY

'I'm sorry for calling you back so quickly, my friends,' Jarl said, 'but Brennus has returned and it would appear that things are moving quickly. The Forest Reivers have been spooked – their rangers are talking of demons in the Cheviots and wolves in the fells.'

There was a chorus of alarmed voices. Sam and Emily pressed their faces against the books, trying to hear every word.

'I'm sorry to burden you with such news, but these reports have been validated along the whole of the borderland. The Way-curves are silent, so we remain blind to what moves against us. That is why I have asked you back here. It is essential we are not caught sleeping. I will let Brennus tell you the news he brings.'

Sam edged a little further to his left and through a gap in the books he could at last see those gathered around the table. To his amazement, one of them was his mother.

Professor Stuckley stood before them. He looked ten years older than he had yesterday. A great weight seemed to rest on his shoulders.

'The boy is in great danger,' he said. 'We can ill afford to let him out of our sight.'

He paused, letting his words wash over the assembled company.

'I warned him this morning not to venture into Northumberland,' Jarl said.

Sam let out a long breath. At his side, Emily put her head into her hands.

'It is clear the enemy is moving,' Professor Stuckley continued. 'In the last few days alone it has sought to neutralise our charge in Oxford and has moved quickly to cut off our path to the one thing that can guide our next move. If it succeeds, we will pay dearly.'

'Then what chance do we have here in Gosforth?'

'It is a good question, Morcant, and one I cannot answer. I do know there will be days when we won't trust one another. I also believe we face not one enemy, but two – possibly more.'

An uneasy murmur arose from those seated in the circle.

'There is a new danger that stalks the boy – a Shadow I have seen for myself.'

Despite their predicament, Sam heard Emily let out a little gasp of disbelief.

'We have been caught unawares and we have no defence against it. The boy is in danger and we have little time to move him. I sought counsel whilst in Oxford and now I must seek answers from the Dead Water.'

Consternation filled the room.

'I thought we said we'd never return to the Dead Water!' exclaimed Sam's mother.

Morcant was on his feet. 'Why the Faeries, Brennus? None of them can be trusted!'

'I sought counsel from the Keepers and that is what they advised. So that's where I'm going.' Professor Stuckley was adamant.

'This is madness!' Morcant cried out. 'Your fear makes you reckless, Brennus.'

'If you *don't* fear this thing, Morcant, *that* is truly reckless.' Professor Stuckley met his gaze calmly. 'There is a new malevolence out there.'

Professor Whitehart now stood, his cards flicking from hand to hand.

'Tell them what happened to you in the house of the Keepers,' he said. 'Tell them, brother. Tell our good friend Morcant what you suffered and what you gave of yourself.'

Brennus shook his head. 'Drust, now is not the time…'

'Of course!' thought Sam. 'That night in the Fellows' House Professor Stuckley called Whitehart Drust!' He tried to meet Emily's eye, but she had her head turned away.

'I've been following the boy for almost a year,' Drust said firmly, 'had him under close observation for months, and still we've been negligent, we've been caught asleep, we've let this abhorrence walk right past us.'

'Drust,' warned Brennus.

Drust ignored him. 'There is nothing in this world that could have unpicked our defences at Magdalen, or walked into the Keepers' house. I see your shock, friends, but shock will not defeat it, and there is every chance that it will follow us here. The calm has now passed and we must await the storm that will bear down on us all. Oscar visited the boy and told him the Circle was broken and a Shadow was moving through the Otherland. If that doesn't chill your hearts then we've become fools in our complacency.'

There was stunned silence.

Brennus broke it. 'There is something that worries me greatly – the Keepers say that we could face several enemies. It is important that we understand where this new one crossed. I must travel to the Dead Water.'

One by one, he looked at the faces of those gathered.

'Later this evening I will meet the boy and will ask him to go there with me. You must make sure the way is safe.'

'You'll take the boy there?' Morcant cried out. 'You'll take him north as our enemy moves south? Wouldn't it be wiser to take him back to Oxford? Or to some other place?'

'If the Fall is diminished, he won't be able to outrun the Otherland and no place will be safe. It is time to do the unexpected, take the enemy by surprise. This is our only hope.'

Morcant let out a long sigh. 'We've spent nineteen years doing nothing and now we can't do enough in no time at all.'

Drust laughed. 'Yes – come along, brother, you must have an inkling why!'

Brennus sighed. 'I'm sorry I can't raise a smile to your humour, Drust, but I'm tired. It has been a long few days and protecting the boy is very much on my mind. You know the Fall is trying to speak to him and that she speaks to those touched by the flow. *You* know that better than most. We have to protect and nurture him.'

'Yes, but do you actually know how?'

'I do know,' said Brennus carefully, 'that the enemy will have learned much from its encounter. It knows the boy does not walk alone and it knows what protects him. It won't seek a confrontation directly, but will come upon him by stealth.'

Sam could barely control his anxiety. This was a conversation that he and Emily shouldn't be overhearing. He took no satisfaction in her baptism of fire – he was too frightened by the knowledge that he was caught up in all this more deeply than he could ever have imagined.

'He may not walk alone,' Drust replied, 'but it was chance that he survived – chance that brought him safely to the Keepers. That's all.'

His eyes were glittering in the light cascading down from the windows high above.

Brennus was calmly observing him. 'That is your conviction, but it is not mine. I have more faith than that. Come now, we need to prepare for the journey ahead. I am to meet Sam later this evening and I'll persuade him to come with me then.'

'I don't want Emily travelling with him.' Jarl's voice was low and Sam could hear his anxiety. 'Are they even going to be safe tonight? Should the boy stay with me?'

'That is a good point, Jarl, but why not allow him one more night in his own bed? It may be his last for a while. And then let's hope that both faith and chance travel with us.'

'We may regret this, but—'

Jarl broke off as a pile of books went crashing the full length of the wooden floor.

'I see we have company – why don't you join us?' Professor Stuckley said smoothly.

He smiled warmly as the plume of dust settled and Sam and Emily got to their feet.

As they shuffled nervously forward, Sam could hear Emily trying to swallow. Briefly he felt her hand touching his. She looked over at her uncle, but he too seemed suddenly uncomfortable in his own skin.

'Emily,' he said, gathering himself together, 'I really don't know what you're doing here and I'm afraid you can't stay. Brennus would like to speak with Sam in private.'

'Oh, no,' thought Sam. He could imagine what her response was going to be to that. But her usual cheekiness seemed to have sunk to the bottom of her feet. Then she spoke.

'All right. But before I leave, Uncle Jarl, I'd like to know...'

It seemed her embarrassment had simply delayed the inevitable. Sam wondered how she could be so brazen. But before she could continue, Brennus interrupted her.

'She would like to know,' he said, with a hint of a smile, 'why I go by different names in different places.'

'Yes! I've never heard anyone call you Professor Stuckley, but Sam seems to think that's your name.'

Sam sighed. But Brennus was smiling openly now.

'I am known as Professor Stuckley in certain places.'

'Not in Cherwell College, though, because no one at Oxford has heard of it!'

Sam winced. But Brennus's smile remained.

'I understand your frustration, Emily. There is much to say and little time to say it in. What I can say for certain is that Cherwell College is real. It meanders through places in time, not unlike the river itself, places that cannot be easily remembered by the many, or forgotten by the few. It is a kind of physical and metaphysical crossroads.'

This time he let the words settle upon her with the weight he had intended.

'I understand that blind faith can lead you down blind paths and that without questions there can be no answers,' he continued. 'But know that it wasn't by chance that I happened upon Sam in Oxford. If you can suspend your disbelief for a moment, you might begin to understand that the world is far stranger than you could possibly imagine.'

Sam could feel Emily prickling at the professor's words. He had stolen her thunder almost without effort. Her cheeks were flushed and Sam couldn't help but think she looked even more beautiful like that.

'Now I must speak to Sam in private, Emily, and you must not feel hurt.'

Without a word to anyone, Emily allowed her uncle to put his hands on her shoulders and propel her out of the room.

* * * * * *

Brennus emptied the room apart from himself, Sam and Drust. The space suddenly felt much bigger.

'Sam, come and sit with us and I will explain what I can.'

Sam placed himself down on a hard wooden chair.

'We have news that the Shadow is no longer imprisoned in Magdalen.'

'Where is it?'

'We don't know for sure, but there's no doubt where it's heading.'

Sam felt his mouth go dry. 'How long do we have?'

'It isn't a question of how long we have,' answered Drust, 'but when it chooses to strike.'

He was sitting quietly, his eyes following the incessant flow of his cards passing from finger to finger.

'The Shadow has access to the Otherland,' he continued, 'and therefore time has little meaning anymore. The one advantage we had was taken away by your meeting with Oscar.'

He stopped his card play and looked at Sam. In the harsh light, the wound to his forehead seemed longer and deeper than it had the day before.

'A good point,' said Brennus, 'and we can ill afford to have a repeat of Oxford. We need to understand how it can be defeated. There is a place where we can seek help. I have travelled there myself over the years to seek counsel. And they have never let me down.'

'I'm guessing we're talking about the Dead Water?'

'Yes, Sam. I think it has become our only option.'

'Didn't Oscar say it was lost?'

'We're not sure about that. Paradoxes are hard to break. Oscar could have been doing nothing more than repeating your words to the Keepers. After all, they travelled to meet him in Alnmouth and gave him the letters to give to you. There may actually be no truth in it.'

'And if you're wrong?'

'Admittedly, we could be wrong. We thought you would be safe in Oxford.'

'You can't keep it from him, brother.' Drust had resumed his card play. He kept his eyes on his cards, turning them over one by one, but there was an edge to his words, a tension that Sam could hear.

Brennus took a deep breath. 'Listen, Sam, the Shadow passed through Gosforth in the early hours of the morning. We lost it in the woods north of here. We have no time – we must leave for the Dead Water tonight. We cannot wait until the morning.'

The words swam through Sam's mind, but he couldn't grasp their meaning. How could the Shadow have travelled three hundred miles in such a short time?

'What if we don't find a way to stop it at the Dead Water, professor? What if it catches us on the road there? What if it can never be stopped?'

He felt chilled by his own questions.

His words had struck a note with Drust. He stood, a fierce look in his eyes.

'Sometimes, Sam,' he said, 'you have to face your nightmares in the dark. You have to face your fears or you will forever be in their shadow. Your only chance now is to travel with my brother Brennus. He will protect you.'

'But do we really have to travel tonight? In the dark? I think it will increase the danger.'

'If we don't go this evening,' Brennus said, 'I can't guarantee your safety. Also, if we stay, it won't be just you in danger, but those who wish to protect you. The woman who came to you before the gates of Magdalen is real. I believe the answers are to be found from her kind, at the Dead Water.'

Sam felt as though every word was pounding him into the ground. He covered his ears with his hands.

'Sam, you must listen to me,' Brennus continued. 'This Shadow, it is a foe whose strength and power I've never felt before.'

'Enough!' shouted Sam. '*I* know its strength and power. *I* faced it under the Fellows' House and at the gates of Magdalen, and believe me, *I* know we have to find a way to stop it. I want to do that. And then I want to go back to living a quiet life with what remains of my family. I don't want to be afraid every minute of every day. And now I want to go back to my house and sleep there for just one more night.'

Brennus stood and put a firm hand on Sam's shoulder. 'I understand.' His face softened as he held Sam's gaze. 'We'll meet at first light.'

With that, he turned and walked towards the door.

Sam felt Drust pat him lightly on the back as he too left the room.

* * * * * *

Sam sat there for a moment in silence. It had been a crazy few days. At least Emily now knew some of the truth.

His eye was caught by the tapestry on the wall. It was back – how come he hadn't noticed that before? And it was spellbindingly intricate. He marvelled at its colour and depth. Quite what it portrayed was more difficult to say. He'd thought it was a map earlier, but perhaps not. He got up and went a little closer to it.

He was trying to decipher the long-faded outlines when something caught his eye. A subtle movement – the tapestry was swaying as if caught by a gentle wind.

All at once, a swarm of invisible hummingbirds were darting through the reading room. The air was crackling and Sam felt an unseen hand ushering him away from the wall and down the steps onto the wooden floor. Static electricity brushed against his skin with a million little spikes and his hair was standing on end. A sulphurous hiss was making his nose run and all his senses seemed heightened. The reading room was coming alive, even as it was fragmenting before his eyes.

The tapestry began to dance, its woven strands unravelling in a blur of movement. The hummingbirds broke up into a thousand vibrating shades of moving colour and exploded against the tapestry in a pixelated shower of light. Sam was transfixed as a mesmerising flow of images passed before his eyes.

A steep hill with a castle appeared, ebbing and flowing with each turn of the swirling birds. Fascinated, Sam felt himself reaching out to the rippling material, unable to stop himself from touching it. Instantly, a vibration ran through him, a cold resonance that hummed and flickered in his mind's eye. A room appeared, full of light that flooded the canvas with a warmth that Sam could almost feel, a radiance that formed around a figure standing motionless at the centre of it.

The room was the very one that Sam was standing in and the figure was Oscar.

'*Sam!*'

In the clamour of the kaleidoscopic sea, the voice anchored his feet to the floor and he remembered who and where he was.

'Why have you called me? The Way-curves are no longer safe.'

The words fizzed and popped in his head. He opened his mouth, but his words were already there in the weaving streams of colour.

'I have been asked to go to the Dead Water.'

Suddenly the colour and light drained out of the tapestry like sunlight draining from the sky at twilight. In the blink of an eye it went black. Sam felt the pressure in the room drop. For a moment he didn't know which way was up or down. Darkness swirled around him and he was back in the river Cherwell, cold and afraid.

Then movement caught his eye. A deeper darkness was taking shape and a place he did not recognise was flickering out of the tapestry weave. A single figure was hunched in the gloom. It had its back to him, but Sam felt a new panic boil up through his stomach. He knew what it was before its image had fully formed. It had heard Oscar's words and was standing slowly, a black-hearted stalker reaching for him through time and space.

A single word reached him, spilled black against the streaming light: '*Druidae.*'

Then it was gone.

Light flooded back into the room and the air hummed and hissed with a hundred thousand tiny wings. Oscar was standing once more in the shifting colours of the tapestry. Or was he here with him in the room?

'I told you the Way-curves were no longer safe.' He seemed to be breathing heavily and looked exhausted. 'Quickly now, listen.'

His words waxed and waned in the charged air that swarmed across Sam's face, prickling with energy.

'You cannot go to the Dead Water.' A picture of a mountain range gleamed against the glowing shards of light. 'The enemy killed your father on the shores of the Dead Water. Now it knows you are going there. Do you want history to repeat itself?'

An angry roar exploded and somewhere far away the noise of shattering glass echoed in the darkness. Sam stood in the middle of the streaming light whilst the vision of Oscar momentarily fluttered.

'The Keepers came to me in the mouth of the Aln. Set your path to Warkworth and find me in Birling Wood. The Forest Reivers will come down from the hills seeking counsel. Your paths will cross.'

And then the swarm of pixels broke up and he was gone.

* * * * * *

Sam felt the solid floor beneath him and he was no longer riding waves of light and colour. The tapestry was blank, the tiny humming-birds still. Then he heard a snap high above him.

A thin crack appeared on one of the giant panes that covered the glass dome of the reading room. There was another snap as a second pane cracked. Figures were scurrying backwards and forwards on the domed roof.

Sam stood in the middle of the room, both transfixed and terri-fied, watching as dark shapes thudded down on the glass far above him, opening up a myriad of smaller cracks.

Behind him the door opened.

'Sam, I am to accompany you and Emily,' Jarl began, then stopped as he followed Sam's gaze. 'What's happening?'

'There's something up there.'

Without taking his eyes off the splintered panes, Jarl took Sam by the shoulder, twisted him round to face the door and led him out.

Back in the long corridor connecting the reading room to the spiral stairway, Sam watched Jarl close and lock the round door before racing off down the ill-lit corridor, seeming to forget Sam was there.

'Wait!'

Sam hurried after him.

As they reached the spiral stairway, the air was filled with the noise of shattering glass. Whatever had been on the roof had broken through.

Sam stopped, eyes wide.

'Leave it,' Jarl snapped. 'Come quickly.'

He disappeared down the spiral staircase at frightening speed.

Before he had hit the bottom step, he was shouting, 'The reading room is breached!'

The professors and Emily were standing in the foyer.

'Take Emily back to Sam's house,' Brennus said quickly. Then, without another word, both professors were running towards the staircase.

Sam felt Jarl's grip on his shoulders, propelling him and Emily towards the back of the shop. At the back entrance, Jarl placed his key in the door and started turning it. Then he stopped.

'What is it, uncle?'

But Emily's uncle didn't answer. Instead he quietly pulled the key from the lock and stepped back from the door.

'Uncle?'

This time Jarl pressed a single finger to his lips, signalling to Emily to be quiet, before leading her and Sam back into the main foyer.

Shadows were moving against the blinds of the shop front. With one grim look in their direction, Jarl led Sam and Emily up the spiral staircase to the third-floor landing.

Sam was familiar with this floor. It was one long room with chairs of all shapes and sizes strewn haphazardly in all directions and dark shelves filled with second-hand books on ancient history.

Silent and unsmiling, Jarl marched him and Emily to the far end of the room, where a window overlooked the roofs and chimneys of the nearby houses. In the distance they could see the trees of Elgy Green. Somewhere between here and there was the safety of Sam's house.

'Stay here.'

There was an edge to Jarl's words, a bluntness that froze Sam and Emily to the spot. They watched the big man limp back through the leather seats and worn chairs.

'What's going on?' Emily whispered.

Sam hesitated. He didn't want to scare her out of her wits. Then again, would she believe it anyway? How could he even begin to tell her about the tapestry? But at the very least she had to know what was happening now.

'I think we are being attacked.'

'*Attacked*? By who?'

Twilight was fading fast, throwing the long room into darkness. Sam shivered.

'You know who. Or what. I'm not saying another word – I'm not giving you another chance to tell me I'm—'

He was struck dumb by the sight of the creature that pressed itself against the window. Without thinking, he pushed Emily away, onto a leather chair. It tipped over and they fell together, with his hand instinctively clasping her mouth. Upside down, they stared at each other in the darkness, their breath loud in each other's ears. Then came the screech of claw against glass.

Any minute the black feathered creature would be in with them. Sam forced Emily to her feet and pushed her back from the window towards the stairwell. They stood in the dark corridor, listening to the distant sound of shattering glass.

Sam wasn't sure whether to go up or down. He thought the noise had come from above, but other noises were starting to drift towards them, muffled shouts that were faint but disturbing. Still, there would be safety in numbers.

'Quick,' he whispered, 'we'll go up and join the others.'

With Emily now gripping his hand with a strength born of fear, he led the way up the staircase.

When they finally reached the seventh floor, he paused. The corridor was empty, but they could both hear desperate shouts from within the reading room.

'Who are these people?' Emily asked, her face pale.

Sam shook his head. There was no time to figure that out. He just had to get Emily to safety.

'Is there any other way out of here?'

Emily nodded. 'You can cut through into the other shops from the loft. It runs the full length of the street and brings you out in the Quaker meeting rooms.'

'Where is it?'

This time it was Emily who led Sam, gripping his hand tightly as she pushed past a double door to a square loft hatch just beyond their reach.

'Somewhere there's a pole,' she muttered, looking around frantically. Then, as further sounds of splintering glass reached them, she gave up and called, 'Sam, lift me up!'

Sam didn't waste a moment in lifting Emily's slender frame towards the hatch. She hooked a finger through the metal ring and pulled. A plume of thick dust burst down on them, followed by a wooden ladder. Emily clambered up, with Sam only a second behind. He reached back and with a grimace pulled the ladder back up behind them and replaced the hatch.

Darkness and dust rolled over them. Emily coughed, then stuffed her hand over her mouth as muffled noises came from below. They grew closer, then disappeared. The corridor fell silent.

A single light bulb flared.

'That's better.' Emily looked around her. 'If I remember rightly, there's a small wooden pathway that joins the lofts together.'

Just as she spoke, the bulb popped in a spark of light that sent flashes across Sam's vision.

'Oh no!'

Emily continued her search in the darkness. Every now and again there would be a screech as she bumped into something. Sam stayed still, steadying his breathing, trying not to think about what might be happening down below.

'I've found it.'

Sam followed her voice, scrambling on all fours, his hands sinking into decades of dirt and grime. Unsure of where she was, he bumped into her. Just for a second she held him in the dark and he had the wild feeling that he was safe.

As his eyes grew accustomed to the gloom, he realised they were both on a wooden ledge. Crawling on all fours, they made their way slowly along it, through the loft of the Seven Stories and then through a small dividing wall that separated it from the next building.

As they moved from one building to the next, Emily kept calling back to Sam, making sure he was all right. He was surprised by her bravery, although he knew she still didn't fully appreciate their predicament. He was alone with that.

His options seemed more limited than ever. He couldn't go back to Oxford and it was clear that he could no longer stay in Gosforth. Professor Stuckley wanted to take him to the Dead Water, but Oscar had warned him against it. Was that because the enemy was already there? Hadn't Professor Stuckley mentioned that they'd let the enemy get ahead of them?

Sam sat back on his heels and shivered, despite the stuffiness of the loft. What was he supposed to do? He was running away again, but how could he turn and fight? He didn't even know who the enemy really was. The thing he had seen at the window was different from the Shadow he had faced in Magdalen and he shuddered as he remembered its feathered face.

Pushing the thought aside, he set off again, only to hit his head on Emily's behind. She had come to a sudden stop.

'What is it?'

'The ledge has come up against a wall. I think we are over the Quaker house. We just need to find a way down. There'll be a hatch somewhere.'

They couldn't see a thing, so there was no option but to run their hands through the matted woollen insulation of the loft. Every now and then Sam would touch something furry and dead and pull his hand back in disgust. Not far away, Emily couldn't hide her distaste and kept letting out little screams that made Sam jump.

'Can you stop that?' he hissed.

'I can't help it. Hang on, it's here.'

A blast of warm air met them as Emily raised a hatch and lowered herself down a flight of wooden stairs. They gave onto a short corridor that led to a grand staircase. Emily knew it well, as on her lunch breaks from the Seven Stories she would often go to meetings in the Quaker house. She swept down the staircase and on through the quiet house.

As she walked, her uncle's face kept coming back to her. She'd heard his voice amongst the shouts in the reading room. There was starting to be something very real about this. She reached out and took Sam's hand. It made her feel safe, but she also wanted to reassure him that he was not alone.

She led him on through a number of double doors until at last she brought them to the large oak doors that would lead them straight out onto the road. They were locked solid.

For a moment, Emily and Sam leaned against the doors, still holding hands. Emily had an unsure look on her face.

'What is it?' Sam asked quietly. 'Don't worry – there's bound to be a window we can open.'

'It's not that. I'm scared. I saw the look in my uncle's eyes earlier on and he was scared too. So I have to know – what are we involved with and who can we trust?'

'I'm not sure,' Sam admitted. 'So much has happened in the last five days it's all got jumbled up. But Oscar says we have to go to Warkworth, so that's what I intend to do.'

'Can you trust him? There are so many different opinions – someone has to be wrong.'

'I know, but someone has to be right, and the Dead Water seems like a step too far. I don't know where it is, or where Professor Stuckley is now, and I don't know what Oscar meant exactly about history repeating itself, but I don't like the sound of it. We both know Warkworth and we can always go and stay with your cousin Eagan.'

'My cousin Eagan? He spends most of his time chasing fairies in the woods!'

'That doesn't sound too crazy after this week.'

Somehow, they both managed to smile.

THE GRIM-WERE

Once again Sam and Emily were drinking tea in Sam's kitchen, this time in silence.

Despite his earlier words, Sam was inwardly debating whether he should take the advice of a man he had met only briefly or that of the professors who had saved him in the Fellows' House. What had Ronald counselled in his letter? Beware of false prophets and wise men taking decisions based on fear? Was Professor Stuckley making such a mistake? Or was Oscar?

Emily kept opening her mouth as if to say something but then thinking better of it. What *could* she say? Professors Stuckley and Whitehart had said it all. Sam was being pursued by something that could not be stopped. There was something fantastical about it all, but she had just fled on her hands and knees from an attack on the bookshop, and who could tell where Brennus, Drust and her uncle were now? Where was Sam's mother? There was definitely something going on and there was no longer a sensible way of denying that Sam was in the middle of it.

'Do you still have the letter I gave you in the bookshop?' Sam's question interrupted her train of thought.

'It's here somewhere.'

She fumbled in her pockets and took out the envelope. Already crumpled, it was now looking even more bedraggled.

'Read it out loud.'

She opened the envelope and drew out the letter, surprised by the elegance of the handwriting with its intricate loops and the fact that even though it was battered and faded, the insignia of Cherwell College could still be seen on the headed paper.

'Look, Sam, there's a tree here in a circle.'

'Just read the letter, Emily.'

'I know I've seen that somewhere before.'

'*Emily.*'

'All *right.*'

Emily took a deep breath and read:

Dearest Sam,

We hope this letter finds you well.

Oscar came to us again seeking counsel. He tells you spoke with him using the Way-curves on the second night after you left Oxford. There is a chance that these words may not find you until it is too late. If you read them now then take great heed. Professor Stuckley will ask you to go with him to the Dead Water. The enemy knows you are taking this path and will be waiting.

There is a new threat that stalks your protectors. With the fading of the Fall, the creatures known as Grim-were have awoken in the Underland. They will await their mistress when the Dead Water is finally lost. The Underland is moving and the Otherland is again seeping into this world. You can ill afford to delay your departure.

The way ahead will sometimes appear to be the way back, but it will be the only way.

With good wishes,

Ronald

'It's completely different!' cried Sam. 'It bears no resemblance to the letter I read in the Eagle and Child!' He paused. 'So the enemy definitely knows I'll be going to the Dead Water. I can't go there.'

'I thought you'd already made up your mind to go to Warkworth,' said Emily, frowning over the letter.

Sam took it from her.

'Listen, I'm leaving tonight and I think you should come with me.'

'Sam, you can't just pack your bags and go in the middle of the night! If you aren't safe in your home, then how will you be safe travelling across Northumberland?'

'Well, I'm not safe in Gosforth. The bookshop's already been attacked. I'm not staying here, Emily, and neither should you.'

'And where's this going to end? Once we reach Warkworth, where then?'

'I don't know, but if I find Oscar, I'm sure he'll be able to help. If the enemy is at the Dead Water, that's our only option anyway. We pack, we get what sleep we can and we set off at first light.'

'And how do you propose we get to Warkworth with all this going on? We can't even travel to the bookshop without running into trouble.'

Emily was fanning herself with a cushion, her face flushed with worry.

'We get the 6 a.m. train to Alnmouth and then it's a five-mile walk to your cousin's.'

'And what do we say to my uncle and Brennus? Even supposing they've got out of the bookshop in one piece?'

'Nothing. I don't think we can trust anyone. Every time the professors have turned up, trouble's not been far behind. And Oscar said there was a traitor.'

'Oscar! What if *he's* the traitor? What if he wrote the letter? What if he's leading you into a trap? Wasn't it Brennus and Drust who defended you in Oxford? You can see from their faces that they were in some kind of fight.'

Emily took a big gulp of tea and put her mug down rather hard. This was all sounding ridiculous again.

'You're making your decision off the back of a letter delivered by a stranger,' she said anxiously. 'Didn't you say it was Oscar who introduced the idea of a traitor anyway?'

Sam sighed. Emily's words only added to his confusion. He had yet to tell her about his conversation with Oscar in the tapestry. But her logic could be extended to that too. Suddenly he felt exhausted by it all.

'I need my bed. I don't know about you, but I'm so tired.'

'So am I,' Emily said, 'but the letter tells you not to delay. If you *are* going to follow it, I don't think you can pick and choose which bits you accept and which bits you ignore. If we're going to Warkworth, shouldn't we go now, after all?'

It was a rational argument, but all it did was make Sam feel even more tired.

'I can't think about it now. I'm sorry, I just need to sleep.'

'You just don't know *what* you're doing,' said Emily grumpily.

* * * * * *

They retired to bed, Sam climbing the stairs as if in a daze and Emily following on behind, heading for the spare room on the second floor as Sam climbed up to the third. He fell onto his bed with thoughts still going around in his mind. What if Oscar was wrong, what if he was the traitor and by not going with Professor Stuckley he was putting himself and Emily in danger? He fell asleep still in a whirl.

Emily was washing her face in the large family bathroom. Looking at herself in the mirror, she realised how tired she looked. It had been a long day.

It had been a long summer, for that matter. With her mum and dad fighting, she'd spent almost the whole summer staying with her uncle and aunt, either in Gosforth or their house in Warkworth.

And she hadn't even had chance to tell Sam about it – that was how crazy today had been.

Taking one of Sam's old T-shirts from the airing cupboard to sleep in, she walked back down the quiet hallway, undressed and fell into bed.

Hours later, she woke, heart thumping. Faceless black creatures had been throwing themselves at the window. 'It's just a dream, Emily,' she told herself.

But as she lay there, now wide awake, she couldn't help but worry. What had those creatures been? Had they attacked the bookshop because Sam had been there, or was it because of her uncle? She'd watched his mood grow blacker this past year and the strange folk coming and going from the bookshop, their accents and clothes becoming more unfamiliar as spring turned to summer.

One day a group of Forest Reivers had arrived. They were hard-faced and spoke little. Their dialects were hard to fathom anyway. She'd heard terrible rumours about the Reivers. They were thieves and murderers, or so the stories went.

The Reivers' visit had coincided with Brennus and Drust briefly appearing at the bookshop. Now she thought about it, it had also coincided with Sam's supposed transfer to Cherwell.

Now Sam was back, life had definitely taken a turn for the ludicrous. This wasn't what she'd expected at all and she still didn't really want to accept the day's events. But no matter how hard she tried to reject them, she'd been shaken by the attack on the bookshop. Even though she hadn't seen the creatures, she'd heard them and seen her uncle's fear.

Then there were the crows. She'd seen this behaviour once before, on her father's farm – swooping towards the house and then turning just before the walled garden. She'd spent a week with Angus in Edinburgh too, and he'd told her about his close encounter with the crows.

Now here she was contemplating helping Sam find a man who'd briefly visited him in Oxford with a strange message. It was clearly all connected to the mysterious Shadow. The thought of it hunting Sam was almost too much to think about. But the question that no one was asking was *why* was it hunting Sam? And why now?

With all this going through her head, she couldn't go back to sleep. She got up and stood looking out of the window. Thankfully, the road outside was quiet.

How long she'd been staring at the open gate before she realised its significance, she didn't know. Quickly, she took a step back from the window, butterflies fluttering through her stomach.

Elmfield Road was still quiet, its pavements empty, its long avenue of trees unmoving. But something was wrong.

Quickly she sprang up the stairs to the third floor and knocked on Sam's door. There was no reply. Frightened now, she opened it.

Sam was lying, still in his clothes, spread-eagled on top of his bed. It took a little shaking before he was sitting up, looking at Emily through groggy eyes, his hair sticking up in all directions.

'What?'

'One of the front gates is open.'

Sam came wide awake. 'What? I locked it and my mother always locks it too. If she has come back, she won't have left it open. She's got very security-conscious lately.'

In an instant he was up and making his way to the front-facing dormer window. It was a long way down to the gates from the third floor, but he could see one of them standing open.

He stood still, waiting for the dark chill that came when his silent stalker was near, but there was nothing but Emily's breath catching the side of his face as she stood next to him. And yet ... there it was, a faint chill that didn't come from the air.

'We should have heeded the letter.' Emily's voice cut the silence in two.

Sam felt guilty.

'I hope I haven't brought trouble to my home.'

He moved to the back window, which gave him a view of the long garden backing onto Elgy Green. All was quiet. Just a hint of light was coming back into the eastern sky. His bedside clock gave the time as 4 a.m.

'I don't think we should wait any longer,' he said softly.

'I think you're right.'

They quickly got their things together and packed small rucksacks. Sam wrote his mum a short note to say that he was staying with Emily in Warkworth and would be back in a couple of days.

They made their way quietly through the dark house to the side door. Sam felt apprehensive as he opened it and looked to the left and right across his neighbours' tree-filled gardens. Then he grabbed Emily's wrist and pointed wordlessly with his other hand. The arched gate at the side of the house was also open.

Which way should they go? Leaving Emily by the side door, Sam inched forward so he could get a better view of the front of the house. Panic was rising in him and he took a deep breath before peering round the corner.

There was nothing other than his fear peering back.

He edged back along the wall towards the arched gate, fear pricking him with every step. The warmth of the day had long vanished and a cold breeze met him as he came to the gateway and slipped through into the back garden.

Out towards Elgy Green, the dark trees stood like watching giants. For a moment Sam felt paralysed with terror, unable to take another step.

A sudden movement near the old oak tree caught his eye. At first he couldn't pinpoint its position, but then he saw it again. Someone was climbing the steps of the tree house.

Shivers tingling down the full length of his spine, Sam dropped low, using the mature herbaceous borders for cover as best he could. Straining both his neck and eyes in the darkness, he approached the giant oak.

Cold danger was now encircling him and he couldn't shake off the overwhelming feeling that he was being watched. Briefly he glanced back at the dark windows of the house, but there was no one there.

He was now ten feet from the tree house. Was this crazy? Why wasn't he running away? He paused, confused.

'Sam – quickly,' came a voice no more solid than his frozen breath.

Sam rose to his full height, relief flooding through him. 'Professor Whitehart! I'm so pleased to see you!'

He ran up the wooden steps leading to the now crooked tree house. As he bent to enter it, he found Professor Whitehart crouched against the far wall of the single room, looking through the unglazed window over the wall towards Elgy Green.

Before Sam could say a word, the professor turned to him and pressed a finger to his lips. 'Quiet now.'

'What happened at the bookshop?' Sam whispered.

The professor didn't reply, but turned back to the window.

'Professor, are the others okay?'

Still the professor kept his face turned away from Sam. 'You must be quiet or it will hear you,' he breathed. 'Where's the girl?'

Sam edged forward, trembling. How cold it was here.

'Professor, we need to get back in the house now. We shouldn't be outside. There's something really bad nearby, I know it. What are you watching?'

'Where's the *girl*?' The professor's words now had a ring of urgency to them.

Sam shrank back, shivers running down his spine, his stomach knotting into sickness. The professor turned to face him and instantly he felt the chill emanating from him. There was no deep cut on his forehead. And behind him, through the window, Sam saw a sea of silent shapes on the far side of the green, some standing, but most hunched over on all fours, dozens in number, waiting.

'Who are you?'

Sam didn't know why he had said it, couldn't remember even thinking the words, but they were out in the cold air.

The professor replied with a terrifying mewl. In response, the chilling sea of shapes leaped forward, bent and dark. The trap was sprung. And the professor was laughing, with a deep guttural growl that contorted his face into a menacing mask.

Sam was up and running, flinging himself down the wooden steps and falling onto the cold grass as something slammed against the brick wall with a sickening noise. It came again and the wall burst in a cloud of slivers of brick. Shrapnel swirled through the air and yet not one shard found its target. Sam lay on the lawn, a silent observer, as the dust settled around him. Through the breach in the wall, a dozen forms, hooded and faceless, watched him.

Sam couldn't breathe. His legs wouldn't move. He was crushed by an unknown hand, slaughtered in his own secret garden, in a place he loved. What was happening? Why hadn't the neighbours heard the wall falling? Why wasn't anyone coming to help him?

And still the shapes on the other side of the shattered wall did not attack.

'Sam!' He heard Emily calling to him and turned his head. She was standing by the arched gate, looking out over the lawn.

A hideous form stepped out of the tree house, no longer resembling the professor but feathered and twisted, its face beaked and grotesque, the creature that he had seen through the window of the bookshop. Sam felt it rising before him, chilling and dangerous, ancient and malicious, its strange darting features now fixed on Emily.

Others now burst through the broken wall, surging forward through the rubble. Sam was overwhelmed by a kaleidoscope of black feathers, twisted faces and misshapen bodies. A thousand shrieks erupted around him in a tempest. He was lost in a maelstrom and then a slender hand rested on his shoulder and he thought for a moment there was a tall and beautiful angel standing beside him.

'Sam, the Grim-were cannot stand against you here.'

The voice was the one he had heard before the gates of Magdalen, a voice not of words, but of light shot through with silk, a commanding voice urging him to use the light that was flowing all around him.

He was thrown backwards by the force of a blast. The twisted shape heading for Emily was now a blurred human form, now a giant winged one. A murder of crows took off into the air, several bursting into flames as lightning flashed across the sky. Thunder boomed out and burning crows were falling all around Sam, turning to empty air as they hit the ground.

As he got to his feet, the sky was lit by a thousand burning lights. Then nothing remained other than the after-images that left him blinking in the now quiet night.

8

THE ROAD TO WARKWORTH

'They've gone.' Drust entered the reading room, a dark look on his face. 'They've left a note saying they're going to Warkworth.'

'And you are happy for him to disappear with Emily?'

Jarl was sweeping the remaining pieces of glass into a small pile. The sun was streaming in through the broken windows, a stark reminder of what they had faced last night.

'Brennus, is this what you want – the boy defenceless and travelling with my niece? She's in my care, you know. You should have stayed with him at the house last night. Coming back here was a mistake.'

'I have a sense of what travels with him. If it can't keep him safe then nothing can.' Brennus seemed untroubled. He was sitting at the table, bent over a map of Northumberland.

Jarl looked at him, unsure. 'They may well seek out my son.'

'I'm sure they will.'

With a grunt of disapproval, Jarl resumed his sweeping.

'What were these creatures, Brennus?' he asked after a while, looking at the little black piles of dust amongst the shards of glass.

'Crow-men,' Drust answered for him as he stepped through the carnage and came to a stop at the now-shredded tapestry. 'They knew what they were doing taking out the Way-curves.'

He shook his head, wondering if things could get any worse. It had taken less than a week for them to lose their grip on events and the situation was growing more perilous by the day.

'I've seen some strange things in my time,' he sighed, 'but nothing like this. We need to go after them.'

'No.' Brennus shook his head and for the first time that morning looked up from his map.

'The crow-men have no use of the Way-curves. They were sent here as a distraction. They have joined the hunt, for they too will be wondering about the Shadow. I have to say I'm surprised to see them so far south, for they dwell in the Underland beneath the borders.'

'So the Underland really is awake,' said Jarl.

'These are strange days,' Brennus sighed. 'And it weighs heavily enough upon me that I have placed you in the middle of this.'

He turned so he could see both Drust and Jarl.

'The crow-men didn't come here to kill us,' he said firmly. 'If they had, we would have been sorely tested against such numbers. Their curiosity has been aroused, that's all.'

He turned back to his map.

'Our enemies will be watching us. We have to do the unexpected. I told you that earlier. What I didn't say was that I left Sam here last night so Oscar could speak with him.'

Jarl stopped his sweeping and Drust's cards went still.

'Brother, the Way-curves are not safe – you could have brought the Shadow to him!'

Brennus raised his eyes and looked steadily at his brother. 'I think Sam is being helped – I am sure of this.'

'What are you saying – that you don't trust us to keep him safe? That the safer route is to abandon him?'

Drust's words were meant to sting, but still Brennus did not lower his eyes.

'I think Sam will find his own way. We were touched by the Shadow, you and I, and who knows what effect that will have? Tell me you don't still feel its touch and I won't believe you, for I feel it still. It isn't a question of trusting each other, it's a question of not trusting myself.'

Jarl felt himself gripping the handle of the sweeping brush. 'But if we don't follow Emily and Sam, who will protect them? Would you leave it to Eagan?'

'We are up against an enemy that is relentless and grows in strength and intent,' Brennus said calmly. 'It is only a Shadow in this world, but I believe it is a reflection of an enemy that we know only too well. The Fall is dying. So if we stay and hide, then all hope will be lost. And from what I saw in Magdalen, we cannot stop and fight. So we must seek counsel at the Dead Water. What else would you have me do?'

Jarl was silent.

Brennus turned to his brother. 'We need to be sure that the Shadow follows us to the Dead Water. You know you can draw it to you – no one can use the flow as you can. But you know what that means. You know what I'm asking of you.'

He stopped suddenly, unable to go on.

Drust looked at him for a long moment, then gave a half-smile and nodded.

'Drust,' Jarl's voice was strained, 'from what you tell me of this enemy, it is beyond our skill and understanding. If you face it by yourself, there will be no going back. You will be sacrificing yourself!'

Hearing the blunt words, Brennus seemed to change his mind. 'Yes, it's true,' he muttered. 'Are you sure that you don't want to reconsider? You are my brother and I fear for you.'

'Then you should turn your fear into strength and make sure that my sacrifice is not in vain.' Drust smiled again, but his expression was serious. He flicked his cards from hand to hand.

Brennus stared at him and just for the briefest second seemed to plead with him, but Drust turned away.

'There are others who will be sacrificed before this is over,' he said, looking down at the cards flashing from hand to hand, 'others who will be hunted down until they have no breath left and nowhere to hide. I do not intend to be one of them. I have felt it already and the end will be quick. Come, let us travel with the sun at our backs and make for the Dead Water.'

* * * * * *

When the day finally broke, it revealed the extent of the fallen wall and the bricks lying in a wide arc across Elgy Green. Sam and Emily took a taxi from the red-bricked Elmfield Road down Grandstand Road, with its long corridor of yew trees clasping their branches to create a shady arch. As they passed the giant town moor, with its grazing cattle, and Cow Hill stretching out in the distance, for a second Sam remembered the days he'd spent sledging down its steep slope without a care in the world. The days walking across the hill with his mum now seemed on the edge of his memory, pushed aside by the torrid flow of the last few days. Oscar, the Shadow pursuing him through Oxford, the attack on the bookshop, the attack on the house…He could feel danger rising on all sides as the taxi sped through the early morning streets, heading for the station.

There were just so many unanswered questions. Where had his mother been during the night? What had been happening at the bookshop? Where had the neighbours been? How could you not hear a wall bursting asunder?

There had been so many other things lately that seemed surreal. How could you communicate with the past? And what part did he and Emily have to play in what was happening? He looked sideways at her pale face and remembered the chill words of the imposter Whitehart. The Shadow might have been searching for him, but the feathered men had come for her.

Emily, too, was puzzling over the events of the night. What had she really seen? There had been movement along the fallen wall, indefinable figures, haunting voices, and Sam lying on the grass with just a hint of someone standing beside him, a flicker of light before the thunderstorm broke.

In front of the imposing architecture of Newcastle station, they hoisted their rucksacks onto their backs before entering the almost empty concourse. It was a quiet Sunday morning and few people were catching the first train to Alnmouth.

They sat waiting side by side. They had said almost nothing to each other since leaving Gosforth, but their thoughts flowed strangely together, a single question keeping them silent and pensive. Were they doing the right thing?

They were both relieved when the train pulled in on time. They sat across from each other in an empty carriage and gave each other a half-hearted smile as the train jerked slowly north in the early morning sun.

* * * * * *

It wasn't long before they'd left the bricks and mortar of Newcastle behind and were entering the deep green world of the Northumberland borderland. The train gathered momentum as it looped around the medieval market town of Morpeth and headed deeper into an alluring landscape full of hidden villages. Before long, the green shimmer of the North Sea was away to the east and the long beaches of Druridge Bay dropped unseen over the arched horizon.

Sam and Emily watched the familiar places pass by in a blur. They had travelled this route many times. But this time the train juddered after crossing the river Coquet and seemed to turn sharply to the east, towards Warkworth. Emily looked up in surprise as it juddered a second time and the smell of its brakes wafted through the carriage before it came to a long slow stop.

'I didn't think there was a stop before Alnmouth.'

'Neither did I,' Sam replied, looking out of the window. It was a station that he had perhaps glimpsed before, he thought, but he'd never stopped there.

They waited for the train guard to announce the reason for the unscheduled stop, but none came. Sam walked the length of the carriage and then the adjoining one and quickly found they were alone. When he came back through, Emily was hauling her rucksack off the train.

'We might as well get off here,' she said, nodding towards a rusty and faded sign announcing that they had arrived at Warkworth station.

'Why not?' Sam shrugged and joined her on the deserted platform.

Behind them the engine revved suddenly, making them jump, and then the train slowly pulled out of the station, gathering speed as it rounded a corner and disappeared.

Sam and Emily stood a little bewildered in the deserted station with its antiquated stone building thick with moss. There was a real stillness to the place, a placidity that was caught in the deep blue sky glistening with the still-rising sun and the cirrus clouds that gently etched a sea of patterns moving north. Sparrows flew from the open fields across the railway line and darted over the station's roof, and in the distance there was a faint hum of a diesel tractor lost in the rolling hills that framed the farmland surrounding Warkworth.

Sam and Emily breathed in the early morning freshness and looked round them at the scented flowers still clinging to broken pots and the flags and broken benches that were slowly being reclaimed by the Northumberland landscape.

'What is this place?' asked Emily.

'Warkworth station.'

'Yes, I too can read the big sign in front of us – I was thinking more along the lines of why have we always caught the train from Alnmouth when this has been so close to the village?'

'It doesn't look used to me.'

'It's 8 o'clock on a Sunday morning, Sam – most sane people are probably having breakfast and wondering what they are having for lunch.'

Sam smiled at Emily, remembering just how much he liked her.

They walked from the platform through a set of double doors whose paint had all but faded and entered a waiting room full of chairs piled high. To the left was an abandoned ticket office whose blinds had fallen into disrepair. The wooden floor was loose and creaked as they walked across it. The further they looked, the more ramshackle it appeared.

The door on the far side was unlocked. On opening it, they found themselves at the top of what had once been a grand stone staircase leading down to a short horseshoe-shaped drive with an overgrown lawn. It was north-facing and they quickly noticed the air was colder here, which was a shock after the morning sun on the platform.

They were looking at a narrow pot-holed road. On the other side of it was a thick bushy hedgerow and beyond that a solitary roof with a wisp of smoke that floated lazily into the crisp air.

'I think we are northwest of the village,' said Sam. 'I've come this way once or twice and the road loops to the right, eventually entering the village from the north. It can't be more than a couple of miles and in this weather it will be a pleasant walk.'

Emily was only half listening.

'You know, I've been coming to these parts all my life. How come I've never stopped at this station before?'

Sam felt uneasy. He'd already been asking himself why the train had stopped at a station that had obviously been derelict for an age. But that was one more question that could not be answered.

'I don't know. Come on, let's enjoy the walk in the sun.'

They left the neglected station and walked down the bumpy road towards the village. Emily slipped her arm through Sam's and at that moment it was as if time had stopped and a great distance had opened up between the sunny morning and the drama of the previous night.

Sam's spirits rose. Perhaps he'd made the right decision after all.

* * * * * *

They didn't see a single person on the road. After crossing a small stream whose waters barely trickled through trees choked by the slow creep of ivy, they passed a working farm on their right and a field ploughed by molehills on their left, then came to a number of large Georgian houses set back from the road. High stone walls kept prying eyes from private lives.

Moving on, Sam noticed the decade old bricks gave way to century old stone. The architecture changed, as did the colour and texture. It was as if they were stepping back in time. Even the trees switched from Ferns to watchful Yews; the older the stonework, the greater the tree. They came to a crossroads with a sign letting them know that to the left were Alnwick and Alnmouth and to the right Amble and Warkworth.

The view that met them as they turned towards Warkworth was sublime. The village had been there since ancient times. King Ceolwulf of Northumbria was said to have given it, along with its church, to the monks of Lindisfarne in the eighth century. At the far end of it stood the castle atop its steep hill like a dragon jealously guarding its kingdom and now sending long primeval shadows cascading down into the heart of the village.

At the other end of the village, Warkworth Bridge greeted them like an old friend. Sam stepped onto the stone bridge with lightness in his heart. The shackles of his fear seemed to break and for a moment he felt almost happy.

At this hour, the village was just waking up and people were walking over to the shop to buy their Sunday papers. As Sam and Emily entered the village square, the Greenhouse was already open for business. It felt as if the shop had always been there. It sold just about everything you could imagine and already had metal flamingos and an assortment of finery outside in the morning sun.

'Let's get something for breakfast,' Emily said. 'It's a bit early to go and bother Eagan.'

They entered the cool interior of the shop, bought some food and drink and paid the shop assistant, then returned to the village square and walked back the way they'd come. As they reached the bridge, they turned left into the road that led down by the river to the old school house.

'Are you sure Eagan won't mind us staying with him?' Sam asked.

Emily laughed. 'He'll probably hate it – you know he loves his own company and prefers it when my aunt and uncle are staying in Newcastle. But I've been staying there a lot this summer anyway.' She paused. 'Don't worry, I know to handle him. We just need to tell him we aren't staying long – we're just passing through.'

'Well, we *are* just passing through. Though I have to say I don't know how long it'll take to meet up with Oscar.'

Emily spun around. "We need to tell Eagan a little of what's been going on. He might be just a little strange, but at the moment, Sam, he would fit into our company only too well. I'm sure we can stay here. There's nothing to rush back home for'. It was the first time Sam had heard Emily hint at her mother and Father's separation. She had spent almost the whole of summer staying with her Uncle and Auntie moving between the bookshop and Warkworth.

Completely ignoring the question, 'Well,' Emily continued blithely, 'I think Eagan is a little scared of me, so we'll just stay until we decide to leave.'

Sam could see how Eagan could be just a little intimidated – although Emily was only 17, she acted much older. She had an air of confidence that could even appear a little arrogant, though Sam knew this was not the case.

They continued along the road, which eventually opened onto a small green with wooden benches every hundred feet. They decided to stop and eat their picnic there, alongside the river.

The tranquil waters of the Coquet were broken by brown trout feeding, sending ripples across the smooth surface. On the far side of the river, a steep bank full of trees and mature bushes led up through Birling Wood, where the Reigns had an orchard full of apple and pear trees.

How peaceful it was here, Sam thought, as he watched a huge grey heron standing motionless on the far side of the river. Then he shivered. There was something just a little unnerving about herons – about the way they would move swiftly without warning. It reminded him of the Shadow, a silent stalker hiding in the edge-lands, watching and waiting. What could he and Emily do against that? And he wasn't just involving Emily now, but also Eagan. What darkness was he bringing to their door?

Emily interrupted his thoughts. She had moved to stand at the river's edge.

'You have to love this place,' she said, looking down into the water.

Sam left his sandwich and stood alongside her. To his surprise, she slipped her hand into his and pulled him closer.

'I'm going to look after you,' she said.

Sam felt uncomfortable and thrilled all at once. Emily smiled mischievously as she watched his cheeks flush.

Trying to extricate himself, he dropped her hand and turned back to the heron, but it had gone.

Slowly, a rowing boat was approaching. In the middle of it, rowing effortlessly, was a young man with his back to them, wearing nothing more than a pair of swimming trunks, blue Wellington boots and a straw hat.

'He's not all there, you know,' commented Emily loudly.

The man paid no attention. He didn't even seem to notice them.

'*Eagan!*'

As if waking from a dream, he turned his head towards them and gave them the briefest of smiles. Then he pushed the oars into the water and brought the boat to drifting stop.

'Emily! Just when I thought I'd got rid of you.'

'Have you missed your favourite cousin?'

Eagan smiled more broadly. 'Maybe, but definitely not your snoring. You know it's been impossible to fish around here when you've been in the back room.'

'Hmph!'

Eagan threw back his head and laughed. 'Hey, Emily, meet me back at the house and you and Sam can cook this.' He held aloft a large trout.

'He *knows* I'm vegetarian,' Emily muttered under her breath.

Eagan took the oars again and started rowing with intent. The boat skipped along the water and Emily and Sam jogged along the bank.

Before long, the light stone of the old school house emerged from around the long twisting river. The house had literally been built beside the Coquet. It had magnificent gardens on either side and at the back there was a short lawn leading down to a small wooden jetty.

Sam and Emily stood waiting for Eagan to alight from the boat and let them in through the door at the west end of the house. When it eventually opened, they were met by Eagan still in his Wellington boots, although Sam was relieved to find he had put on a tight-fitting tartan tunic that thankfully covered his groin.

'Do come in. Make yourselves at home!'

Sam had to stoop to miss the door's original wooden frame. The inside of the old school house was a living homage to the Reigns' travels through ancient places of the world. If the Seven Stories was orderly, this was a chaotic muddle, a jumble of ornaments that stretched back three or four generations.

Eagan led them down the low-ceilinged corridor and through a round door into a grand room that had a large Georgian garden room leading off it. There were stunning views from here across the Coquet and Sam was ready to fall into one of the welcoming chairs, but Eagan was moving on.

He took them down a second corridor that joined the west wing with the east and brought them into the old library that housed the Reigns' private collection of first editions. It had once been the school hall. It was always a joyous moment for Sam to enter such a splendid room.

One thing you noticed about the Reigns' home was the natural light. It was the most impressive aspect of the house, and the library was no different. Sam came to a standstill looking up at a glass dome that was the same shape and structure as that of the reading room at the Seven Stories.

'Come along, Sam, keep up,' Eagan called as he passed through another round door and into a kitchen that had a vast round island in the centre of it. At the far side, beautifully crafted doors opened onto a small patio with steps leading down to the river.

'Where exactly are you taking us?' Emily didn't bother to hide her irritation.

'Cousin,' Eagan turned with a grin, 'patience is a virtue. You should know that more than most, and you should also know that my favourite place in the world is my little patch of bliss down by the river.'

'Where you paddle up and down like Toad!'

'You mean Ratty,' corrected Eagan, gathering up three glasses with one hand whilst opening up the fridge with a deft touch of his Wellington boot.

There was something about Eagan Reign that Sam couldn't help but admire. Tall and handsome, he was his father's son for sure, but there was none of Jarl's ruggedness about him. He was clean shaven and had a mop of jet black hair, the darkest eyes and rings to match. There was a touch of theatre around everything he said and did. Even his speech was different from that of most Northumbrians.

Now, carrying a large jug of lime and lemonade along with the glasses, he took Sam and Emily into a private garden full of fruiting apple and pear trees. Skipping down a short path, he made for a small picnic table and poured out the drinks.

'People ask us why we stay here,' he said, waving an arm dramatically, 'when we have been flooded twice. You sometimes have to take the good with the bad. Some weeks the days can be more bad than good, though, especially when all you seem to do is mop the sludge from your favourite rug.'

Emily wasn't impressed. 'We know you write poetry, cousin, but must everything be poetry?'

Eagan laughed, and the sound was as uplifting as it was loud. Sam relaxed as he sipped his drink. The morning was warm, though there was just the slightest breeze prancing across the Coquet.

'Poetry is a little like this river,' Eagan was saying. 'You can never tell what's going on beneath the surface until you submerge yourself in its flow.'

Emily was shaking her head, but it had little effect on Eagan. He turned to the river, took off his hat and flung his arms wide.

'You are so cynical! The world is poetry – don't let the scientists pretend anything else.'

Emily glanced at Sam and he could tell her patience was wearing thin. But Sam couldn't help being captivated by Eagan. There was just no one like him. He kept to himself and spent his days travelling up and down the Coquet and the Aln on his rowing boat, the *Celtic Flow*, journeying deep into the Cheviots and the border forests. He had been head boy at the Royal Grammar School and could have made the British swimming team, but had met the Forest Reivers and given it all up to tend the Reigns' orchard and sell the fruit in Alnwick market. He rarely travelled further south than Amble or further north than Holy Island. He was as enigmatic as he was charismatic, and Sam knew there were times when he preferred to sit quietly in his rowing boat and reflect on nothing.

'Come along, Sam,' he was saying now, 'I won't bite. Tell me why I have the pleasure of your company.'

Sam felt a little uncomfortable, but Emily jumped in first.

'Oh, we're just going to spend some time in Warkworth before Sam is due back in Oxford at the end of September. We won't disturb your frolicking, or your sordid little trips with the Reivers.'

Sam winced. He couldn't understand why Emily was being so offensive.

Eagan seemed unperturbed. 'There's no need to be rude to your host, Emily,' he said calmly. 'The Forest Reivers are my friends and I will treat them as I treat you and Sam. I'm travelling up to the orchard a lot right now and I'd welcome your company. And your help. It's been a favourable season and the fruit will keep the wolves from the door during the winter months.'

'Thank you,' said Sam quietly, with a pointed look at Emily.

She turned away.

Sam was feeling at home in this hidden garden nestled so close to the wide and gentle river. On the other bank the grey heron was back, prowling with its long neck and piercing beak. He watched it walking slowly, head bent, alert for any movement under the still surface of the water.

'I've spent the last three summers on this river,' Eagan said, 'following it for many miles as it has turned and twisted like a captured snake. I've rowed many of the rivers in Northumberland and the borders, and there is none as mysterious and thought-provoking as this.'

He took a sip of his drink and tossed back his dark hair.

'Its waters run south for a while, then drift east, passing Rothbury, and you find yourself moving from familiar valleys and woods into something far more remarkable, if a little haunting.'

Sam felt as if Eagan was leading them somewhere he wasn't sure he wanted to go, not after the past few days.

'You move through the Barrow Burn, a place where the river turns sharply north, becoming treacherously shallow but fast in places. It moves underground and you have to drag your boat for a half a mile before you find it again. You are also watchful that the barrow doesn't hurl stones down upon your head, for there are rumours of giants hiding beneath the hills.'

'Is there a point to this?' Emily was looking exasperated.

Sam was glad of the interruption, for even in the quiet garden he could feel his anxiety notching up a level. But Eagan continued regardless.

'At the top of the barrow, the river again runs south. When I came at last to the Blindburn two days ago, I was tired and my rations were almost gone. It was hot and I may even have been a little delirious, for there was an old man there, drinking the clear waters of the river. At first I thought he hadn't seen me, but he bade me good day and when I looked upon him I realised his great age. He had a wrinkled and weathered face that distorted who he might once have been.'

Eagan raised his hand, not in the mood to be interrupted by Emily.

'There I was, quite literally in the middle of nowhere, with no villages in any direction. And there was a man who could quite easily have touched a century, walking alone with nothing more than a stick and a pair of sandals. He asked me whether I would be kind enough to sit with him for a while, as he'd been travelling all night to meet me before I met the Reivers.'

Eagan was now still.

'Your faces don't come close to the surprise that must have been etched on mine. So we sat alongside the Coquet and he bathed his feet in the waters and didn't once gasp at their icy flow. All the while I was wondering how he'd managed to get to that place. It's inaccessible to all but the most ardent fell-walkers and there was no boat but mine.'

Sam was now hanging onto to Eagan's every word, watching him weave his tale.

'We sat there in the sun and he told me that he lived in the borderland, in a place that I'd probably not heard of and that was of no importance today. He spoke sometimes in an uncommon tongue, drifting back into an English I could barely understand, revealing a message that was as confusing as it was worrying.'

'What was the message and what has it got to do with us?' Emily had beaten Sam to the question.

Eagan leaned forward and looked her in the eye.

'He said I should expect two unexpected visitors, visitors who would need shelter against a gathering storm. I met him two days ago and he said that on my return the visitors would be waiting for me.'

Sam should have been shocked, but somehow he wasn't. The last few days had put paid to that. But Eagan himself looked shocked. He put his drink down on the table.

'I have long travelled through those lands. I know the fells, woods and dens. There was no way for the old man to have travelled to the place where I found him without a boat.'

When he spoke next, his voice was low and inquisitive.

'The Forest Reivers have a fireside story of an old man wandering the borders, warning travellers of unseen dangers. Whether you believe such stories or not is neither here nor there. What is surprising is that the old man's words have proved prophetic.'

'You know I don't believe in fairy stories,' Emily said, pushing her glass away.

'It's not fairy stories you should be worried about,' Eagan said. 'It's when they become real that you have a problem. I was sent to seek the Forest Reivers by my father. He wanted me to bring them to Warkworth. He said in the days ahead we would need their help. I don't think he expected you to come here, or I would have known.'

He looked curiously at Sam. But once again Emily spoke first. 'We came here for a rest, Eagan. We've had a long night with little sleep. Today isn't a good day for more stories.'

Lack of sleep was indeed stamped in the dark rings beneath her eyes.

'Apologies, Sam,' Eagan muttered. 'I can see you are both tired and I am being a poor host. Forgive me. Father has been acting a little strangely of late and I'm worried about him. And the Forest Reivers speak of skirmishes along the whole of the borders. I've never seen them fearful in their own lands before.'

He stretched, as if his own words bothered him.

'These are hard folk, not easily frightened. But when I met them, they were travelling in force through the secret ways, following the river east to the Cheviots and their spiritual meeting-place, the King's Seat. They have called the heads of the four main families together.'

Sam had been hoping that they would outrun such grim news, that Warkworth would offer them a haven whilst he consulted Oscar. Perhaps it had been wishful thinking.

'There are other things that you need to be aware of.'

Emily had turned her head away from the table as a sign that she didn't want to hear any more. Eagan ignored her, his dark eyes focused on Sam.

'There have been queer folk passing through Warkworth this past year. Folk I've never seen before. The Pauperhaughs' eldest son was attacked on the old road between Alnmouth and the coast. By a wolf.'

Sam's blood ran cold at the mention of Morcant. There was just a little bit of him that thought he probably deserved to be attacked.

Eagan drained the last of his lemonade.

'Look,' he added more gently, 'why don't you get some rest? Have the run of the house. I'm going into Amble so I can have the pick of the vegetables for this evening's tea.'

He made his way back up the slope towards the old school house.

Silence fell. Sam watched the hypnotising flow of the water as he thought about what Eagan had said. Every now and again the heron flapped its wings and made a harsh croaking sound. Emily was looking down at her feet, seemingly working herself further and further into a black mood.

Then there was the splash of oars and Sam turned to see the *Celtic Flow* cutting quickly through the water. Eagan, wearing what could only be described as a woolly jumper, waved to them as he moved off in the direction of Amble harbour.

'Wouldn't it be quicker if he walked?' Sam asked.

'Oh, everything he does is for attention – the way he talks, the way he walks, the way he dresses!' Emily exploded. 'He spends far too much time with the Reivers. He's brought suspicion on our family, not to mention brought himself to the attention of some unsavoury characters from Amble. Don't be fooled, Sam, that nonsense about the old man is an attempt to put himself firmly in the middle of whatever is going on. He will have overheard Uncle Jarl talking and been upset by the fact that it had nothing to do with him.'

'He's always been perfectly polite to me. I know he's different and flamboyant...'

'That's all part of the façade. He thinks tending a wild orchard is work and he pretends to live off the land. He didn't tell you that he was arrested in connection with the attack on Morcant, did he?'

'What?'

'Morcant was found bruised and battered in Birling Wood and Eagan's blood was found on his clothes. Eagan was arrested and it was Uncle Jarl who got the charges dropped. You know there's history between the Reigns and Pauperhaughs that goes back several hundred years? Well, that's opened it all up again. My uncle's tried to get the Reigns, Pauperhaughs and Hoods all talking, but if you ask me, Eagan's determined to rock the boat, especially now he's befriended the Forest Reivers.'

Sam thought about this. 'So am I right in thinking that the people who've been meeting at the bookshop are representatives of each family?' he asked.

Emily gave a brief nod.

'What hope do we have if the people who are meant to help us can't even trust each other?' thought Sam. Leaving Professor Stuckley suddenly felt premature, and they'd come only thirty miles. Where was the Shadow now? If it attacked, there would be just him and Emily left to face it.

She had turned to look at him.

'If this is all real, Sam, have you ever thought why you? What does the Shadow actually want from you?'

'I think it wants me dead.'

'But why?'

'I don't know, but when it stood before me at the gates of Magdalen, I could feel its intent. I know you don't believe me about the woman, but she's the only reason I escaped. I don't know where she comes from, but there's a change when she is nearby, an energy that prickles my skin, and she has a power that has been able to keep the Shadow at bay.'

Emily frowned, remembering the flicker of light she'd seen on the lawn. 'It just sounds so weird, but – oh, I don't know any more, Sam. I'm so tired. I'm going to sleep for a bit, okay?'

She walked off to her room.

Looking at the sparrows hopping across the lawn and the ducks paddling lazily in the river, Sam pondered her animosity towards Eagan. He knew she could be prickly, but very rarely was she spiteful. There had to be something else at work.

Perhaps it had to do with the company Eagan was now keeping. Very few people had anything positive to say about the Forest Reivers.

9

THE TRUTH ABOUT OSCAR

'**I** am doing you the most amazing omelettes and salad with a touch of homemade mustard!'

Eagan was on all fours, sticking his head into a cupboard, looking for a frying pan.

Sam looked across at Emily, who was busy shaking her head at him. Ignoring her, he said, 'Eagan.'

'Blast! Sorry, Sam – did you say something?' Eagan withdrew his head and looked up enquiringly.

'I'm thinking about going up to the orchard this evening.'

For a split-second Eagan's face was clouded by concern, then he pushed the hair from his eyes and disappeared back into the cupboard. When he resurfaced, he was clutching the frying pan.

'Why?' he asked, as he got to his feet.

'I want to go and see a man called Oscar.'

'Oscar?'

'Yes. I want to talk to him. I met him last week in Oxford.'

Eagan paused. 'There's only ever been one Oscar around here as far as I know. Are you sure you have the name right?'

'Definitely. He told me himself.'

'Someone's been playing a joke on you,' said Eagan, placing the frying pan down on the stone top. 'The only Oscar in Alnmouth was there in the fifties, possibly sixties. He was one of the Inklings, though he was on the periphery of the group. We have a few first editions of his work in the library. Father used to read them to me when I was little. I'd be very surprised if he was hanging round Oxford now.'

He laughed.

'Well,' said Sam, 'it definitely sounds as if it was the same man. I bumped into him in Magdalen. He'd come to give a message to Professor Stuckley.'

'Professor Stuckley?'

'*Brennus!*' Emily said triumphantly. 'You didn't know Brennus was there, did you?'

'Why is Brennus going by the name of Professor Stuckley? Does Father know?'

'Yes.' Emily couldn't get the word out quickly enough.

Sam felt a little uneasy at the way she was enjoying her advantage over her cousin.

'I think Professor Stuckley and Professor Whitehart – that's his brother – were in Oxford trying to make sure that I was safe,' he explained.

The atmosphere in the kitchen had suddenly turned cold. In the silence, Sam could hear the kaark of the grey heron as it took off from the riverbank.

'Someone needs to tell me what's been going on,' Eagan said flatly.

'I'm sorry,' Sam said hurriedly. 'I shouldn't have mentioned Oscar. It would be good just to get a little sleep and then I'm sure we would welcome the opportunity of accompanying you to the orchard tomorrow.'

'Well, I'd like to know how you met Oscar in Oxford, for a start,' Eagan continued. 'He's been dead for over a decade.'

'What? But I gave his message to Professor Stuckley and Professor Whitehart and they never mentioned he was dead. I'm sure they would have told me.'

'Perhaps it wasn't the same one, after all.' Eagan picked up the frying pan and moved towards the stove. 'Who knows? Why don't we have lunch and you can tell me your strange tidings and I can tell you what I know?'

* * * * * *

It wasn't long before they were back at the little table at the bottom of the garden overlooking the river. There were now a few light clouds in the sky, but it was still a fine day. Eagan had prepared what could only be described as a small banquet. Sam couldn't deny that he was a superb cook. The omelettes had been light and stuffed with potatoes, mushrooms, cheese and tomatoes, and the salad had tasted as good as it had looked.

'You have to admit,' began Eagan, as they cleared the last morsels from their plates, 'even you, Emily, that I make a nice salad.'

Sam couldn't help but laugh and even Emily's pout almost became a smile.

'I think it's time we all came clean,' Eagan went on. 'It's clear you're in some kind of trouble and I can't help you without understanding what it is.'

'This is going to be tricky,' thought Sam. He looked at Emily, but she was sitting with folded arms, looking down at her empty plate.

'Do you want to start with Oscar?' Eagan prompted.

Sam took a deep breath. 'I met Oscar last Tuesday night,' he began. 'He had a message for Prof– for Brennus and Drust. He mentioned a Circle that was broken and a Shadow that was moving through the Otherland. He told me the Dead Water was lost and the Fall was dying. He said the professors had to seek the help of the Three.'

Eagan was watching him closely. 'What did he look like?'

'He looked tired. And he'd been in some kind of accident. He had blue eyes, grey hair and a grey beard. He was quite strongly built. I'd say he was no more than sixty at a push.'

'You see, there's the problem.' Eagan sat forward in his chair. 'Oscar would be in his eighties – it can't have been him. As for circles and shadows and Otherlands, there are rumours, of course. I have, however, heard stories about the Dead Water. The Forest Reivers say it is an edgeland where wild things dwell, creatures not from this world but from a world that lies on its western shore.'

'And you believe the fairy stories of the Forest Reivers?'

Eagan couldn't help but sigh. 'Oh, be quiet, Emily. Go on, Sam.'

'He was with a man called Culluhin.'

'Culluhin?!'

'Yes – who is he?'

'He is mentioned in the Forest Reivers' folklore. He is a knight of the Druids. Protector of the Garden of Druids.'

'The Garden of Druids,' thought Sam, 'just what it said in the letter.'

'What is the Garden of Druids?' He tried to make it a casual question, but he couldn't stop his cheeks from flushing.

Looking at him curiously, Eagan explained, 'The Reivers say it is where the Druids came from. But again, we are in the realms of myth.'

The letter was definitely real, Sam thought. He wondered how far he could trust Eagan. Did Emily have a good reason for her behaviour?

Keen to change the subject, he said, 'Tell me more about the orchard.'

'The orchard?' Eagan was surprised. 'Why, you know about it already, Sam! What more can I tell you? It's very old – it's been there since before the castle was built. It's been in the Reign family for generations. It was originally in the hands of the Hoods, but then it was seized by the Pauperhaughs, only to eventually end up with the Reigns. By all accounts, that's why there is so much mistrust between the old families.'

'I don't understand why you would have people fighting over an orchard.'

'I think they used it as a lookout point or something. On a good day you can see Alnmouth from the top of Birling Hill. Very few people go there now, but Father says it's where the Marcher Lords used to meet.'

'Marcher Lords?'

'Surely Emily's told you about them?' Eagan was looking at his cousin and she was shifting uncomfortably in her seat.

'No, I don't think so.'

'I've heard Uncle Jarl speak of the Marcher Lords, that's all,' Emily broke in. 'Mercenaries, by the sound of them.'

Eagan shook his head, a light laugh escaping his lips. 'Come on, cousin, you're half a Reign – you should know the history of the Marcher Lords. They were the defenders of the borderland, Sam. They would come together with the Forest Reivers once a year to vow their allegiance to each other. They would camp in the orchard, fish in the Coquet, pick the fruits from the trees and make merry. Then they would defend the realm from the Underland. They brought peace to these lands – or so the story goes.'

'Peace! They were all villains!'

Eagan shot Emily a glance. 'I don't think they were villains. And the Reivers certainly aren't.'

'They bring trouble everywhere they go!'

Emily had clearly had enough. She left the table and stomped back towards the house.

* * * * * *

Eagan took his hat off and pushed back his hair. 'I don't know why she believes all that, Sam. The Forest Reivers' reputation is ill-deserved. They have been guarding these lands for generations and the only thanks they receive is suspicious looks if they venture into the markets.'

'I think she's scared and doesn't want to admit to it. That's all. I'm sorry she's being so rude to you.'

'Oh, she's been like that all summer. She blames me for the breakdown of her parents' marriage.'

'Why? What's it got to do with you?'

'According to Emily's father, I tried to kill Morcant.'

'And did you?' Sam felt a little foolish as he said it. Eagan was hardly likely to tell him if he had.

'No,' he replied, 'but a lot of people don't believe that. I've been warned to stay away from the village shops. Most of them are owned by the Pauperhaugh family. No one goes in or out of Warkworth without them knowing.'

'So what did happen?'

Eagan turned his face towards the river, watching its currents gently twist and turn.

'One evening in early summer I decided to pay a visit to the orchard to check the trees. There are only one or two of us who know the path to its gates. I always go part of the way by boat so that no one can follow my tracks. That day when I was on the path, I quickly realised that I was being followed, so I doubled back through the woods. There's no man alive who could have followed me through those woods, and yet there was Morcant Pauperhaugh. I could tell something was wrong with him by the look in his eyes. And he was carrying a long knife.'

Eagan looked back at Sam.

'As soon as he caught sight of me, he exploded with anger. He rushed me and that's when the wolf appeared, snarling, all teeth and feathers.'

'Feathers?'

'Well, that's what it looked like. It barged me out of the way, knocked the knife from Morcant's hand and rushed past him, knocking him unconscious.'

'There are no wolves in England, Eagan.'

'All I can tell you is what happened. I carried him back through the wood and rowed him all the way to Amble. I was thanked by being arrested and put in jail for a couple of nights. Very unpleasant, I can tell you.'

With Emily out of the way, Eagan was opening up. His extravagant manner had disappeared and Sam could see a stern young Jarl looking back at him.

'Morcant spent a couple of days in hospital,' Eagan continued, 'and says he doesn't remember anything other than me attacking him. But they dropped the charges. Emily's father thinks my father called in some favours and had me released. Of course he's on his nephew's side. But I was released because the bite marks on Morcant's arms and legs didn't match my rather small mouth.'

Eagan smiled grimly.

'There's a strange mood in the village. I've never known so much mistrust between the families. Father's attempt at reconciliation seems to have failed completely. Before he left for the bookshop the other day, he told me to be careful. He wants me to get a message to Braden Bow, the current leader of the Forest Reivers.'

Eagan leaned across the table, keeping his voice low.

'He thinks the Reivers will be needed in the days ahead. Braden will be on his way here after meeting the other clan leaders at the King's Seat. I'm meeting him at the orchard this evening.'

He took a quick look around as if he was speaking out of turn.

'There are rumours that the Reivers have lost control – that they are no longer in charge of swathes of land. You don't have to spend long with them before they start talking about the darkness that is seeping out of the borders. I know Brennus and Drust are trying to re-establish the old alliance between the borderland and Northumberland. What I can't understand is why Brennus would spend time in Oxford when the borders are in chaos. Sam, you're going to have to trust me and tell me what's been going on there.'

Standing by the river's edge, Sam told Eagan about the night in Oxford and the appearance of the Shadow. Whilst he was speaking, Eagan kept his gaze on the river, though every now and then he would turn to ask a question. In particular he wanted to know how Sam had escaped from the Shadow and who had rescued him.

Sam found himself strangely reticent about the woman and his conversation with Jack and Ronald. Some things were just too fantastic. Also, he wasn't entirely sure he could trust Eagan. When he eventually described the events in the Seven Stories, he didn't tell him about the vision of Oscar in the tapestry either.

When he came to the feathered men who had attacked the bookshop, Eagan went pale. Without warning, he grabbed him, pulling him closer so they were facing each other.

'Tell me you're not hiding anything about Father from me!'

Although Sam was physically bigger, Eagan's strength was like iron.

'Let go of me! I don't know what happened to him. That's all I can say.'

Eagan released him and turned back to the river. 'You'll have to meet the Forest Reivers,' he said quietly, 'for they have a story of the crow-men who used to live under the Cheviot Hills.'

Sam found himself thinking about what he had seen in his own back garden. 'Crow-men' sounded a very satisfying name for them.

They had been standing beside the river for nearly an hour when a crow appeared, flying low along the river. Instantly, Sam threw himself to the ground and scrambled behind the table.

'Sam – that's just a crow.'

Eagan was still by the water's edge. Sam waited until he was certain the crow had gone before regaining his feet and warily making his way back down to him.

'Before the attacks in Oxford and Gosforth, crows were behaving in an unnatural way.'

'Unnatural way?'

'Almost as if they were intelligent, as if they were drawing an invisible map.'

'Crows are very intelligent, I'll give you that. Come to think about it, a couple of weeks ago there was a murder of crows roosting on the fringes of Birling Wood.'

'That sounds too close for comfort, Eagan. You know, I'm no longer sure I should have come to Warkworth. But it doesn't seem that anywhere's safe.'

'I'm just surprised that Brennus didn't keep you with him, that he let you come here when he knows there is so much unrest. A lot of this doesn't make sense. Unless…'

Eagan stared unmoving into the depths of the river. Sam waited. Across the shimmering waters it seemed as though the grey heron was waiting too.

Then Eagan raised his head. 'That's it, Sam – Brennus is playing decoy! He's giving you time to escape.'

'But I don't really know *how* to escape,' Sam whispered. 'The Shadow follows me everywhere.'

'I understand,' Eagan said gently. 'And I'd still like to know what it is and why it's following you.'

'Oscar said it was moving through the Otherland.'

'The Otherland?'

'Professor Stuckley spoke about it. It stands outside time and between places. He spoke of it as being entangled. I'm guessing it's a place that can link two places simultaneously. The Shadow must have used it to find me in Oxford.'

He felt himself toying with a question. Once or twice it almost fell from his lips but each time he sucked it back in. Then, almost without his volition, it rolled from his tongue.

'What do you know about the *Druidae*?'

'The Druids?'

Sam felt the reply slam against him and for a moment he was dizzy. He stepped back from the water's edge.

Eagan was watching him with renewed interest. 'What is it?'

'Nothing – I'm just a bit warm and the crow...'

'Come off it – when I said the word "Druids", you went drip white.'

Eagan's words rattled around Sam's head like burning marbles, making his thoughts wheel like the angry crows from last night. For just an instant, dark clouds were approaching, moving over the horizon like an angry herd of buffalo. Sam again found himself stepping back, whilst Eagan watched him with a look of puzzlement turning to concern.

'What now, Sam?'

Sam was breathing deeply, but it was like watching jigsaw pieces being swept up by the wind, only to fall, piece by piece, into their rightful places. In that moment the old school house, the garden and the river seemed to fade to grey whilst his thoughts were like threads of vibrant colour.

'The Shadow is trying to destroy the Otherland. If it does, then all communication with the Keepers will be lost. If you think about it, without the Keepers, there would have been no message to Oscar, who came to warn Professor Stuckley that the Shadow was coming.'

'But who are the Keepers?'

'Listen, the Shadow could be seeking *Oscar*, not me!'

Eagan was mystified. 'But Oscar's no longer around to be pursued by anything.'

Overwhelmed with relief, Sam wasn't listening. 'I could have just been in the wrong place at the wrong time! I could just be caught up in this because I happened to be the person who carried Oscar's message to the professors!'

It was an intriguing thought. If he hadn't met Oscar that day, he wouldn't have found himself in this predicament. It was, after all, his own words to the Keepers that had found their way to Oscar and the sequence had started again.

Eagan was trying to keep up. 'And the old man in the Blindburn?' he asked.

But Sam couldn't answer. A crow was flying upstream and turning west. Sam bobbed down behind the table just in time, or so he hoped. He remained there whilst Eagan followed the bird's path, watching it until it had disappeared over the bridge.

They waited in silence, but no further crows came. Eventually Sam had the confidence to rejoin Eagan at the edge of the river.

'You need to take me to the orchard,' he said. 'I think that's where I'll find Oscar. We need to stop this happening.'

Eagan shot Sam a hurried glance. 'You won't find Oscar there, and I'm not sure what *is* happening.'

Sam's mind was back with Professor Stuckley's lectures on quantum mechanics.

'What if it was my choice to visit the orchard and therefore my responsibility?'

'I would stop you.' A flicker of anger crossed Eagan's face as he turned back to look at the slow-moving water. 'There's no point to it. Oscar isn't there. He has gone, just like the Druids.'

He walked towards the small wooden jetty, signalling that the conversation was over.

Climbing into his boat, he called, 'I'll take you to meet the Forest Reivers tomorrow – they may be able to shed some light on your story. If I were you, I wouldn't wander much beyond the village in the meantime.'

Thoughtfully, Sam walked back towards the house.

* * * * * *

Sam found Emily in the library. It was now mid-afternoon and they decided to go up to the village.

On the way, Sam decided to leave the conversation about Emily's mother and father for another day. Instead he told her about his belief that the Shadow could be hunting Oscar and not him.

'That would be such a relief,' he said.

'That's something of an understatement,' Emily remarked.

Sam actually laughed.

But then Emily added, 'Only how would it help us now?'

'I'm not really sure,' Sam admitted. 'That's why I have to talk to Oscar. I have to get into Birling Wood and find the Garden of Druids. I'm sure, from what Eagan has said, that it's something to do with the orchard. I don't understand why he doesn't want to take me there now.'

'I don't trust him at all,' Emily muttered.

* * * * * *

She cheered up as they entered Warkworth. The village was busy with the last days of the summer holidays. The small tearooms were overflowing with people travelling south towards Amble and north to the Northumberland coastal route, and for a while Emily and Sam enjoyed being lost in the hustle and bustle.

They stopped for tea at a little tearoom at the bottom of the steep hill, then walked the full length of the small high street and started to climb up to the castle. Every now and then Emily would pop into one of the picturesque galleries that lined the way. Sam couldn't believe the amount of time she spent studying the paintings and sculptures, but he was pleased to see her enjoying herself after the horrors of the night before.

It was early evening when they reached the top of the hill and stood looking up at the castle, which was catching the last of the sunshine. It was said the foundations of Warkworth Castle had been laid before the Norman Conquest. It had stood there for a thousand years, watching people come and go, their fortunes rising and falling.

Sam and Emily were drawn to the views from its walls. From their vantage point high above the slate rooftops, Warkworth was spread out like a fine watercolour with streaks of red vibrant on the skyline. They could almost see back to the arched bridge and down to the old school house. In the east the faintest flicker of the sea sent the light scattering, whilst the Coquet now appeared like a giant serpent snaking through the deep green of Birling Wood.

They stood next to each other and Sam felt his fears melt away in the sun. Emily gently slipped her hand into his.

'I hope you find your answers.' She squeezed his hand.

Sam felt the sting of tears. To hide them, he looked over at the dark line of trees.

'They're somewhere in that wood.'

'Are you sure? I've been there dozens of times and there's nothing there but trees.'

'That may be how they are protecting the way to the Otherland. I was in a circle of trees when I met Oscar in Oxford. I think that's got something to do with how he travelled there.'

'If I were you, I'd just keep your head down and hope Brennus and Drust are still alive and can find the answers for you.'

'You know what the letter says.'

'Yes, but we don't know who's writing the letter. We don't even know if it really *was* Oscar you met. And let's not forget the traitor. If we can believe that part.'

'We *can* believe,' said Sam, 'that the Shadow has something to do with the Druids.'

Even in this place his throat felt suddenly dry. He would not forget the word it had said beneath the Fellows' House and in the tapestry.

'It said their name. Twice. I need to know why.'

'And when you do find out why, what then? I mean, there aren't exactly a lot of Druids running around here nowadays.'

Trust Emily to put her finger on the weakest part of any argument, Sam thought.

'Well, we can at least tell Professor Stuckley, or your uncle, or someone else who can do something about it.'

'Mmmm.' Emily didn't sound terribly impressed.

Moving on quickly, Sam said, 'I just need a way to distract Eagan tomorrow, so I can sneak off to the wood and try to find the Garden of Druids. Any ideas how?'

'No, Sam, and don't look at me, I'm not distracting anyone.'

Sam couldn't help but laugh. 'You distract *me* often enough!'

There was a moment's awkward silence, then Sam managed a smile.

'Come on, Emily, I'm sure you'd love to put one over on him.'

Emily turned Sam to face her. Her dark eyes were lit by the sunlight and she had a slight flush to her cheeks.

'Are you trying some reverse psychology on me, Samuel Wood?' she asked, laughing. 'Well, if you are, all right, it's worked. I'll do it, but just remember what I told you about Eagan. The rumour is that Morcant was in a bad way. I might not like him, but they say he spent a good few days in hospital and that he had deep wounds to his neck. So be careful.'

Sam leaned forward and placed his hands on the castle's time-worn stone. Hadn't that attack taken place when Eagan was on his way to the orchard? Perhaps Morcant knew about the Garden of Druids. He shivered suddenly. He didn't like that thought.

The late summer sun was fading now and a chill seemed to be seeping into him. He looked around. The castle was almost empty. There were one or two people on the far wall, but they were making their way to the stairs.

Somewhere far off, music was being played. It was almost imperceptible, as if filtered through the stone Sam was standing on. The harder he tried to focus on it, the more obscure it became. He felt a little unsteady and found himself pressing his hands into the hard stone for support. A gentle fluttering vibration passed from it to his hands and then his whole body, and he began to understand the music, as if it were a language. A voice was calling to him.

'The enemy is amongst you. Great danger is coming. Come to me.'

Was it Jack's voice, or perhaps Oscar's, or even that of the Garden of Druids itself? As Sam listened to the words trembling through his mind, he felt that whoever it was, somewhere in the wood, the Garden of Druids was calling to him. At that moment he knew that the answers to the riddles that had played out over the last few days would be found there. The clarity was like the flow of water from a mountain spring. He could see it swirling past him and through him. He could feel it, like warmth in his heart.

'Emily.' He felt himself reaching out to her.

'What is it?' Emily had been gazing at the wood.

'The Garden of Druids *is* the orchard.'

'What?'

'I think it just called out to me.'

'What are you on about?'

'I have to go there soon, Emily. Great danger is coming.'

As he repeated the words, he looked around him. All the sightseers had gone. Suddenly he felt they had made a mistake climbing to the top of the castle.

'I don't think we should be in the open. It isn't just the Shadow looking for us, but the things from the bookshop. The Reivers call them crow-men.'

'What? That's a fairy story.'

'You know it's not, Emily.'

He took her hand and pulled her after him down the steps. They were soon off the wall.

'This way.'

Instead of taking the main village road, Sam led Emily across the road to a long stairwell that led from the top of the village down to the river. All he could think as they descended the steps was how foolish they had been, acting as though they'd come to Warkworth for a break.

Reaching the bottom of the steps, they crossed a dirt road and came to a stone wall.

'I don't understand how one minute you're enjoying the scenery and the next we're running from our shadows,' Emily muttered.

'Don't joke – it's not funny.'

'I wasn't—'

She stopped in mid-sentence. Sam pushed himself up against her, trying to flatten them both against the wall. Three black shapes were flying low over the river, coming from the south, the direction of Amble harbour. They were spread across the river and when they grew closer Sam could tell they were scouring the banks. There was no doubt in his mind that they were looking for them.

They passed by not more than a hundred yards from where they were hiding, calling to one another every so often.

'It's building,' he whispered. 'Just like the evening in Oxford.' He could feel the tension in the air. 'Whoever attacked the bookshop and the house is looking for us. They won't stop looking for us. I have to reach the orchard and talk to Oscar. I'll ask Eagan the way. I'll *make* him take me if I have to.'

'But what if the man you met wasn't Oscar? What if the letter is a lie? What if Eagan is the traitor?'

'I don't—'

Sam got no further before Emily grabbed hold of him and slapped her hand over his mouth. A moment later the distinct sound of crows calling to each other came to them from the far side of the river.

Sam daren't move. The calls were loud and excited and he could tell the crows were flying in numbers.

It seemed to take an age for them to pass by. Even when the last of them had gone, Sam and Emily remained standing there. Then she dropped her hand and he put his arms round her. She raised her face to his and he saw tears in her eyes

'I'm so scared, Sam,' she whispered. 'I don't think I can do this anymore. I just want to go home.'

Sam felt a mix of emotions swirling through his body. Fear was there, along with anger and defiance. He was going to find the answers that would bring an end to this.

'Everything's going to be all right, Emily. I'm frightened, but I'm no longer overcome by it. I really don't blame you if you decide to go home. But I'll sort this out somehow, I promise you.'

Taking cover behind a long line of trees, they made their way slowly back to the old school house.

CROW-MEN

Twilight fell and Eagan still hadn't returned. Emily retired to bed early, looking exhausted by the day's events. Sam sat in the garden for a while, but tiredness rolled over him without warning and even the chill breeze couldn't keep his eyes open. It wasn't long before he made his way back to the house.

He ended up in the silence of the library. It spanned the full width of the old school house and its bookcases stretched from floor to ceiling. At the far end was a round desk made from a light wood in front of a large arched window looking directly onto the sloping lawn and river. On the far bank the heron was back, its harsh call ringing out.

Sam's tiredness was forgotten as he found himself walking the length of the room, stopping every now and again to reach for a book. The library was a treasure trove of first editions – *Where the Wild Things Are*, *Swallows and Amazons*, the Famous Five stories, *The Railway Children*, *The Wind in the Willows*, *Goodnight, Mister Tom*. Sam took each from its place, feeling its weight, spellbound by its colours and catching its dusty smell as he opened its pages. Some were perfect, others less, so but they were all here, the great and the good.

Taking a copy of *The Secret Garden*, he seated himself at the desk, looking out over another sort of secret garden. Every now and then swans would glide by, apparently without a care in the world, but he knew they would be paddling beneath the surface. He managed a smile as he lit the lamp and turned the book over in his hand.

Life wasn't like fiction, he thought. In fact, it was all a bit of mess. First Oxford, then Gosforth – all the places that had provided him with solace had become unsafe. Perhaps this one would too.

His thoughts turned to the professors, out in the wilds of Northumberland somewhere. He hoped they would find a resolution to what was going on. How could he find out?

Of course! He found himself reaching for the letter Oscar had given him. Then suddenly he was nervous. This time he wanted it to have changed, but what if it told him that Eagan couldn't be trusted? Or that the Shadow had found him? What would he do then? He shivered, despite the warmth of the library.

He turned the letter over in his hands, almost irritated with it. The envelope looked old and battered in the light of the lamp. He opened it and half withdrew the letter, then stopped. Then he withdrew it completely, but laid it face down on the desk.

It reminded him of a lecture Professor Stuckley had given during his first week at Cherwell. The professor had spoken about a famous thought experiment called Schrödinger's cat. The imaginary cat is locked in a box and its life is determined by the state of a radioactive atom. Quantum mechanics suggests that before you open the box the atom can be in many states – a 'quantum superstition' as the professor had so eloquently described it. So the cat can be both dead and alive at the same time. It is only on opening the box that the atom is in one state only and you can be certain the cat is either dead or alive.

What if the letter from Oscar was acting in the same way? At the moment it was face down and Sam couldn't make out any letters. What if its meaning were entangled, a wave of probabilities that would collapse into one certainty as soon as Sam turned it over and began to observe it? And what if he had a part to play in that meaning?

He sat back in his chair, drumming his fingers on the desktop. His eye was caught by the circular pattern in the wood's grain. When he sat forward he could no longer see it, so he began to gently rock back and forwards, making the circle disappear and reappear at will. It was only when he was at a 45-degree angle that he could see it completely.

That was another thing, thought Sam. All the doors in the Old School House were solid round wooden doors when he thought about it a moment longer, the whole of the Reign's family home had the same architectural coloration, the same feel and look as the seventh floor of the bookshop. Though this wasn't odd considering it was owned by the same family he had seen this arrangement before and it was the sudden and jarring comprehension that stopped him in his tracks. The design of the doors, the bookcases, the windows and even the furniture recalled the Fellow's house at Magdalen, the Eagle and Child and one other place. It had been prodding him from the deep places on the far edge of his sub-conscious, it had evaded him only because the past week had been moving at such a pace, but no he had seen these doors at his home. The circular design had been the elephant in the room, an elephant made of the same wood he had touched in the Fellow's garden the night Oscar appeared.

This was ridiculous, he thought. He was just wasting time.

He took a deep breath and turned the letter over.

He didn't have to read it to know it had changed. He could see at once it had been written by a different hand. There was a new message waiting to be read. Whatever it was, if he read it, it would change the course he took. What if he chose not to read it?

What if he chose to ignore the Shadow altogether? Would it stop existing or would it creep up on him without warning? Could he afford to ignore such messages from the past – or were they from the future? Hadn't the night in the Eagle and Child created a paradox – one that was almost impossible to overcome?

Impatiently, he leaned forward again and picked the letter up.

Dearest Sam,

We can only guess your bewilderment at the turn of events. The moving parts are now in free fall and it is difficult to offer counsel at this time. We are only too aware of the paradox that grows in the telling.

Though we regret the hurt our words will cause you, know that we have long deliberated and found we must tell you that Brennus and Drust are journeying to the Dead Water and are pursued relentlessly by our enemy. You cannot expect them to return to you.

We ask that you prepare to leave at short notice, but only when the Forest Reivers come down from the hills.

Know that the Dagda seeks you. We do not know what part he has to play, but he will find you.

We are sorry.

Jack

'*You cannot expect them to return to you.*' Sam let the letter fall back onto the desk, not wanting to touch it a second longer.

The professors were drawing the Shadow to themselves, sacrificing themselves so he could escape. How could this have happened? Who could he tell? What could he do? Was it too late to change their fate? He thought about the terror he'd faced in Magdalen. The professors would be facing that same terror in the dark hills of Northumberland. No, he couldn't bear it!

He jumped to his feet and started pacing across the wooden floor. The light from the lamp seemed to intensify, but he didn't notice it. The professors were walking into a trap!

Sizzling with adrenaline, he crossed from the west wing into the main hall and ran up the stairs.

'Emily! Emily!'

'Sam?' Emily appeared from the back bedroom, bleary-eyed and clearly not happy at being woken up. He grabbed her by the arm and pulled her along the corridor.

'The letter's changed again! The professors are walking into a trap and they won't return!'

'Slow down – what's happening?'

Emily swung Sam around and took his hand off her arm. 'Show me the letter!'

He led her back to the library and handed it to her.

Emily's face went pale as she read it. Then she looked up at Sam. 'What about my uncle? He was with them. It doesn't mention him.'

'No. What does that mean?'

They stared at each other.

Then Sam said firmly, 'Look, I think we have to tell Eagan about this.'

'No, Sam!' Emily howled. 'I've already *told* you he can't be trusted. He's already upset half the village, he's hand in glove with the Forest Reivers and what about that business with Morcant?'

'Jarl's his father – surely he has the right to know?'

Exasperated, Emily waved the letter in the air. 'This warns you to leave when the Forest Reivers come down from the hills. It warns you to have nothing to do with them, Sam! Indirectly, that means Eagan too.'

'It doesn't say that, Emily. It could equally mean that they will bring us news that will help us.'

'The Forest Reivers help no one but themselves.'

Emily laid the letter back down on the desk with an air of finality.

'Well, I'm still going to try and find Oscar in this Garden of Druids,' said Sam. 'What else can I do?' He sank into a chair. 'I can't send any help to the professors – I don't even know where they are.'

Emily frowned. 'If Brennus and Drust can't take care of themselves, then no one can do it for them. I think we have to use the time they have given you to get those answers from Oscar. Then we can decide from there.'

* * * * * *

It was late evening before the *Celtic Flow* came into view. Then the peerless figure of Eagan was lifting his oars and grabbing hold of the wooden jetty.

Sam and Emily met him at the door, but to their surprise, instead of greeting them he walked right past them and into the library.

'What's he up to now?' Emily asked.

'Who knows?' Sam answered. He felt just a little perturbed by Eagan's grim expression.

There was nothing for it but to follow him into the library. They found him standing by the desk.

'When were you going to tell me that you talk with the dead, Sam?' His voice was loud and had lost all of its good humour.

'I don't know what you mean,' Sam replied, feeling the blood rush to his face. 'Are you telling me something about Oscar? Whatever it is, I don't much like your tone. What's happened?'

Eagan placed both hands on the desk and leaned over it, looking back at them with eyes that suddenly blazed with anger.

'You don't like my tone. Well, let me tell you, there's a lot *I* don't like! Look at you – you turn up at my home uninvited, you eat my food and you do nothing but criticise me. I'm kept in the dark by my own parents about who you really are and I'm even thrown in jail because of the wretched Morcant Pauperhaugh's treachery. Do I deserve that?'

Sam and Emily exchanged quick glances.

'I tend the orchard and rebuild relations with the Forest Reivers,' Eagan went on, slamming his hand down on the table, 'and even my own father refuses to tell me the truth. In fact, no one has the *decency*, let alone the *courtesy*, to tell me anything! Why didn't you tell me about the letter?'

Sam froze and his hand instinctively went to his back pocket, but there was nothing there. Of course, they'd left it on the desk. There was no sign of it now.

Eagan let out an odd laugh.

'And why won't you tell me anything about my father? Is that my thanks for my hospitality to you?'

Sam shifted uncomfortably.

'I know who wrote this letter.' Eagan held up the now ragged piece of paper. 'I would just like to know why the Keepers of the Ruin are guiding you.'

Sam was taken aback. Was that who they were? But what did that mean?

'And Emily,' Eagan continued, '*I* didn't cause your mother and father's break-up. You need to stop being so insolent or I swear...'

'Swear what, Eagan? That you'll rip my throat out too?'

In one swift move, Eagan had leaped over the table and before Sam could think what to do he was standing over Emily with a menacing snarl, fist raised.

Then he took a step back, breathing heavily.

'I want you to leave, Sam. I know who you are and they'll never leave you alone. Already you have put my family in great danger and it's only just begun for you.'

Sam went pale.

Eagan turned back to Emily. She was looking petrified.

'Your mother and father are splitting up because a Reign and a Pauperhaugh should never have got married in the first place. You keep believing it's down to me and you'll be as big a fool as your father is. Now go and don't come back.'

Sam moved between him and Emily and took her hand. Her grip was tight and tense. Making sure to pick up the letter, he led her out of the room. As they walked into the hall, they could hear Eagan calling after them, telling them to leave Warkworth for good.

Sam closed Emily's bedroom door and rested his head against the thick wood. He was shocked. Emily had clearly been right. They couldn't rely on Eagan at all.

'What actually happened back there?' he asked.

'He's always had a temper. It used to get him in trouble at school and with the neighbours. But I've never seen him like that, Sam. I thought he was going to hit me – perhaps worse. I know you'll still want to go to Birling Wood and find the orchard, but if he finds you in there, who knows what he'll be capable of?'

The thought had already crossed Sam's mind.

'I don't think I have an option.'

'Of course you do. That's what he wants. He'd like nothing more than to find you in the wood. And me too.'

She rubbed her hands over her face.

'I don't think I can do it, Sam. I'm sorry, but I'm going back to Newcastle. You can come and stay with my mum in Jesmond.'

'No.' Sam shook his head. 'Eagan's going to have his hands full this evening. Those crows will bring trouble with them tonight. I can't wait any longer. Can you get me to the orchard?'

'I can get you there, but we'll need to avoid the Forest Reivers, otherwise they'll alert Eagan.'

She looked at Sam and he could see fear in her eyes.

'Listen,' she said quietly, almost pleading with him, 'are you sure you don't want to catch the train back and forget about all this?'

'I don't think I *can* go back. You go if you want. I think Oscar is my only hope.'

* * * * * *

Eagan sat in the garden with only his guilt for company. What he had done to Emily and Sam was almost unforgivable, but it was the only way. He owed Sam an apology and hoped that when they realised what was about to happen, they would forgive him. Still, he hadn't enjoyed his final performance. He sat there heavy with guilt and resignation.

Reading the letter had simply reinforced his suspicions. He'd known his father, Brennus and Drust were prepared to lay their lives down for a cause they didn't fully understand. He took a deep breath and slumped back in his chair.

As daylight seeped out of Warkworth, the edges of Birling Wood became into black walls. Eagan hoped that Emily and Sam were already clear of its edges and making their way to the orchard. Would Sam really find Oscar? Surely not.

He felt the strain of the last few weeks in his neck and shoulders as he rested his hands on his lap and waited. The air was cool. The garden was still and silent. He could hear the gentle roll of the river and make out its twisting shape against the now shadowy banks. He took another breath, taking little comfort from the cold touch of the chair against his back.

He stood and stretched and walked the short distance to the wooden jetty. The *Celtic Flow* was pulling against the knotted rope, creaking and groaning. The odd car was trundling across Warkworth Bridge on its way south and a blackbird was skittering across the lawn, signalling to Eagan that he was still alone and the enemy had not yet arrived.

He knew he had been kept in the dark about Sam's true nature, but he accepted that. It wasn't his place to know. Brennus had tried to protect everyone as well as keep together the old alliance. He had even tried single-handedly to recreate the Keepers, for the Keepers had been the faithful partners of the Druids, studying their lore and the magic they had brought to the Mid-land. But the enemy had grown in numbers and confidence. And the new alliance had been built on sand, on the flawed relationships between the old families of Northumberland.

Eagan sighed. His father had suspected there was a traitor amongst them. Morcant was the main suspect, but there might be more than one.

He wished he could have been more open with Sam, but the school house had been watched for a number of weeks. The old man he had met in the Blindburn had warned him that a Grim-were had appeared from the Underland with its own questions about the emergence of the Shadow. It would take the form of a grey heron in the daylight and its true shape at nightfall.

Eagan found himself shivering at the thought. The heron had indeed appeared across the river. It was never far from the garden now, walking up and down the riverbank in what appeared an endless search for food, yet finding nothing. But Eagan had used that to his advantage, purposefully bringing Sam to the water's edge so he could tell him and the listening enemy that only he could take them to the orchard. He had put on quite a performance, he thought, for the watchful heron.

It saddened him to think about the friction with Emily, but he also knew that her dislike of him would mean she would take Sam straight to the orchard. The only problem with his master plan was that, like the Hoods and his father, he had become the bait.

The old man had told him far more than he had admitted to Sam. The enemy would attack on the first night. They would come in great numbers, both crow-men and the Grim-were, who could take any shape, including that of those it had slaughtered. He would need the strength of the Forest Reivers, whom he had summoned from their secret places in the forest borders. Uncertain times called for the certainty of great allies, and there were none more powerful than the Forest Reivers.

As evening turned to night, however, he found himself wondering if they would come to his aid and whether it would be enough to turn back the tide that was creeping silently through the lands. As the time continued to flow, a horrible thought occurred to him: what if the enemy hadn't been fooled and whilst he was standing there Sam and Emily were being hunted like animals?

Then hair on the back of his neck rose and he found himself crouching down, almost sightless in the darkness. There had been just the tiniest of splashes in the river.

Alarm surging through his body, he started walking slowly backwards from the wooden jetty whilst reaching behind him and sliding two long knives from the sheaths fastened tightly to his body. There were white ripples in the darkness of the river and he could make out movement on the far bank. Something was dropping from the edge of the wood where the tree roots drank from the river.

When the first bent and twisted shapes, feathered and black, hauled themselves out of the water and lurched onto the bank, Eagan was hit with the bitter realisation that he was out of his depth. In the darkness their wicked beaks and eyes were glittering. How many were they? How had Emily and Sam faced such a threat and survived?

Less than a hundred feet away, they stood and mocked him with a hideous noise. He could smell their poison even from this distance, a foul and fetid reek that spoke of evil to come. Then the lines of misshapen forms went quiet and a figure stepped out, bloodied and torn.

Eagan knew this was not his father but an apparition sent to ridicule and torment him. Still his long knives were suddenly limp in his nerveless fingers.

'Where is the girl?'

That wasn't what Eagan had expected.

'First tell me who you are.' His voice sounded weak and jittery.

'She *was* here,' the voice grated.

He was silent, waiting for a sign from the dark wood, but nothing came. The Forest Reivers were not coming to his aid.

Then the crow-men's unnatural clamour broke out again, freezing Eagan's blood. They attacked without warning, quick and hungry.

Eagan was swift and powerful. The force of his blows took them by surprise. He rolled and span, but as he swung his knives down upon them, opening up their bodies, he knew they meant to capture him alive, for several let themselves fall. He danced amongst them, their blood stinging his arms. They were herding him away from the house, down towards the river.

For all his strength and speed, a deep gash to his back sent sparks of pain gushing through his body and his breath exploding out of his lungs. Still he danced on, parrying and cutting, and still they fell, but soon they had encircled him in a tormenting wall of misery. They began to hold back, allowing him to feel the venom surging through him. His throat was beginning to burn with the poisonous flow.

The thought of being captured by them turned his stomach. He couldn't let it happen. As his vision begin to slip and slide, he turned his knives towards his own chest. Gathering all his strength, he thrust them inwards.

There was an explosion in his mind, a pain that blinded him, and then he was falling forward into a cold anguish.

* * * * * *

Sam and Emily had been walking along the river for nearly an hour. They had reached a part where the waters were clear and the trees on either side were alive with birds preparing to roost for the night. A slight breeze was rustling the leaves and joining the river's song.

Emily knew what she had to do. Over the years she'd spent several summer holidays helping Jarl and Eagan pick the fruit for Alnwick market. But this would be the first time she'd gone to the orchard without either of them.

She stopped beside a boat. It was a small rowing boat not dissimilar to the *Celtic Flow*.

'Whose is this? Why have they left it moored so far from Warkworth?' Sam was looking over his shoulder anxiously.

Ignoring him, Emily said, 'We need to cross the river.'

'Shouldn't we have just crossed the bridge?'

That was a good question, thought Emily. She ignored that one too.

She held the wooden mooring post and put first one leg and then the other into the boat, then fished around for the oars.

'Do you actually know whose boat this is?' Sam asked.

Emily gave him a little wink and proceeded to grab the oars and place her feet into the single set of riggers.

'If you want me to take you to the orchard and make sure no one can follow us, just get in.'

Sam felt a little uneasy about taking someone's boat, but Emily had made a good point – no one could follow your scent across a river. He gingerly climbed in and took the opposite seat, looking back the way they had come. He watched as Emily raised the oars and pushed off, gaining the centre of the river with great finesse.

'I didn't know you could row like that.'

'You don't know everything about me.'

She was settling into a rhythm, making sure she was rowing down the very middle of the river, away from the banks.

Birling Wood was now thick and dark on either side of them. The first autumn leaves were beginning to fall, gently twirling down all around them. The further Emily rowed under the broad canopy, the stronger the wind seemed to become. The banks drew closer together and the trees leaned in around them.

Emily had been rowing no more than thirty minutes when she started making for the far bank. Sam looked on in admiration as she manoeuvred the boat into a small culvert where a wooden stake and thick rope were lying waiting.

It took them only a few moments to moor the boat and make sure it was secure against the current, which had strengthened as the river had narrowed. Emily's cheeks were flushed and her hair damp against her forehead. Sam felt just a touch guilty for not offering to help, although he guessed he would have been more of a hindrance.

'Right.'

Standing on the bank, Emily faced the river and took a small compass from her pocket.

'We need to bear northwest and head over towards the Cauldron.'

'Cauldron?'

Emily ignored him yet again. 'It shouldn't take us too long to get to the orchard. I'm guessing it's less than five miles from here. Let's leave our rucksacks in the boat.'

They set off. Emily carried a bottle of water, but before long she was wishing she'd brought a torch and a coat as well. The day had been warm, but with night approaching it had turned altogether colder.

They walked together but spoke little, concentrating on following a path that might once have existed but had been swallowed by the slow march of tree and undergrowth. The further they walked, the more the wood seemed to close in, and they felt stifled by the smells of damp earth and rotting bark.

Trudging through the gloom, Emily could barely make out the compass readings and started stopping every couple of minutes, spinning around and looking up into the dark night, trying to ascertain their whereabouts.

Sam was beginning to feel claustrophobic and a little disorientated. He could feel the strain in his legs as he walked, but Emily kept on pressing ahead. The alder and willow by the river's edge had given way to oak and ash, and they were now passing beneath the dark foliage of giant yews, trees that had been around for hundreds of years, perhaps thousands.

In the first clearing since leaving the river, they came to a stop.

Sam couldn't hold back any longer. 'Are we lost?'

'Yes and no.' Emily was pressing her face against the compass.

'What does that mean?'

The last thing Sam wanted was to be lost in Birling Wood at night with only a bottle of water as provisions, not forgetting what could be following them.

'It looks familiar, but there's a rope bridge that takes us across the Cauldron and we should have been there by now. I think we may have come a little too far west, but we can correct it.'

Emily tapped the compass whilst Sam frowned. He still didn't understand why Emily had brought them this way when surely they could have crossed the bridge at Warkworth and come into the orchard by an easier route.

Outside the clearing it was pitch black and eerily quiet. Sam could barely see beyond his hand.

'How do we know the Shadow isn't out there?'

'I think it would be impossible for it to track us once we crossed the river.'

'Not if it was moving through the Otherland,' Sam thought. If it was doing that, it could be very close indeed. In fact, wasn't he heading towards the very place where it could find him?

They set off again, with Emily taking them north. The way seemed to be blocked by bushes thick with thorns that snagged their clothing and grazed their exposed arms, but finally they arrived in a part of the wood where the trees were more widely spaced.

The air was thick with a musky scent that made their noses run and the back of their throats tingle. Sam was breathing heavily after another sharp climb, whilst just ahead Emily was muttering to herself about the elusive rope bridge.

The further they went, more it was becoming clear to Sam that they really were lost.

'Perhaps we should find a place to shelter and start up again in the morning,' he suggested. 'Then you'll be able to see the compass more easily. Or we could always try to go back.'

'We can't go back, Sam. I just don't understand how we've missed the bridge.'

'Well then, let's go on.'

They set off again and, after clambering up a short ridge, stumbled upon on a path of finely cut logs.

'At last!'

Sam could hear the relief in Emily's voice.

'Who made this path?'

'Eagan.'

'It would have taken ages. Surely he had help.'

'No, he cut each log and brought them all here himself. Now whatever you do, don't step off the path. There are traps running all through this place.'

'How do you know?'

'Eagan put them there,' came the answer.

The path seemed to start in the middle of nowhere and lead through a group of shadowy elms. Sam couldn't guess how far they reached skyward, but their trunks were like titans standing guard over some lost world. It was unnerving moving through them on a path of logs that couldn't have been more than two feet wide, knowing there were traps to either side. He could see no more than a couple of steps ahead and to his left and right was a sea of blackness.

The river had been full of birdsong and life, but this part of the wood was quiet and imposing. To Sam, it was as if they were trespassing through a place that should have been left in peace. He shivered. The breeze had turned chill.

Ahead, Emily had come to a stop between two giant elders. It was as if they had been planted to create a natural gateway.

'What is it?' Sam carefully squeezed himself alongside her.

'The bridge is just ahead.'

Sam had expected the gloom to lift, but he was still blinking back the darkness from his eyes, whilst all around him a fuzzy blackness swarmed around his head.

Emily led the way to a rope bridge and set off across it, walking slowly and placing her feet firmly one after the other.

As Sam stepped onto the bridge, both the air and the smell changed in an instant. He still could not see, but knew that somewhere below a cavernous space had opened up. It seemed as though they were crossing a gorge.

'What is this place?' he asked, his hands gripping the rope handrail.

'I don't know. I've never crossed this bridge before.'

'What? I thought you'd visited the orchard with Eagan many times!'

'I have, Sam, it's just that,' Emily wiped cold sweat from her eyes, 'the way to the orchard is never quite the same. The bridge doesn't even feel like this in the daylight. I don't think this is the same one at all – it's changed somehow.'

'You really aren't helping matters, Emily.'

Feeling the bridge bouncing with every step, Sam increased his grip on the rope.

'Stop moaning, Sam. I don't like this any more than you, but it's the only way to get to the orchard.'

'This orchard is pretty hard to find. Whoever planted it obviously didn't want anyone *to* find it.'

The truth of Sam's words struck them both in the darkness.

Emily came to a stop.

'Go on. We should keep going,' Sam urged. He could no longer hide his discomfort. They were swinging on a rope bridge in absolute darkness.

'It all feels different.'

'So you keep saying, but we have to either go forward or go back. And this bridge feels as though it hasn't been used for decades, so we ought to make a decision *now*.'

Sam's voice had risen and there was a touch of desperation to it.

Emily edged forward again, then gave a cry of relief. She was across.

Sam followed her and found himself hugging her in the darkness. To his amazement, she burst into tears. Then she loosened her grip just enough to speak.

'I just want you to know I thought you were very courageous back there.'

Sam looked at her, amazed. She must have been scared – it was the first compliment she'd ever given him.

* * * * * *

It was still pitch black in this part of the wood. Looking back to try and see something of the way they had come, all they could see was the end of the rope bridge.

The darkness seemed to be moving with them, Sam thought. When he tried to peer up through the trees' canopy, any possibility of seeing the twinkle of stars was quickly extinguished. And the place felt haunted somehow.

Emily was again looking at her compass, but it was first pointing one way then another, and no matter what she did it wouldn't settle.

Fortunately, there was a clearly a path of sorts. It led them through some tangled bushes and up and over a hill. Down the other side they went, stumbling through the darkness, and found themselves in an open space. For the first time in hours they could see more of their surroundings.

They had arrived at a short waterfall which tumbled over a sheer rock face into a small pool. From it, a fast-flowing stream wound its way back into the dark wood.

Sam had almost reached the water's edge before he noticed the old man. How long he'd been waiting for them, he never would find out.

'Come and sit with me.'

He was hanging his legs over the side of the rock and letting his feet dangle into the pool's clear waters. His face was furrowed and lined, his hair was white and his eyes were ringed like ancient oaks. He wore a simple brown habit like that of a monk and his sandals were placed beside him. Sam knew instantly he was the self-same man that Eagan had met in the Blindburn.

'I last saw you eighteen years ago, Samuel,' he said with a warm smile.

Somehow Sam wasn't surprised he knew his name. The surprise was that they had met at all.

'You won't remember. Your father brought you to see me and I was glad that he did. I didn't think we would meet again so soon. It's a shame we couldn't have met for a stroll in the high woods or swam together in the source of all these rivers, but alas, the shadows grow long and it must wait for the beginning.

'Now, Emily, come here, child, and let me wash those tears from your face.'

Emily found herself sitting next to the old man whilst he gently scooped up clear water from the pool and washed her face with it. It was cold, but the moment it touched her skin, she felt as though she had drunk an invigorating elixir bursting with light and life.

The old man smiled and said, 'Both of you, bathe your feet in the pool.'

The moment his feet touched the water, Sam felt his weariness rise from his feet to the top of his head and disappear.

'I can spend only a little time with you,' the old man said, 'for there are others who need my help and I must go to them before the night ends.'

Sam and Emily did not question his words, for it seemed as though he was only saying what they both already knew.

'There is now much in darkness,' he continued. 'The world turns and there is no longer certainty that morning will follow night. The Fall is dying and a Shadow has passed through. We do not know its name or where it has come from, other than it is a servant of the Ruin.'

They understood his words. They had always known he would speak them.

'One other has awoken in the deep places. Her hatred of the *Druidae* runs deeper than seams of gold under the hills and great treachery will be in the heart of those who fall under her spell. Men will listen to grand words with only hollow deeds behind them.

'I asked Eagan to bring you here and I am grateful that you came. The way ahead is unclear to me, but there are others who walk the Earth and they will help you along the way. I have sent my daughters into the world and they may aid you.

'Go seek your answers in the Garden of the Druids and remember that chance must play its part, as must faith. You are not alone in this world. The road ahead will twist and turn, and in the dark hours help will be there if you ask for it.'

The old man smiled again, then raised his arm and a giant king-fisher swooped down and landed on it. It had the deepest orange and blue colouring and its beak was silver and long. It spoke to the old man through melodious whistles, then launched itself into the air and turned in midflight before vanishing in a blur of colour.

'It is time for you to go. The Grim-were has found your boat and will be here soon.'

'But where are we? What is this place?' It was Emily who had woken first from her dream.

'A place that is not for meant for the living. Follow the stream and it will bring you back safely to the wood. In the uplands, the orchard will find you.'

* * * * * *

They walked for a while, each with their own thoughts. It was Sam who spoke first.

'I think it's safe to say that this has been an interesting walk in the woods.'

Emily laughed. 'I still don't quite know what happened back there,' she said softly, 'but I feel invigorated somehow. Whether it was the old man or the water…'

'I'm just glad he is on our side,' Sam added. 'It feels at long last that the Shadow has an equal.'

They carried on following the stream, but it wasn't long before it disappeared underneath a steep slope thick with trees.

'What now?' Emily asked.

'Let's go up.'

When they had scrambled to the top, they realised they had climbed a hill that looked out over Birling Wood. The night sky was ablaze with starlight. To the north they could see the faint twinkle of

Alnmouth, though to the south Amble harbour was nothing more than an obscure haze.

'Where's the orchard?'

'I don't know, Sam, but listen.'

From east to west, the wood was beginning to stir, coming alive with sound and movement. Horses were neighing and gruff voices were drifting on the air. On the far slope, shadowy figures on horseback were emerging from the wood in long lines.

'Quick, Emily, this way!'

But it was too late. Figures on horseback were approaching from all sides. There were hundreds in number and not all were men. Most sat astride their horses without saddles and used only coarse-looking reins. These people were unmistakable.

'Forest Reivers,' Emily whispered.

Then a voice was calling for them to be silent.

A SHADOW ON THE WALL

He had said his final farewell on the edge of the Jedburgh road. Now a cool wind soothed his scarred face as he walked across the darkening landscape. He had cleared his mind of all emotions and could feel the flow tingling through his fingers as the cards flashed from hand to hand. He was going south as Brennus and Jarl went east. He had to make the hunt last as long as possible to give them time to reach the Dead Water.

He had resolved to seek out the Faerie who dwelt in the crags in the wildest parts of Hadrian's Wall. He had kept this hidden from Brennus, for he wasn't sure what his reception would be. She was one of the Three that Oscar had mentioned in his message to Sam, the three daughters of the Dagda. They had fought alongside the Keepers over a century ago, but the alliance had long been broken.

Twilight flowed across the Northumberland landscape like sand falling through glass. He had been walking for near on ten hours, a slight figure trudging through field and valley. Stopping beside a line of trees, hidden from any watchful eyes in the sky, he took a long drink of water from a small flask. He leaned against the firm bark of an oak tree and looked around him.

From his vantage point he could see the ridge he had just descended. Down below, Chollerford was falling into darkness. He had to decide whether to take the stone bridge that crossed directly into the village or the stepping stones that were all that remained of Chester Bridge, which crossed the river half a mile south in the crumbling remains of a Roman fort.

He noticed the wind was now blowing from the north and he scented an autumn storm approaching from the borderlands. He was still alone, but this would change, for the Shadow would come. That was as inevitable as the changing seasons. Taking a deep breath, he moved out into the open.

The years he had spent with the Forest Reivers had prepared him well. He had journeyed through their forest homes deep in the borders, places where none of the old ways were inked in on the maps. He had been Eagan Reign's mentor, the one who had first introduced him to the ways of the Reivers, for Brennus had believed Eagan to be the one. The boy could feel the flow, could use it to his advantage, and was one of the few who could enter the Garden of Druids. Both he and Brennus had come to believe that the flow was in the boy's blood, but it was a different skill Eagan possessed, one that he could barely control. Drust remembered the boy's pain at being told that he could no longer live in the lights of the city, that he must retire to the woods and hills of Northumberland, away from questions and prying eyes, a place where his secret would go unnoticed.

He climbed the last fence and could hear the river in the distance. To his left, there was just a suggestion of the arched splendour of the village bridge as the night drew in. He approached the fast-flowing river with caution. He had never crossed the stepping stones in darkness.

He had used the land and a little of his magic to hide his passing, but he would stand little chance against the enemy in this place and without help. Whether that help would remember him was debatable. But there was a part of him that did not want this week to be his last.

He stopped at the edge of the river, where he could feel the current moving swiftly below the surface. It was wide, for this was the Tyne surging down from the Northumberland hills and nothing would stop its journey to Tynemouth in the east. He stood there for a while listening to the water flowing, breathing deeply, letting his eyes adjust to the darkness. He could just make out the first stepping stone, no more than four feet away, thrusting its jagged peak out of the noisy river.

His focus was suddenly pricked by a fluttering feeling that passed through and over him. He instinctively flattened himself against the ground, his hand going quickly to the long knife that was his weapon of choice. He kept his breathing slow and steady. The feeling returned. It was as if a giant dark light had passed over the field from one end to the other, sweeping across every nook and cranny.

He didn't allow whatever was searching a third attempt, but rolled upright and without a second thought leaped for the broken stone, scrambling to stay in the centre of it as all around him the river swept past, throwing up icy spray.

He could see the second stepping stone now and realised it was slightly lower in the water. He would have to be careful not slip or he would be in the river in an instant.

The dark light from the field swept across him like the gentle breeze from a hundred butterflies circling around him, a fine spider's web caught in the wind. He felt himself trying to wipe it from his face. But no sooner had the feeling disappeared than a second crept across him and he knew the Shadow had found him.

He held onto the stepping stone in the darkness, looking back towards the shallow bank, whilst every now and again the fast-flowing water spilled over the stone, spraying water into the air. He couldn't help but smile at his predicament. Had he really expected to outpace such an enemy? An enemy that had easily swept him aside in Oxford? He and Brennus had only survived that night because they hadn't been the prey, but that had now changed.

As he leaped, his feet slipped ever so slightly and he landed heavily on the second stepping stone, but his strength allowed him to balance on its rough surface even whilst his eyes searched for movement on the far bank. He had hoped to at least have reached the wall before revealing himself, but as he clung to the wet stone, he brought the flow to his hands, weaving a thin veil between himself and whatever was hunting him.

Instantly something shuddered against it, sending sparks sizzling into the fast-flowing waters and nearly making him lose his footing. In that second, balancing on the hard stone whilst trying to resurrect his shattered spell, he wondered again how Sam had stood against the Shadow at Magdalen.

He didn't linger on such thoughts, but threw himself into the darkness and the thick mist that now covered him from head to foot. His timing was perfect as he leaped to the third, fourth and then fifth stepping stones whilst his hands tingled and burned as they found a way to make him invisible. He stood there in the night like a shadow himself, perhaps the most powerful since Oscar, for no one could speak to the flow like him. It was he who had driven back the crow-men in the reading room. But recently, he had been amazed by Sam. He'd never seen the flow so powerful in one so young.

When he'd first met Sam at Magdalen, it was clear he was his father's son. It wasn't just his flaming red hair, blue eyes and physical size that gave it away, it was something far more subtle – a slight dance of light that played around his hands, an ability to see things. He had seemed unaware of it, but then Brennus had related how the flow had presented itself to him as a blend of colours and the voices of the Magdalen choir the afternoon before Oscar had appeared to him.

They had been at a complete loss as to how the Shadow had let him live that night, first beneath the Fellows' House and then before the gates of Magdalen. None of it made any sense, and when the first wave of relief had dissipated, the searching questions had started.

He believed Sam would go on to be far more powerful than any of those who had been sent to teach and protect him. If only he could reach the Faerie tonight, perhaps they could face this enemy together and he could live long enough to see Sam come to maturity.

He was breathing heavily now as he landed on the sixth stepping stone and scrambled for footing on its ragged surface. He was still regaining his feet when the blast shattered his spell into a thousand tiny flares that hissed as they hit the dark waters.

The force took him by surprise. Shaking the dizziness from his head, he peered back across the stepping stones. He was visible now, but the Shadow was no longer pursuing him in the physical world, it was searching for his connection beneath its surface.

He leaped for the last stone and fell hard against its sharp sides, clinging to it as the cold waters of the Tyne whipped through his legs, threatening to sweep him away. Wet and half-stunned, he dragged himself onto the stone's slippery surface. Then the next shuddering vibration knocked him clean into the fast-flowing waters.

For a moment panic gripped him as the current dragged him beneath the surface and the river tried to swallow him whole. But then he was breaking the surface, gasping, choking, holding onto the long reeds that lined the riverbank and pulling himself slowly towards the shallow embankment.

He hauled himself onto the muddy bank, but there was no time to rest. He felt the shock pounding him through him, but still he managed to call softly to a flow that had never been part of the river. He wasn't prepared to be found just yet. He wanted one more night of freedom.

He had emerged from the river no more than thirty feet from the stepping stones, and although night had descended on Chollerford, the enemy was physically distant. He took a deep breath and shivered in his wet clothes. He still had some time.

As he ran from the edge of the river towards the remains of Chesters Fort, the heavens were gleaming with an infinite dance of stars. Briefly, he wondered whether he would ever see them again. He came to the Roman ruins, a place of haunting stone walls, their history now lost in time's endless arrow, and passed ghostlike amongst the ancient remnants, his hands now flashing white.

It was no accident he was travelling through this place. Long after the Romans had departed, a great battle had been fought here between a Northumbrian army led by Oswald of Bernicia and an army from Wales. It was well known to the Keepers that that had not in fact been a Welsh army, but something far more sinister. The Northumbrians had been joined by Forest Reivers and there had been others amongst their ranks whose names were better left unspoken. The battle had raged for several days along the line of the wall and it would be here that he would join it, for the murmur of the fallen would make it difficult for the Shadow to see through the flow.

As he emerged from the crumbling fort, cold and tired, directly ahead was Walwick Hall, with its magnificent circular lawns and watchful turrets. He would have liked to have spent the night there, perhaps taken a stroll through the walled garden that reminded him of the Fellows' Garden where he had spent so much of the summer, but there would be no peace tonight, only the dance of the hunter and hunted.

Across the scented lawns he ran. The main house was in darkness, save for the odd light here and there and the red stone of the walled garden glowing from behind a line of horse chestnuts. He passed through a long archway of wisteria and was showered by the purple rain of a thousand floating petals that popped and fizzed beneath his feet in an autumn chorus.

He emerged on the far side of the gardens through a small grove that opened back out onto the Northumberland night. Not more than a hundred feet away was Hadrian's Wall, not looking like a wall here but a mound of earth. Many books had been written about the wall originally being built to keep out the barbarians in the north and Drust had often wondered whether those barbarians had ever truly originated in Scotland. He knew the wall was eighty miles from sea to sea and in its day there had been fortlets or mile-castles all along it. In the darkness he could feel its presence and he shivered at its scale and age.

He followed a line of trees that initially concealed nothing more than the slight indentation in the ground where this part of the wall had once stood. It had long been removed, but to the west, the wall still stood on a steep set of ridges. It was here he would seek out the old man's daughter, on the edge of the fort known as the Vercovicium, the place of good fighters, Housesteads as it was called in English. It was said she had chosen to live there in isolation from the world.

To the north the sky had gone black, its flickering stars obscured by dark clouds. The wind was rising and it wasn't long before the first raindrops were beginning to fall.

Drust was leaving the shimmering lights of Chollerford and Walwick behind. Ahead, the vast Northumberland landscape opened up on either side of him and for a brief moment he felt alone and naked in the darkness.

He took little comfort from the scarred earth where the wall had once stood. The wall had been built atop a leyline and its force was distant, but aware of him running through the gully's centre, and uneasy voices were softly calling his name through the wind and rain.

He was moving west into a barren vista where the dark sky blended with the rolling hills of Simonburn. The rain was falling harder and harder and he was still wet from the river. As the first signs of the wall made themselves known, he shook his dark curls out of his eyes, wrapped his arms around himself and quickened his pace.

He had been walking for a couple of hours when the wall turned sharply west and he knew that he had reached Limestone Corner. He couldn't be more than ten miles from his destination. The wall had crept up through the ground without him noticing and was standing silently in the night, and he was thankful that he could walk through a thin copse of trees that shielded him from the gathering storm.

He was tired and his already wet clothing was giving him little protection against the driving rain by the time he at last came to the place that he knew was the beginning of the end. No more than half a mile away was the ruined fort at Carrawburgh, though it was lost at the moment in the swirling rain. It was here that he would no longer fight to keep the Shadow from finding his resonance in the flow.

He stood under a large ash tree, wiping the stinging rain from his eyes, and for a moment he couldn't help but think about Brennus and all he had worked for.

Standing there, he could feel his fear trying to unlock his resolve. If the Faerie would not help, he would fall as all men feared – alone and afraid.

He took a deep breath and left the shelter of the tree. The wind was whipping the rain into long sheets in the pitch-black night. The icy droplets, driven down from the north, were filled with an electric charge he could not identify.

It took him a while before he found what he was looking for. At last he stood beside what had once been a temple to the water goddess Coventina.

There he turned and faced the way he'd come, buffeted by the squall and unable to hear himself think above the raging wind. He clasped his hands together and started gently humming, feeling the flow swelling up, amplified by his position alongside the temple. It wasn't long before the Otherland opened up to him and time dropped away and mattered no more. He stood with his hands burning bright and the storm's fury crashing down all around him, then dropped to one knee, his body drained by the exertion, and waited for an answer.

There was no time passing, only the entangled now of the between places. There were others in this place whose presence he could feel. Far to the north a great light flickered, whilst to the west there was the realisation that no storm could stop him from arriving here. Then everything was shut out as cold terror answered his call. It came like the call of a blue whale beneath the seas, a long mournful sound vibrating through the Otherland.

Drust fell forward, feeling blood running from his nose, and found himself on all fours back in the tempest. The Shadow was close. It had crossed the river.

He sat back on his ankles, blood running down his face. Strength was refusing to return to his body, but he staggered dizzily to his feet and began moving forward, step by step, the cold rain waking him from his stupor.

He found the wall again, bent his head into the wind and went on as quickly as his legs would carry him. Two miles and he would be through Sewingshields and onto the crags themselves. He would have to navigate the Knag Burn Gate, but just beyond it he would make his stand, with or without help.

He had staunched the blood from his nose, but the front of his jacket had turned red, the biting wind was buried deep within him and he could feel himself shaking. He didn't turn around again, for he would know when the enemy was close by, but kept to the wall, trying to quicken his pace but stumbling every now and then, for there were hidden ditches.

Here the wall was built along ridges that rose high above the land. On the first stood the gateway to the spectacular central belt of the wall. As Drust came breathless to the top, the storm threw itself at him, trying to stop him going a step further. He was high up, looking down on sky and landscape entwined in a black embrace. To his right, the earth fell away into darkness. Ahead, the vestiges of a turret long fallen rose to meet him, jagged and broken.

Passing through its crumbling remains proved difficult, as the wind howled around him. He knew that one false step could prove his last. Then he was laughing, shaking his head at the absurdity of such a thought. The danger wasn't here, it was coming up behind him. Falling into the blackness below could be his salvation.

He passed into the madly swaying trees of Sewingshields Wood almost without noticing. Inside the wood, the storm seemed eerily distant, even though he could feel the wind moving through the thick foliage. He stood there for a moment, almost dazed.

'What have we here, lost in the dark wood?'

It was a voice that made Drust's blood turn to ice, a chilling inhuman voice of sharp knives. This was different from the Shadow in Oxford, different from the feathered men who had attacked the bookshop – this was a presence he hadn't felt before.

'I am not lost – I seek the Morrigan.' He hoped his words carried authority.

'There are only the lost here.'

Drust was trying to find the direction the voice was coming from.

'Who are you? Show yourself.'

An inky haze moved only feet from him. Drust instantly went for his long knives, readying himself.

'I am the servant of the mistress. A comfort to her.'

A face that was nothing more than a shade of black appeared, looking at him out of the darkness. It was as horrifying as it was surreal. And yet he knew that something far more threatening was gaining on him every minute he was delayed.

'Why do you seek the mistress?'

'I have news for her.'

How Drust found the courage to speak out he would never know.

'I am Drust Hood…'

'The mistress knows your name. She knows who you are. Knows of the magic that runs through you.'

'Then will she hear me?'

Drust turned away. He could not look at the empty dark face for long.

'You are fortunate that she knows you. Go quickly – you are hunted.'

'Hunted by what?' Although he already knew the answer.

'I am not here to play games. Go. The mistress does not want you here.'

They were the words Drust had feared.

'I have a message I must deliver to her.'

'She asks that you leave. You cannot stay here.'

'Go to your mistress,' Drust said fiercely, 'and tell her that a Shadow has passed through the Fall. But also tell her there is hope, for the *Druidae* are not gone. The old alliance can be renewed.'

Above the wood it seemed the storm lessened as the shade lowered its head.

'What trickery is this?'

'None. Soon I will no longer have the breath to deliver my message. If your mistress does not stand with me then her kind will be one step closer to the precipice.'

The shade was still, as if listening.

'She is beyond the Knag Burn Gate.'

And then he was alone.

* * * * * *

He didn't wait a second longer, but was soon out of the wood and back in the deafening storm, high up on the crags with only the night for company. He was now exposed and watching his footing, for the drop to his left was sheer and the path narrow. The remnants of the wall stopped moving west and took a sharp turn south at this point, and although he couldn't see them, the waters of the Broom-lee Lough were directly ahead.

In daylight the views offered across the lakes and ridges were the most stunning anywhere on the wall. But now it was night and he had at last reached the place where he would face the Shadow. He hoped the Faerie would be waiting for him.

He had always found this place menacing and it was even more so in the bleak night with the storm raging above him. And he knew that it was aware of him.

The wall sat on the very top of the crags and to the west lay the largest of the Roman forts. They had been built nearly two thousand years ago to protect the south from the barbarians in the north. So the story went. The Forest Reivers spoke of a war between two forces whose potency had opened the Otherland, and a bloody battle that had been fought across the borderland. The wall had been built to keep the barbarians from the south, but little did anyone know that it wasn't the wall alone that had kept them back.

Drust bent into the wind and followed the wall along the crags. The going was treacherous, but he at last came to the Knag Burn Gate.

As he passed through the gap in the wall, he knew that something was wrong. He was different from the others – his power was raw and pure and he didn't need ancient words or delicate staffs to speak with the flow. Now he felt electricity coursing down through his arms and into his hands, a delicate haze danced across his fingertips and he watched a colour he had never seen before shimmer and weave its way through his mind's eye.

There was just the faintest crackle in the atmosphere around him and the hair on the back of his neck rose up. The storm seemed to have unexpectedly abated, as if he was stepping out of the squall and into shelter. Yet he was still high up, looking down through the long darkness into the Vercovicium.

He had shut everything from his mind, but now he felt a trembling in his hands and realised he was blind to the Otherland. The Shadow could have been silently stalking him only feet away and he would never have known until it was too late.

There was also something unusual about the night, a greyness that had crept over the fort. He stood still, his senses straining in the gathering dusk, then sank to his knees, closing his eyes and scouring the high walls and hidden places. There it was again – somewhere in the castle there was an impenetrable barrier, and behind it something was waiting…

In the back of his mind he could feel butterflies of doubt take flight. The colours continued to flash and flicker and the new one deepened, suggesting that what waited was neither living nor dead.

When he had first entered the fort there had been empty battlements, crumbling edifices and deserted halls, a forgotten and crumbling past imprinted on the dust that fluttered through the outer keep. Now, as he started to make his way through the vestiges of a complex web of interconnected corridors, the walls were solid and firm and the air clear. Only now did he understand the potency of the creature that he had come to meet.

The corridor came to an abrupt end and he was surprised to find a door leading back out into the night. He found himself in an imposing garden. Then a pile of ancient stones moved and he found himself reaching for his long knives and unsheathing them in one fluid movement.

'Why do you come here?'

Where the stones had stood, now there stood a woman. She was tall, dressed in a simple brown robe and her hair was blood red. Her skin was pale, almost colourless, and he could not easily put an age to her, for her face was flawless, though her eyes were deep wells of wisdom.

'I seek the Morrigan.' His voice sounded tired and grey compared to the lightness and colour of the woman's.

'My father heard your call, but I am no longer involved in the affairs of men. I cannot help you.'

She looked at him and Drust could not tell whether it was a look of pity or indifference. He had to convince her.

'There is an enemy following me now that cannot be stopped without your help. My brother wishes to recreate the old alliance, like our father before him.'

'The old alliance has crumbled into the sea. The Faerie are waning, the Forest Reivers are few and the Marcher Lords are hiding in their crumbling castles. The Underland is on the move and great in number. Their hate runs deep and the Grim-Witch seeks her revenge. The Fall is dying and the Ruin has sent its Shadow into the Mid-land – what hope do you have?'

'It is for these reasons that we need the counsel of the Morrigan.'

'There is no life beyond this life for me. You know that. Yet you would have me sacrifice it for your own ends. You must go – I cannot help.'

Drust stood for a moment unable to move. Without her, he was doomed.

'You can't leave me.'

He sounded desperate – and he was. He didn't want to face the Shadow alone.

'Go.'

He couldn't tell whether she knew she had sentenced him to death. Suddenly he was angry.

'Is that all you have to say? Does it mean so little to you that our forefathers fought with you? They came to your aid and drove back an enemy that was never theirs! It was released into the Otherland through the wars of *your* people, don't forget. Mortal men sacrificed their lives for you then. And all you can say now is "Go"? Call yourself your father's daughter? *He* wouldn't turn his back.'

The woman's face didn't change, though the grey light permeating the fort seemed to flicker.

When she spoke again, she repeated, 'I cannot help you. Your knowledge of the flow can only delay the Shadow. You have called down your own end. It will be swift. Be grateful for that.'

Drust was boiling with frustration. Every moment lost trying to convince the Faerie brought the Shadow closer.

'Oscar and Culluhin have been seen in the Mid-land,' he said desperately. 'We have hope if we stand together. You must stand with me.'

'No, that cannot be true. Culluhin was trapped with the Druids – and there is no way back from the Darkhart!'

* * * * * *

The tempest erupted around him. He was back in the thick of the storm, the wind and the rain howling around him. He staggered back under its onslaught and managed to find the wall. Atop the now wailing ridges there was anger caught up in the gale. He felt hopeless fear burn through him, a wave of despair grasping at his throat.

A second later, the night had taken on the shape of giant wave rising up, ready to engulf him. He drew his long knives and called to the flow as the Shadow took shape on the wall.

He would not wait for the wave to break or the darkness to sweep him from the ridge into the endless night. He leaped down the stone steps, showering the black menace with shards of burning light.

He ran with fear and anger colliding in his mind. Behind him he could feel the Shadow, desperate to rend his heart, growing closer with every second. Why had the Morrigan abandoned him?

There was no time to seek answers. As he reached the small wooden bridge that spanned the ridges near the concealed waters of the Crag Lough, he turned. He would run no more. He would not die with his back to his enemy. He would make his brother proud.

The storm sent its feral winds across the bridge and a wildness raged through the ridges that seemed unnatural. He thought he heard the wind calling to him as it swirled and pounded him, but he stood resolute before the black mist, the sea of roiling despair and hopelessness that had no place in the world of the living. Then the raging tempest stilled and there came a sound that could have once been a voice, rasping, grinding out long-forgotten words. He recognized just one word, a word that was being repeated over and over again: 'Druidae.'

He finally understood. The voice was calling him out in a language that he could only just remember. It wanted him to know that he was defeated and that his death would lay his kind to rest for eternity. The fall of the Druids would be complete.

Through his fear there was a strange satisfaction that he had fooled the enemy and given his brother the chance to reach the Dead Water. He wished he could meet his brother again, have a last day to walk in the sunshine, with the wind at their backs, a day to tell him the truth, a day without fear.

He stood holding the wooden rail, kindling a fire in his thoughts with words that flowed like music. In his mind's eye a thousand will-o'-the-wisps flared across his vision, waiting for the Shadow to make its move. He felt his life flowing into the music, into the magic, and still he waited, facing the servant of an enemy that had been hunting his kind for two thousand years.

At last it came for him, at once ethereal and impenetrable, an unearthly Shadow bearing down on him, filling the bridge with its hatred.

He waited a split-second longer whilst a thousand thoughts and images flooded his mind, then let go of the rail, and with a single word, the flow lit up the whole of the raging night.

* * * * * *

The Faerie was standing on the far bank of the river when the light and boom made her turn. A mile back towards Steel Rigg, a thousand feet up the high slopes, a million fireflies were dancing in the night sky. Then came a crashing sound as parts of the bridge began falling.

She could not have saved him, not against the Shadow.

Her father had asked her to seek out the Marcher Lords and bring them from their secret halls.

From the ruins of the bridge came a long baleful howl, seething with rage.

She didn't wait a second longer, for she knew the Shadow had found that its hunt had been in vain. The Druid-Fall had not ended with this man's death, for he was not the last Druid.

THE DEAD WATER

They walked in the silence of their grief, Brennus beside Jarl, the weight of the last few days carried in the darkness beneath their eyes. The autumn sun was beginning to set and a light wind was blowing from the north through the hills of Northumberland. Animals were scurrying away in the twilight and now and then they would hear the almost silent wings of a bird of prey passing over-head.

They had first gone east along the Jedburgh road as far as Belsay, and then Drust had gone south. Now Brennus was taking the old Roman paths east into the wilds, hoping they would be less easily followed. They were walking alongside the coarse hedges and copses that were the remnants of an ancient Northumbrian forest, with the Tyne river to the south and the fells to the north.

The landscape was bathed in the orange hues of the setting sun and yet there was a cold darkness settling over Brennus that had little to do with the approaching night. The rumours had first started trick-ling out of the borders no more than twelve months before. Perhaps he should have acted more quickly, but he had thought Sam was out of harm's way in Oxford. The old alliance had fragmented during his leadership along the same family faultlines that had splintered it down the generations. Things had come to a head in spring when Eagan Reign had supposedly attacked Morcant Pauperhaugh. Oscar's mention of a traitor in their midst made sense.

They had been outmanoeuvred in every sense. It was clear that whilst they had grown weaker, the enemy had grown stronger and more cunning. Though he hadn't said it openly, they had let Sam down, and this journey to the Dead Water was an act of desperation. The best they could do now was try and deflect the hunt from Sam to them. To Drust.

The pain of what he was about to lose made the ground beneath him swim for a second.

'Everything all right?' he heard Jarl say.

'We should have stayed together. How could I let my brother face such evil alone? I feel ashamed.'

They came to a halt beside a crumbling stone wall, looking down a long field towards an open valley on the horizon. Behind them the landscape was falling into shadow.

'I think you both know what is at stake and the consequences for everyone if we fail,' said Jarl carefully. 'The stakes are impossibly high. And Drust has the gift – who knows what he is capable of? Didn't you say it was Drust who saved you all in Oxford?'

'The Shadow wasn't interested in either of us, though – its focus was Sam. It is beyond us, but I still feel its touch in my heart. I've never known such cold hatred.'

'Drust will find a way back, Brennus – you must trust in that.'

'There is no way back for the dead. You know that.'

Jarl looked at his old friend and knew there was nothing he could say to comfort him.

They were silent for a moment, then Brennus spoke again.

'The plan must remain as we agreed. The Forest Reivers should be on their way to Birling Wood by now. You must represent me at the King's Seat and tell Braden that the weakness of men has prevailed and there is at least one traitor amongst us. I must go on to the Dead Water alone. I have been touched by the Shadow once; I fear it will come for me again before my journey is at an end.'

'Then let me stand with you.'

'No. You must meet Braden – you two are Sam's only hope.'

'Eagan is more than capable of looking after him.'

Brennus met Jarl's eyes and nodded. 'I know, Jarl – he has your way and that makes him a good man. But I want you to go to Braden.'

They reached High Green as twilight spread from east to west. Brennus would now follow the snaking body of the Tyne to Greystead, whilst Jarl would head northeast to the Cheviots and the King's Seat.

They stood at the edge of a garden, looking down the long valleys out towards Kielder, and even in the gloom they could make out the giant hills of the borders.

'There's a storm coming down from the north,' began Brennus. 'We shouldn't delay any longer.' He paused. 'I am troubled, Jarl. I still cannot understand what the Shadow really is. And there may even be more than one of them.'

Jarl felt a shudder go through him. 'Is that possible?'

'After this week, I'm not sure you can say anything is impossible. So go quickly to the King's Seat. If the enemy comes upon you, let it see what secret is in you.'

They hugged before turning to their chosen paths. As they made their way down from the high lawns back into the wild vales, each wondered whether they would see the other again.

* * * * * *

It wasn't long before the last of the day vanished and a cold night settled in. Brennus moved quickly, keeping to the hedges and following a small river that he knew would eventually lead him to the Tyne. Thoughts of his brother loomed large in his mind. If there was more than one Shadow, then Drust's diversion would have been in vain.

He was beginning to doubt his leadership and the decisions he had made. The night in Oxford had shaken his belief in his own abilities. From out of nowhere, the Shadow had nearly caught Sam. He should have listened more closely to Eagan and his messages from the Forest Reivers, but he had been convinced they could protect Sam at Magdalen. The last thing he had expected was a dead Druid to appear in the Fellows' Garden with a warning that a Shadow had broken through the Fall. He hadn't expected to see a weakening of the Fall in his lifetime. What would come through next? Would he have to defend Sam against the almost unimaginable terror that the Keepers said had been driven out for good?

The appearance of the crow-men in Gosforth had reinforced just how bad things had become. Until yesterday they had been part of Northumberland mythology, one of the reasons Hadrian's Wall had been built in the first place. There could be other things lurking in the borders, too, for this wasn't just a border between England and Scotland. And here he was, travelling to the very place where the Shadow had first appeared, to see the old man. Would he have the answers on how to stop the Shadow? Or was this all futile?

He passed Greenhaugh without incident, making sure he couldn't be seen by any prying eyes from the small hamlet. Passing a thick wood to his left whilst keeping the small river to his right, he moved with great stealth through the landscape. He came upon the Tyne with a strong wind blowing from the north and the river running loud and fast. He was now in the middle of a shallow valley with the river uncoiling its long body into the night. He would reach Kielder a little before midnight, but not before the storm caught him in the open.

He again wondered what was happening to Drust. Had the Shadow found him? What if there was more than one? Well, he would find that out soon enough. He was also worried about Jarl, who would be crossing south of the borders where the skirmishes between the Forest Reivers and their enemies had been greatest.

The storm came down from the borders like a raging hurricane, hitting just as the lights of Falstone had begun to shimmer in the overcast night. The hills on either side of the river began to rise steadily skyward whilst the river began to narrow, becoming swift and riotous and filling the night with sinister noises. Brennus bent his slim frame into the gathering wind whilst the rain soaked him to the bone. He slipped between Stannersburn and Falstone and kept moving. He was keen to press on.

Ahead was Kielder Water, a vast man-made lake running north-west towards Kielder village. He came to the water's edge, his senses picking their way through the tempest, trying to uncover anything unusual. If anyone was watching the path to the Dead Water, they would expect a traveller to take the path north to the village and then try and make the fells from there. He had long decided that he would turn off that path to the west and cut through Bloody Bush Road instead. In the night with a storm pushing south, the going would be difficult, but it would be almost impossible for anyone to follow him.

He took a short drink, ate some biscuits and then set off again, skirting the lake's choppy waters, careful to go unnoticed, as every now and then he would pass pockets of houses, some still with lights shining out over dark lawns running down to the water's edge.

The storm was bearing down now and the rain was coming straight at him from the north. He again thought about Drust. He would be some forty miles south now, whilst Jarl would be heading northeast. Where were Sam and Emily? Perhaps he should have accompanied them to Warkworth, after all. But even as the thought trickled through his mind, his sharp logic pricked it. Oxford had proven they were no match for the Shadow. The enemy had gained the advantage over them. In the next few hours he hoped to reverse this, but if the Dagda could not help, then all he could think of was to keep the Way-curves closed and Sam moving from safe house to safe house.

It had been a long slow climb along Kielder Water to Lewis Burn, where his path turned west, leaving the frothy waters behind. He was breathing heavily as he climbed up the steep bank and turned down Bloody Bush Road, which ran almost parallel to the murky waters of the burn.

Not that this was much of an improvement. The road cut through the gap between two rolling hills and was no place for anyone but the hardiest hill-walker. There would not be many attempting it mid-storm. With the rain stinging his face, Brennus turned to look up the narrow incline.

Bloody Bush Road was grim, steep and frightening in the stormy night. The hills on either side looked foreboding and there was a wild loneliness to the place that made Brennus feel vulnerable. He could be on the verge of failing not only Sam but also his brother and all those relying on him. Oscar had been an impossible act to follow; the responsibility had begun to crush him and it felt all-consuming alone in the middle of this desolate place.

With every step, he felt the storm come bellowing through the valley, unrelenting and raw, and then he heard a sound that froze his blood. Somewhere in the tempest, probably not too far away, crows were cawing angrily. There must have been hundreds for their clamour to rise above the wailing wind.

It was unusual for crows to fly during a storm – most birds would have been sheltering – although Brennus knew these were more than crows. The feathered faces from the bookshop came back to him. He had heard about them from the Keepers, although the Forest Reivers had also spoken about the dark men of the Underland.

He was now feeling just a little desperate. Despite the cold wind, the climb was making him sweat.

He was tired and a chill was settling across him by the time he arrived at the Bloody Bush stone. It stood fifteen feet tall, dark and unfeeling in the shadow of Larriston Fells, a monument to those who had once passed through this exposed landscape.

Brennus knew he had reached more than a physical border crossing between Scotland and England. The Dagda would be aware of him the moment he set foot on the north side of the stone. He would soon know if he would let him pass.

He braced himself against the gale and stepped forward. Instantly, the storm abated and the road ahead became clear. For a second he was disorientated, the hush loud in his ears. When he turned to look at the way he had come, it was silent and still. He took a deep breath. It was as if he had woken from a long dream and was looking upon a world he only half-remembered.

The Dead Water was hidden in the borders thirty miles northeast of the Broad Flow and the hanging stones. Few now travelled there. Not even the Forest Reivers. There had been whispers of fell voices carried on the wind. Brennus started slowly picking his way through jagged rocks towards it.

In the darkness the pass was treacherous. He was beginning to see flashes before his eyes and a sickness was creeping into him, a fatigue that he could not shake. The moment he had passed the stone, he couldn't think back to how he had reached this place. He looked at his compass, but it simply whirled, incapable of telling him whether he was heading north or south.

In the darkness he thought again about Drust, but quickly blocked him from his mind. He could no longer think about his brother's plight.

Below him, out of sight, was a vast uncompromising landscape. His senses were jumbled and he could neither see much beyond his hands, now bloodied from the razor-sharp rocks, nor hear much beyond his own breathing. He was going even more slowly now, watching his every step, for to his left there was a sudden drop. If he fell, he might not survive.

Somewhere far below in the night, the Dead Water waited for him. At the thought of it, a momentary flicker of uneasiness flared in his throat, but he quickly brought it under control. He had to know more about the nature of the Shadow and how it could be stopped. Over the years he had thought that they were safe, that the Otherland had been sealed for eternity, but obviously he had been fooling himself.

He wanted to get over the pass as quickly as possible. He couldn't be certain the crows hadn't been searching for him and there was every possibility that this place was being watched. He stood on the little winding path, breathing deeply and trying to sense anything unusual, but there was nothing but bleak silence around him.

He began making his way down before absolute darkness descended and he was stranded on the side of a mountain. He stood on the little winding path, breathing deeply as he reminded himself that three feet to his left was the now hidden chasm. He stood there and tried to sense anything unusual, but there was nothing but the bleak silence of the Dead Water. His descent through the gloom was slow and frustrating, but at last he came to a broad ledge and knew he was down. He found himself blinking into pitch-black darkness and waited for a few moments for his eyes to adjust, relieved he was off the mountain path.

It took a while before he realised that this was an unnatural darkness. He should have been growing used to it by now, but instead it was getting blacker.

The situation began to unnerve him; he was vulnerable to attack and a cold wind was beginning to blow. What if this place was in the hands of the enemy? What if he could no longer summon the old man? Then he remembered his brother's sacrifice and found himself stepping forward into the oppressive darkness.

He had only taken a few steps when he felt a warm wind wrapping itself around him, darting across every inch of his body. He reached for the short sword concealed in his long coat, but the wind had gone as quickly as it had appeared.

He walked on blindly, unable to see or hear beyond one or two feet in any direction. What was creating this eternal night? Were the Dagda or the Faeries using it to defend the Dead Water? Or was it the enemy? He recalled grimly that Oscar had warned the Dead Water was lost. Was he on a fool's errand?

He had no idea how long he'd been walking when he bumped into a large stationary object. He reached out with his hands and realised it was a small tree. The Dead Water had a copse on its southern shore – he was nearly there.

He entered the wood with his hands outstretched, stumbling and sightless. Branches of all sizes were stabbing at him in the darkness and there was a thick smell that stung his nose and made his eyes water. It was all he could do not to retch. Each step took him deeper into misery. He no longer understood why he'd come here, only that he had to escape.

Then the trees came to an abrupt end and he fell to his knees, his head hanging loosely between his shoulders. When at last he raised it, the suffocating darkness had receded, revealing a short pebbled beach and the wide expanse of the Dead Water. He was ten feet from its shores. He took in the clear sky and breathed in the cold air. Then, shivering, he hauled himself to his feet and walked to the water's edge.

He stood there in quiet reflection, waiting for a response, but none came. Uncertain what to do, he turned back to the wood's distorted edge. The trees were huge and unmoving. Then there was movement. A feathered form staggered from the wood and fell, gasping for breath, as he had done moments before.

Brennus drew his sword.

At first only one or two forms staggered out of the dark wood, but gradually more lurched onto the beach. Soon black feathered faces were being raised. Guttural croaking broke out as the creatures regained their feet and spotted their prey. There was a madness in their eyes that sent a shiver into Brennus's heart. It seemed he had been followed all the way.

The Dagda would never have let these creatures past – it was clear the Dead Water had been abandoned and the enemy had set a perfect trap.

Them the first wave came crashing down on him, trying to crush the life out of him. Quickly his blade flashed, tearing them open. Their howls shattered the air and there were half a dozen twisted bodies on the beach before a searing pain in his leg made him stagger.

The enemy renewed the attack, trying to press home their advantage, but once again they were met by the cold unblinking steel of his short sword.

Up close, he could see their wrathful faces and smell their hideous hides. Then the pain of a second wound, this time to his back, washed over him and he stumbled back, dizziness making him reel, but still he did not fall.

Once more the creatures withdrew, for many of their kind now lay dead. But this time they were watching him, chattering to each other and occasionally sniffing the air. He felt a numbness in his chest and realised they had delivered a poison deep into his body.

All he could do was stumble back into the still waters, his legs deadened, his arms growing heavy. He dropped to his knees and there were gleeful howls from the beach. He gritted his teeth as he felt the poison reach his hands and watched the sword fall from his fingers. The creatures were clawing at each other in triumph as he felt the dizziness take him and fell back into the freezing waters.

* * * * * *

He lay still, expecting the end to come quickly. But it did not come. A strong current took hold of him and he felt warmth spreading through his body even as he was drawn out into the cold emptiness of the Dead Water. He floated there, drifting, as if in a dream.

He didn't know how far he had travelled when he felt himself gently bumping against the shore. Slowly, he came back to himself. There was a burning sensation in his stomach and then it broadened out and pushed the numbness from his limbs.

A few moments later he was sitting looking at a gnarled wood bordering a pebbled beach – a mirror image of the place he'd just come from. He clambered to his feet, astonished to find his clothes dry. His mind was clearing and his vision fully restored. He could still feel the gentle throb of his wounds, but it was a dull healing pain. He felt bewildered, but somehow at peace – a peace he could not easily describe.

'Why do you summon me?'

The voice was crisp and strong and there was a music to it. It had come from a figure standing a few feet away on the shore. Her dark elegance was striking. Her skin was pale, but her hair was like the blackest coal and no light could escape from it. Her eyes were darker than the midnight sky. She was naked save for the night that doused her with ink.

Brennus could sense a great power bathed in her ruthless beauty. He found himself struggling to speak. Finally, he muttered, 'I seek the old man.'

'The Ruad Roshessa serves only himself,' came the cool reply. 'Why have you come here?'

There was a heartless ring to her voice that frightened Brennus. Had the Faeries turned their backs on them? A shiver ran down his spine.

'I seek counsel.'

There was silence. Brennus did not know what to expect. He gazed at the dark woman, his mouth dry with apprehension.

'Then you come too late.'

The words seemed to flicker in his mind and he wasn't sure whether they were sounds at all. They were crushing and yet he was entranced. There was something very disturbing about the Faerie woman. He felt a desire to do her bidding, no matter what the consequences might be. He was swept away on a river of emotions that he couldn't understand.

'We have seen what enters the world of men and know you have no answer.'

Again the words flickered in Brennus's mind. They were edged with melancholy and he had the desire to console, to comfort, to feel and touch.

'A terrible Shadow passed through here. The old man fought it in the fells and the caverns, in the deep places, and could not defeat it.'

Brennus seemed to wake to why he was there.

'It is a servant of the enemy that has been hunting your kind down since the beginning,' he said softly. 'So, surely the fight isn't ours alone? Join us!'

He smiled.

There was a sudden stillness, a thoughtful silence. Then the answer came.

'The Ruin is coming for us all. You know the *Druidae* locked it away beyond time, but its servants hid in the darkness, under the hills and in the hidden places, and they are rising. Their waiting is over, for the Fall is dying and the Druids' bloodline grows thin. The

Ruin's servant is coming even now and you are ill-prepared. The old man has blind faith in men, but he cannot be your saviour.'

Brennus went cold. He had risked the lives of those he loved for this? But as he looked at the woman he could not be angry, only frightened by the desire she had awoken in him. She was both the light in the darkness and the shadow in the light.

'And the creatures who attacked me on your shores?' he asked. 'I thought the crow-men were tales told to frighten children.'

'As the Fall dies, the Otherland seeps into the world of men. Soon the last of the Druids will pass away, just as your brother has done.'

The words seemed heartless, cold and without pity.

'Please tell me my brother is safe,' Brennus pleaded. Then he was shouting. 'Tell me my brother is safe!'

He thought he heard an icy cackle.

'Your brother met the Ruin's servant and met the fate you intended.'

Brennus looked down, overcome with grief.

The woman stood watching him for a moment.

'The pain you feel is only fleeting,' she said coldly. 'Mine is for eternity.'

Then she took a step forward and Brennus felt her touch. Warmth flooded through him and the touch of the Shadow was extinguished.

'We seek a girl from the Mid-land,' the Faerie said softly. 'She travels with a boy. Do you know where they are travelling?'

'Warkworth. The Garden of Druids.' Brennus found himself unable to stop the words tumbling out.

As soon as they escaped his lips there was a vile laugh that echoed through his being. The woman was stepping back, her laughter ringing through the night.

As the pain returned to him and the numbness flooded back into his body, he thought he saw a winged shadow take to the air, but he was already sinking to the ground, helpless as a wave washed over him and the current drew him back into the centre of the Dead Water.

* * * * * *

He awoke to guttural sounds and the splashing of water as the creatures hunted for his body. He was floating helpless in the darkness. The croaks were growing closer. Any moment now it would be all over and he would have failed all those dear to him. He should have never come here. It was a fool's errand and he had learned nothing of the enemy.

He felt iron-like talons grab hold of him and heard the sounds reach a crescendo as he was dragged to the beach. A jeering crowd had gathered at the water's edge. Fear ran through his helpless body as they hauled him into a sitting position. What did they mean to do to him?

His ears popped as the air pressure suddenly dropped. What was happening? There was a new noise blending with the jeering, an oncoming roar.

The wall of water came out of the darkness and crashed onto the shore in a deafening explosion. Some of the creatures were crushed by the water's terrible force, whilst others found boulders raining down on them. Those who had survived the first onslaught were seized by twisting currents and quickly dragged, lifeless, out into the churning Dead Water.

Brennus Hood remained sitting, untouched, on the beach, unable to comprehend what had just happened or how he was still alive. All around him the waters were returning to the lake and soon the beach was again empty, save for an old man sitting at the water's edge.

THE GHOSTLY COMPANY

He had left High Green and moved quickly north through Elishaw. The storm had hit as he had been approaching Featherwood waterfall and he had taken refuge under the overhanging rock. Now he was sitting huddled against the wall, listening to the waterfall's flow resonating against the black rocks below.

Suddenly a shape rose out of the spray and mist. He flattened himself against the wall without thinking, glad he had chosen to dress in black.

The figure stopped just beyond the falling water. If this was the Shadow, what could he possibly do?

His mouth had gone dry and he found himself swallowing, trying to keep his breathing slow and even. Whatever it was, he had to deliver Brennus's message to Braden. The Forest Reivers needed to know the seriousness of the situation. He didn't want to think about the Shadow arriving in Warkworth with only Eagan between it and Sam.

The figure was bent over, scouring the floor. Fortunately, the strong winds were driving the rain in long sheets, so Jarl hoped any signs of his passing had been washed away.

A second and then third figure joined the first and within seconds a number of ghostly figures were passing over the falls, departing as quickly as they had appeared.

Jarl now had a fresh problem. They could simply be waiting for him to make a move. Even if they weren't, somewhere in the hills he would have to overtake them without being seen.

Waiting in the dark with the storm howling just beyond the falls, he thought of Brennus and Drust. Sitting here wasn't helping them. He could wait no longer – time was moving against him.

By the sound of things, the storm was intensifying. He slowly walked to the edge of the waterfall and passed through a small opening. Coming back out into the seething night, he flinched as the winds lashed the rain into his face. Climbing the short rock face was almost impossible. He was also aware that he could be walking into a trap, but there was no alternative.

Slowly he made his way up the stone steps that had been carved into the side of the valley by ancient hands now long forgotten. He had passed two hundred steps when they finally came to an end and he made his way through a thick wall of ivy that was wrapping its sinewy body around the surrounding trees, slowly choking them into submission. The smell of rotting wood filled the air as the ivy gave way to him.

It took him a while to find his way out into the open atop the broken path. He had to lean into the wind, for it was sweeping through the narrow valley, bellowing and tormenting him with cold rain. In places the path was missing and he would slip and fall to one knee before heaving himself up again. The roar of the wind through the valley was deafening and still the road took him further into the hills.

In his need to remain hidden, he was heading for the Foulmire. Poisonous gases could bubble up there without warning and kill instantly, but the scent of a traveller would be sucked into the earth within seconds and there would be no trace of their passing.

His mood fluttered with the changing vista, growing darker as he trekked further into the oozing quagmire. In places his feet seemed to dissolve into the ground and he became bogged down. Now and then he stopped to catch a glimpse of his compass.

It was the slight sound of leathered foot against moss that froze him to the spot. He dropped to the ground, lying almost face down in the thick mud. His keen senses pinpointed the noise in the darkness. People were moving no more than two hundred yards to his left. If they were humans, then they were moving almost without sound, their feet barely making contact with the watery bog.

Jarl held his breath and became one with the night. Then something whistled in the darkness and a single arrow fell only feet away from his head. Still he did not move. Whoever they were, they had sharp senses. That arrow had been meant to flush him out, but he knew better than to make any sudden movement.

Now covered in sludge, he could feel his feet beginning to grow numb. He couldn't wait too long. But if he moved too soon, he would receive an arrow for his troubles.

He waited a few minutes longer. All seemed quiet. The ghostly company had gone. Stealing north, he moved deeper into the Foulmire.

* * * * * *

The night crept on and he continued his wearisome trek through the traitorous fen, listening and watching for anything trying to sneak up from the darkness whilst avoiding the odd hidden gully and sinking mud that could suck travellers waist-deep. He grunted up a mile-long hill that rose sharply from the quagmire, coarse grass thick along its edges, and reached the plateau. There he paused. Through the whistling wind there came a cawing sound, far away but growing closer.

He flattened himself against the ground, hoping he would remain unnoticed in the darkness. It wasn't long before a giant murder of crows spilt out of the air on all sides of the hillock. The night sky became a thousand moving pieces of darkness cawing and snapping as they flew east.

Shaking with fear and exhaustion, Jarl watched until the last of the stragglers had disappeared. His limbs were already heavy, but he moved now with added urgency. Thoughts of Eagan, speculations about the nature of the unknown humans and worries about the crows all became blurred behind his desire to arrive at the King's Seat before dawn.

The path through the Foulmire now began to grow firmer with every footstep. Its sickly stench started to thin as a light wind blew from the north, and finally he left the bog and its tortuous route. With his keen eyesight, he could make out the Cheviots standing like monstrous gates between two worlds, west and east, with the unfolding panorama hidden by the dark distances of the borderland.

He could no longer figure out how long he'd been walking; all he knew was that below him the Foulmire had fallen away and he'd reached the spinal ridge of the borderland. Sky and landscape were a now a vast blanket of shifting shades of black and he felt small and exposed to the elements.

The only way to traverse the steep burns and fells running to the east was to pick up a Roman road and follow it north until he found the path running from south of Swanlaws to Windy Gyle in the east. It would be a ferocious walk in such winds, but would avoid the dark passes of the Blind and Barrow burns. If the Forest Reivers were right, these places were best avoided.

He had been fighting the storm for several hours without respite and was now walking into the wind on the bare rock of Mozie Law. There was nothing to shelter him and every now and then he would totter before regaining his balance and setting off again.

The storm reached its crescendo as he approached the summit of Windy Gyle. A faint path led below its summit. On all sides the burns and fells rose and dipped in giant waves, and for a moment he thought he could have been looking out to sea.

A cruel wind raced across the top of the hills like a herd of wild horses, knocking him back and then throwing him to the ground. He lay just below the summit, covering his face with his hands, utterly drained from the long climb to the top of the borderland, but he knew that if Sam and Emily had gone to Warkworth, then Eagan would be in the firing line. He had to keep going.

He gradually regained his feet, braced himself against the storm surge and placed one foot after the other down the east side of the hill, his head reeling from the force of the rain.

He finally felt the path beginning to descend towards the Usway Valley and the wood bordering Davidson's Linn waterfall. He would rest once he was in the valley and out of the storm. Though his pace had slowed, he still expected to arrive at the King's Seat in the early morning hours.

The Usway Valley was a place of waterfalls and stifling conifer woods. Though he could not see it in the stormy night, he knew Shillhope Law would be rising up on his left. The walls on either side of the valley were steep and started to offer him protection from the incessant winds. He was grateful when he picked up a narrow muddy path running parallel to the fast-flowing Usway Burn.

With the storm abating, his senses began to sharpen and he could tell the valley was deepening the further he walked. He was glad he had come down from the hills, where the storm still raged; he wasn't sure how much more he could have taken of the bruising winds before finding shelter. He was limping badly now. It had been a long march since leaving Brennus and Drust.

As the path followed the contours of the winding river, Jarl forced himself to quicken his pace. The burn took a sharp turn, and as he rounded the corner, he was thinking ahead to meeting the Forest

Reivers when an arrow whizzed past his ear and a second and third flew over his head.

He threw himself forward as more arrows went whistling by and felt for his long hunting knife. In the darkness there was movement all around him.

'Go!'

A pale slender woman appeared momentarily at his side. Her was silver, her eyes almost grey, and she had had an unfamiliar accent. In a single fluid movement, she released a flurry of white-feathered arrows from a bow that seemed to curve round her arm.

'Run!'

A dozen shapes were taking up positions in a thin line across the path he was taking and waves of arrows were dancing through the night.

At first Jarl thought the archers were firing indiscriminately, but he quickly noticed the arrows were converging on a point that was slowly moving closer to their line. He felt it before he saw it – a murderous hate that swam through the night, splintering the arrows into a thousand shards.

Whoever these people were, they could not stop the darkness that was taking shape. If he stood and fought with them, there would be no one to deliver the message to Braden.

He glanced at the woman, but she was no longer looking his way. Instead she was focusing on the dozens of arrows raining down on that single dark spot.

He fled north with questions crashing through his mind. Was that the Shadow from Oxford? Why was it following him and not Drust or Brennus? It must have been following him up the burn, and with the noise of the storm, he hadn't heard it coming, or felt its presence. How it had followed him across the Foulmire was anyone's guess. Was there really more than one Shadow or – and this thought was almost unthinkable – had it already caught up with Brennus and Drust?

He ran into a wood of thick conifers clinging to the side of Castle Hill. In the darkness the clawing branches lacerated his face and arms, and his blood mingled with his sweat as he thought of what had just happened. What would happen to those people when their arrows ran dry? Did they know what they were facing? Did they understand the futility of their defence? Did they know they had saved his life?

Then he felt the ground disappearing beneath his feet and he was falling down a shallow hill. Without the strength to stop himself, he tumbled in the darkness and then came to a stop, chilled to the bone, in the cutting arms of a thick bramble.

For long moments, it was enough just to catch his breath. The storm was still raging high above the valley, but here the trees muffled its sound. He sat up, straining his ears in the darkness and shuddering at how close the Shadow had been.

Who were the ghostly company? He guessed they had been the people who had passed him at the waterfall, but he couldn't be sure. Whoever they were, he hoped they knew what they were up against.

The enormity of what they were all facing made him slowly regain his feet. With a grimace, he started clambering back the way he had fallen, exhausted but glad to be alive.

14

THE KING'S SEAT

Braden Bow was looking out over Cold Law, on his way to the King's Seat. The sky was sea-blue, with slow clouds crossing the horizon. The sun hung low and made the whole landscape shimmer in the soft breeze. The first signs of leaf-fall were showing on the giant trees that lined Linhope Spout waterfall. Braden knew the uplands well, from Kershope Burn in the west to Berwick-on-Tweed in the east, as well as all the old roads through the valleys and hills and the secret ways through the woods and forests. Thick-set, with dark brown hair and eyes that were slow to anger, he was head of the Bow clan, one of the oldest remaining Reiver families.

The Forest Reivers had always been different from their border cousins and they had diminished down the ages. There were now just four clans – Bow, Raeshaw, Dun-Rig and Broadflow – roaming the woods. They ventured from their lands only rarely, breaking their isolation to bring news to the Fellowship of Druidae. In recent years, the Hoods had taken over its leadership and the loose coalition with the Reivers had fallen apart. Only Eagan Reign still met up with them regularly – he had spent months travelling with them from Hownam Law in the west to Holy Island in the east. But even Drust had not been seen for a year.

The autumn sun raised Braden's spirits, but he couldn't shake the feeling that the peace that had reigned for a generation was coming to an end. Things had changed when they'd lost Oscar and the Hoods had taken over, and keeping the Fellowship of Druidae going had become an impossible task.

It was winter when things had changed in the borderland. It had started with one of his rangers tracking something he couldn't easily identify. The tracks had disappeared underground and the ranger hadn't been able to follow them.

The first skirmish had taken them all by surprise. Reports had come back to their forest home of a coordinated attack against their posts across the borderland. There were sightings of crow-like creatures and even black wolves. There were rumours, too, of a new darkness, a cunning Shadow that had been tracked all the way to the Dead Water, but spirits were said to haunt the mountain passes and Braden's rangers would not go into such unearthly lands.

The warm sun penetrated his dark thoughts. In the distance were the high hills and many-coloured dales of his homeland. He moved on.

He was fairly close to the King's Seat when the bird of prey caught his eye, sweeping effortlessly through the heavens, a shadow across the sun, an elegant blur of speed and power. It was a giant red kite and it was acting just a little oddly. He watched it climb several hundred feet, turn gracefully and then plummet towards the ground and twist sharply before rising again.

He came to a complete standstill, uneasy now as he watched the streak of red and brown whistle through the clear sky. He found himself crouching down. Almost instantly, the bird of prey pulled up sharply and glided off in the direction he was going.

Where the kite had been swooping, men, or what appeared to be men, were standing. From this distance he couldn't see their faces. He sank further down into the coarse grass, watching intently. When they began to run, they ran unlike any men he had ever seen, hunched over with an awkward gait.

Braden couldn't help thinking that each day brought with it a new and strange event. He stayed where he was a moment longer, scouring the high grass, unsure whether anything else remained hidden, then decided to follow them.

Almost an hour later, he was lying flat on his stomach in the long grass of a small hillock. Sipping from a leather flask, he kept his eyes narrowed on the horizon. The sunset threw the vast landscape into a smouldering haze of half-shadows and shimmering light, but he could still see the men. They had been joined by others and he now counted thirty, all moving with that strange twisted run. They had been avoiding farmsteads and travelling through coppices and hedgerows. Now they were moving quickly and disappearing into the trees of Threestoneburn Wood.

Braden now faced a dilemma. For all he knew, they could be watching his approach. It was open fields from where he lay to the edge of the trees – it could be a trap. But if he waited too long, they would be through the wood and lost. It would be dark soon and difficult to track them.

Without further ado, he took another sip of his water, felt the reassuring metal of his long knife and was up and running quickly down the hill and across the field, focusing on the mature trees of the wood rising up before him.

He broke through into the wood, sweating and breathing heavily, and dropped to one knee whilst his eyes adjusted to the murky light. The hair on the back of his neck was prickling and his senses tingling. In one fluid movement, he drew out the cold steel of his long knife. Blade raised, ready to defend himself, he made his way deeper into the wood.

He was just beginning to think the men had gone when the silence was shattered by muffled screams and high-pitched squawks. He flattened himself against the trunk of a tree, but knew that if they were coming his way, he would be seen.

He could hear the clash of what sounded like metal against metal, but he couldn't be sure. Then they were crashing through the wood all around him, no longer hooded, their black-feathered faces making him recoil with horror. Hunched and twisted, they broke through the trees, quickly followed by whistling arrows with white feathers, which hit them with sickening thuds, killing them outright. Braden had never seen such precision from the bow and arrow.

The wood was quiet once more, but he didn't move. It was likely that whoever had fired the arrows would be coming his way. Then an arrow thudded into the tree inches from his face. Splinters flew from the bark, opening up a cut on his cheek. With blood running freely, he rolled with lightning speed and came to a crouching position.

As he raised his knife, he saw a figure materialising through the thicket. To his surprise it was a woman, her dress flickering in the dull light. She stopped twenty feet from where he was crouching. Her skin was pale and her face untroubled. Her grey eyes met his and he found a sharp intelligence stripping him bare and understanding that he had no intention of dying that day.

She stood there a moment longer, then turned away. As she did so, the wood came alive with ghostly figures. Wiping the trickling blood from his face, Braden counted several dozen forms passing by and gently dissolving into the tangled woodland. He gazed after them, unable to believe what he had just witnessed, grateful that his life had been spared.

* * * * * *

He came to the King's Seat with the sun dipping further in the west and a cold wind picking up. It was known as Birling Hill to the Northumbrians living within its shadow. At its summit was a ring of standing stones. No one quite knew how they had been carried there or why they had been brought there in the first place. There were other stone circles right across the Cheviots, but none quite as significant as this one. Braden had heard his father say that the stones were the remnants of a second wall further north than Hadrian's, a hidden wall that had been built to keep an enemy out of this world. Most of that wall had not been made from stone, but from the magic of the Druids. In the Reiver world, anything that could not be understood was the work of the Druids.

What was known was that as long as there had been Reivers roaming the borders, the heads of the families had been scaling the hill and holding councils at the stones. This was a place of comfort and also a place of safety, a fortress that could be defended.

Braden pondered this last thought as he climbed up the twisting path to the summit of the hill. He could only describe the feathered men he had seen as those from folklore. Why were they here now? Had they even been real? But he remembered the frightening sounds they had made. The smell of their blood was still burning his nostrils. He could tell they had been full of poison.

He reached the King's Seat, breathing heavily from the exertion of the hard climb, and his disquiet eased as the breathtaking view opened up before him, the valleys of Northumberland rolling mesmerisingly away to the south. He remembered coming here for the first time with his father and seeing the stone circle. The thought made him happy and sad all at once, remembering the loss of his father and with it the loss of his youth and innocence.

The sun was falling even lower, touching the top of the distant Cheviots, and the sky was beginning to turn red. Braden moved further into the safety of the King's Seat, keen to tell people what he had witnessed.

The standing stones were waiting for him, their shadows lengthening with the passing of the day. The moment Braden stepped past their ancient guard and into the small clearing beyond, peace spread through him. He kneeled down to feel the earth under his fingers and touch the memories of his forefathers.

He had come fresh from meeting Eagan Reign high up in the Blindburn. It was there that an old man had appeared. He had told Eagan to expect two unexpected guests who should not be offered shelter, but set free to find their own way to the Garden of Druids.

According to his father, the Garden of Druids had been the meeting-place of the Fellowship of Druidae, the alliance that had fought a long war against an ancient terror from another world. It was said that the remnants of this other world had lain dormant beneath the hills of the borders. Eventually his forefathers had named it the Underland. Could this place really have reawakened, Braden wondered. Could the tales of crow-men, Grim-were and wolves be real? Who was the old man? How had he appeared to them in such an inaccessible place?

The old man had turned to him next and said to watch for the red mare in the shadows of his forest home. It would be the sign to gather at Birling Wood.

Sure enough, the red mare had appeared to his people, and so he had sent messages to Jolan Raeshaw, Dwarrow Dun-Rig and the weapons master Ged Broadflow to take their rangers there and to meet him personally at the King's Seat, their spiritual home. Together they represented more than half of the remaining Reiver families and their rangers, totalling several hundred in number.

The standing stones were now losing their shape as the sky turned deep red. Braden sat until dusk had turned to night before lighting a fire in a stone trough and settling down to wait.

* * * * * *

It was the early hours of the morning before the first figures appeared out of the night. Jolan Raeshaw, who led the most northerly clan, was the first. Braden could tell that beneath his travelling cloak the tall slim man wore the light armour of the Forest Ranger.

'It is good to see you, cousin,' Jolan said, slapping him on the back with a heavy hand. 'The Raeshaws send you great health. We answered your call and came quickly through the secret ways of the Blindburn.'

'Thank you. The borderlands grow stranger by the day—' Braden broke off, as two figures stepped through into the stone circle.

Dwarrow Dun-Rig was a giant man with a thick neck who wore a long black coat that covered him almost from head to foot. When he spoke, his voice was deep and reassuring, though a little coarse. He greeted Braden and then stood aside for the other man. He was shorter than Jolan, but as broad as Dwarrow. He wore a black Viking beard and had a shaved head. He smiled only briefly as he shook the hands of those gathered.

These four men represented the four main Reiver clans from across the north: the Bows, Raeshaws, Dun-Rigs and Broadflows. As they stood in the circle, the stones loomed over them, immovable giants whose faces trembled in the light of the fire, their backs turned against the vast darkness of the Northumberland night.

Braden was in a pensive mood. He drew no comfort from the wall of standing stones helping to keep the night at bay. These men were going to be shocked by what he had to say. They might be angry, for he had kept much from them, and even now he could not tell them the truth, for he didn't know it. As yet, he had only fragments of the puzzle.

He looked at each in turn and could see their concern reflected back at him.

'We Forest Reivers grew up on tales of spirits living in the forests and woods,' he began, 'and our elders spoke of a Faerie who dwelt in the Dead Water. Have we not heard that this Faerie takes the form of an old man, walking the fells and valleys of the borderlands, setting those who are lost on their right path?'

He looked round at those gathered. They were silent, waiting.

'I was with Eagan Reign in the Blindburn when we happened upon an old man. He told me to take our rangers to Birling Wood, for they would be needed before this night was over. You know there have been skirmishes along our forest borders. Now the red mare has shown herself in the shadow of the Cheviots.'

'The red mare, Braden – can you be certain? Isn't that a prediction of war?' asked Jolan.

'I believe,' said Braden slowly, 'that the fabled Underland is on the move and the secret ways of our people are in danger of being closed.'

He looked at his friends in turn. Their faces were serious and pale.

'I don't know why you are so shocked at hearing the Underland is moving,' said Ged, moving forward. He had chosen stay out of the firelight, concerned that it could be seen for miles around. 'The forests are quiet – the animals sense a dark wind blowing through the borderlands. The Underland moves through the air and is impossible to track. We have no idea about numbers, or where they are going and what their purpose might be. We followed a horde of several hundred that one minute ran like men, the next scattered into the sky in a murder of crows. How can that be? What magic are we facing?'

He shook his head and stepped back into the shadows.

Braden remembered the strange gait of the men hiding in the grass and their hideous end.

'Today I saw a ghostly company,' he said, 'led by a woman whose skill with a bow I have never witnessed before. They cut these crow-men down with perfect shots to the back of the neck, killing them with one fell strike. Whether they are on our side remains to be seen, but they were definitely not on the side of those they killed, and for that I am grateful.'

Ged reappeared. 'Be on your guard, brothers, for I no longer trust that we are alone. Something is stalking us, I can feel it.'

'That is very likely,' Braden agreed. 'I believe the peace we have enjoyed is coming to an end. We may need to move our people to the safety of Bamburgh and Holy Island. Tonight we will join Eagan at the Garden of Druids and await news from Jarl.'

'My sister Bretta will have reached Birling Wood by now,' began Jolan.

'The Raeshaws will be joined by the Dun-Rigs,' Dwarrow added. 'The crow-men would be foolish to come up against such numbers.'

'Thank you, Dwarrow. I hope you are right.'

'Was there a reason you brought us to the King's Seat, Braden?' Ged asked. 'I am uneasy about the fire you have lit. Shouldn't we join our men and women and await Eagan in a place where we are not so exposed?'

Braden could see Ged's uneasiness, and perhaps he had a point, but there *was* a reason for bringing them there. His elders still spoke of their meetings with Aine, the old man's daughter who had offered them protection in moments of strife, and the old man had said his daughters might help them. He hadn't offered anything more specific, but Braden thought that if Aine was going to offer assistance, she would meet them here. Was he clutching at straws? Perhaps he was. Perhaps the Faerie wouldn't help, after all.

He paused, wondering how to answer, but it was Ged who spoke first.

'Wait!'

Standing on the edge of the clearing, he became as still as the stones themselves. A form was quickly and silently moving up the hill.

A second later the haunted face of Jarl Reign came out of the night. 'Draw your swords!' he shouted.

Braden looked past Jarl in horror. A rippling sea of vague shapes was scaling the hillside. Even in the darkness he could see they were great in number.

Jolan Raeshaw was lightning quick, bounding through the stone circle in long leaps. Braden drew his long knife and as time slowed to a crawl he saw Dwarrow moving to his left and drawing his sword. Ahead of him, Jolan's long knives were already flashing into life and his face was ablaze with fear and determination.

Beyond the stone circle, hell had come to the King's Seat in the form of an unspeakable horde of strange misshapen men. They swarmed in from every point of the north ridge.

Ged was standing alone on the edge of both hill and darkness, firing his bow and arrow, his skill and ferocity keeping him alive. Jolan's twirling knives were sending the enemy backwards, whilst Braden and the giant Dwarrow joined battle with a sickening clash of flesh and steel. Braden found himself face to face with more of the creatures he'd seen in Threestoneburn Wood, their hideous black beaks snapping just inches from him.

The Forest Reivers met the snarling horde with a cold courage, their blades cutting them down, opening up their feathered bodies and pushing them back towards the edge of the hill. Every now and then they would turn to bow and arrow before following up with cold metal.

Jolan was lightning quick, making the crow-men pay dearly as he moved between them with his long cruel knives. It was like watching an acrobat twirling and rolling; his blades were cutting right and left, harrying the inhuman throng, turning them back on themselves. The giant Dwarrow and the fiery Ged were soon fighting back to back and proving themselves to be fearless descendants of those who had made the wild lands their spiritual home. Dwarrow's sabre was sweeping the crow-men away time and time again, whilst Ged was working tirelessly with his bow and arrow.

Still Braden knew they were becoming hopelessly outnumbered. The crow-men kept on coming in a relentless onslaught that would soon overwhelm them. There was a madness in the dark marauders who threw themselves forward without thought, as if possessed, caring nothing for their lives or the terrible weapons of the defenders. Their hatred was spilling out of their cawing throats, their red eyes were bulging with fury in the black night and there was a crazed look about their snapping beaks. Slowly the Reivers were being forced back from the edge of hill and were no longer able to stop more crow-men joining the battle.

Suddenly they were falling back with terror at their heels, almost drunken with the effort. They tumbled into the standing stones, expecting to be followed into the circle and slaughtered. Their eyes searched the darkness between the motionless stones, but the night had gone still.

'Quickly,' shouted Braden, 'circle the fire! It's not our night to perish!'

Jarl and Jolan piled the fire higher, the flames roared back into life and the heat bathed them in hope.

Braden felt his eyes stinging with the fear and effort. He knew there must be a hundred creatures gathering in the darkness. If they came all at once, it would be the end.

Strange barks were coming from behind the watchful stones, and faces were peering at them, but for now the enemy was holding off. He wondered why.

'We can't let them defeat us!' he shouted. It was he who had brought his fellow Reivers to the King's Seat and it was he who would get them off it alive.

His fellowship stood around the fire and took strength from the stone circle soaring around them. And still the enemy did not attack.

Instead, a single arrow whistled out of the night and into the middle of the fire, sending sparks high into the air. As Braden focused on its shaft, he recognised the white feather at its end.

Out in the night, caterwauls erupted, growing louder until after several long minutes the night was silent but for a few distant cries.

In the circle, no one moved for what seemed an age, still half expecting to see the feathered faces in the dark slits between the stones.

Finally, Braden could wait no longer and made his way cautiously into the night, warning, 'It could be a trap – keep together.'

The rest followed, tense and watchful, their weapons poised for action. They came across a sea of corpses, long arrows buried in their hearts. The crow-men had been wiped out by an enemy with a ferocity and accuracy that reminded Braden of the ghostly company in Threestoneburn Wood. He felt repulsed, for the whole of the summit was littered with the dead and dying.

'What is this madness?' growled Jolan.

'How do we know they've gone?' asked Dwarrow wearily, one eye closing from the fight.

'We wouldn't be alive if they were still here. Look at their work.' Braden bent down and examined one of the feathered arrows. 'I've seen arrows like this before,' he added thoughtfully.

Jarl bent down beside him, taking a look at the arrow's shaft. It was made of a wood he had never seen before and was perfectly straight, with a small intricate carving leading down to its point, which was neither made of metal nor stone.

Braden reached for the end, but Jarl quickly grabbed his arm. 'You can't be sure the tips aren't poisonous. Look at the enemy – not one moving.'

'I saw these creatures on the road here,' Braden explained. 'There were a dozen of them. I followed them into Threestoneburn Wood, where they were hunted down by a people I'd never seen before. They used arrows like this – and they used the bow and arrow like no one I've ever seen before. Not even our finest rangers come anywhere close.'

Jarl nodded. 'I have much to tell you,' he said. 'Gather round.'

Leaning heavily on Braden, he waited until the others had formed a tight circle around them. He looked at them in turn. Most were bloodied and all were bewildered and concerned.

'I left Brennus and Drust travelling to the Dead Water,' he began.

'But,' cried Braden, 'those fells and valleys are no longer safe!'

'I hear you, Braden, but Brennus thought he had no option. We had been attacked by an enemy without equal. It appears as a Shadow in this world and we have neither the strength nor the knowledge to stop it. I don't think you can wait until morning before you travel to Birling Wood. The Shadow wasn't far behind me when I left it in the Usway Valley.'

Jarl took a deep breath, unsure whether it would be wise to tell them everything or whether he should wait until he was alone with Braden, for the Reivers were spooked by things they could not understand. He could already see that his words had sent a shiver into their hearts that their hardened faces couldn't conceal.

'What is this Shadow?' Jolan cried. 'Tell us more!'

'Look around,' Jarl said. 'Isn't this evil enough? You can't wait here a moment longer. Great danger will come to the Garden of Druids.'

'And where does this leave Brennus and Drust?' asked Jolan. 'Are we to act like frightened children and desert our friends?'

'Jolan, those are generous words,' Jarl replied, 'but if the Shadow is heading for Warkworth, that's where we must head too. The Hoods are very capable and I have faith they'll find a way back.'

He hoped the Reivers didn't realise how little faith he really had.

'Look!' The cry came from Ged. He had refused to take his eyes off the dead crow-men. They were manifestly unnatural and there had been a colour-magic to their movement that concerned him. Now – were his eyes were playing tricks in the darkness?

'They're moving!' Jolan got the words out through clenched teeth.

At first it was a twitch, then a jolt, then sickening jerks spreading across the entire hilltop as the dead began to wake.

'We cannot fight this,' growled Braden. 'Quickly, we must leave this place.'

* * * * * *

Amongst the convulsing dead, a horrid clamour was rising. Arrows were being withdrawn from flesh and the noise was grating in the Reivers' ears as they wove their way between the trembling bodies and reached the path leading steeply down into the gloom.

A crow-man clumsily reached for Dwarrow and was swept aside, but others were regaining their feet and beginning to shriek as new life flooded into their twisted bodies. Braden felt sick with dread as he realised the path was littered with the returning dead.

At first the reviving crow-men were slow, but soon fighting was breaking out again.

'Go down, Jarl!' shouted Braden, spearing a creature with his sword.

'The way is blocked.'

Ged didn't listen, but hurled himself down the path. Quickly he found himself up against creatures who now had weapons. They were holding the arrows with vile claws, slashing and cutting with a savagery that stopped him in his tracks. Some of the creatures were running at them with the long arrows held above their heads.

The Reivers were once again outnumbered, standing back to back on the edge of the hill. The crow-men leaped at them like frenzied animals. Jarl had an arrow buried deep in his thigh. The pain took him to the ground and if Ged hadn't been near him, another arrow would have found his chest. With astonishing strength, he threw the creatures back and stood over Jarl like a roaring lion.

In the middle of the carnage, the tall willowy figure of Jolan danced between the crow-men, his sharp knives cutting and thrusting.

Braden, already weak from his first encounter, found images of his family racing through his mind, igniting a deep anger that burned through his weariness, and he struck out again and again until his arms were raw and his mind almost blank.

'Keep together – don't become separated!' he heard himself shouting, but the crow-men were now changing their form of attack, almost as if they could sense their advantage, and all across the King's Seat they were throwing themselves against the wall of Reivers.

Despite the Reivers' fighting prowess, they were being pushed back. Jolan went down, crumpled by a sickening blow across the face. For a moment it seemed Ged, now fighting with his short sword, had single-handedly halted the ferocious attack, but the crow-men's strength seemed greater than before, and soon the defenders could feel the last of their own strength draining out of them. Their situation was desperate as they crowded together, with Braden, Ged and Dwarrow protecting the injured Jarl and Jolan. Little by little, they were being forced back towards the standing stones and their escape was now closed off.

'Fall back!' came the panicked voice of Braden, as the sea of reanimated corpses came surging forward like a tempest roaring out of the night.

Then all at once thunderous wings were sweeping across the King's Seat and long claws were grabbing the crow-men and flinging them from the hilltop like broken branches caught in a storm. Red kites, hundreds in number, and larger than anyone ever remembered seeing before, were swooping in to attack.

'What magic is this?' called Braden, but he was quickly silenced by the powerful beat of a thousand wings. In a daze he wondered whether it had anything to do with the kite he had seen earlier.

Then he was calling the Forest Reivers together, for this had given them chance to escape. With Jarl propped up against Dwarrow, and Braden holding the stricken Jolan, he let Ged lead the way. Sick with exhaustion but with grim determination, they opened a gap amongst the scattering crow-men.

Still the birds of prey were wheeling across the night sky and gliding into the attack. Under their protection, Ged and Braden led their weary companions down the hillside and into the fringes of Birling Wood, where they came to a stumbling stop.

'How can the dead come back alive?' asked Dwarrow, horror-stricken.

'What evil do we face, Braden?' asked Jolan, blood running down his cheek.

'Now is not the time to ask such questions,' Braden replied. 'We must hasten to the Garden of Druids.'

Mustering the last of their will, they set off on a desperate march through Birling Wood.

* * * * * *

She watched them go, pushing back her flowing locks of golden hair. She was unlike her sister, who was against meddling in the affairs of men. She had loved a man and spent years searching for his ghost in the forgotten places of the Otherland. Now she would take up the cause he had died for. She would not turn her back on her people's plight.

She knew it would not be easy. It was she who had first felt the Shadow coming and had woken her father from his sleep. She had watched from afar as he had fought it at the Dead Water. And the dark mist still hanging over the King's Seat, filling the dead with an alien energy, was unlike anything she had known in her long years in the Mid-land.

But she also knew the time of the *Druidae* had not come to an end. There was still hope. Oscar had not been the last Druid.

THE BATTLE OF BIRLING WOOD

Sam and Emily stood side by side whilst the people on horseback formed a tight ring around them. In the darkness the horses towered above them and there were harsh faces looking down. These were rugged folk dressed in thick clothes and their voices were gruff and frightening. Sam watched as a woman dismounted and raised a hand, and a hush fell across the clearing. Only the horses continued their nervous whinnying and there was a sea of shifting hooves. The woman threw back her hood, revealing reddish hair, and came to stand directly in front of them.

'What are you doing in Birling Wood at night?'

Though hers was probably one of the youngest amongst the stern faces, her voice was strong and seemed to carry great authority.

'We were just minding our business and enjoying the evening when we were rudely attacked,' Emily replied.

The woman looked first at her, then at Sam, and then broke into laughter, followed by those who were close enough to hear. She shook her head and smiled for the first time.

'Tell me your name, child – if that isn't too much trouble! My name is Bretta, if that helps. We are Forest Reivers from the Raeshaw clan. Now tell me, who are you and what are you doing here?'

Sam got his words out first before Emily could antagonise a people renowned for their fighting prowess and short tempers: 'We are from Warkworth. We are lost.'

'There aren't many who could stumble across this place whilst lost.'

Bretta's eyes were on them, scrutinising them. Sam swallowed hard. Then she seemed to come to a decision.

'Blarus!' Several horses whinnied at her raised voice and a dark-skinned man came forward. 'Take our friends to my fire and I will meet them there.'

'We can't stay,' began Sam, but Bretta gave him a sharp look and his stomach sank.

'You will be free to go at first light. I wouldn't want any harm coming to you in the meantime, especially when we catch the edge of a storm that is coming down from the north.'

'You can't simply imprison us!' implored Emily.

The woman stopped and turned. 'You will be grateful for our company before the night is over, little one. In the morning you might just be thankful.'

She disappeared between the flanks of the horses.

* * * * * *

'I can understand why Eagan likes these people,' huffed Emily.

Sam laughed. Even though he sensed the Forest Reivers were good people, they were rough-looking. Some had dark hair, others were fair, but the majority were red-headed, pale-skinned and thick-set. He couldn't tell how many were assembled, but they must have numbered at least a hundred, perhaps double that.

Blarus led them through the throng of horses and a thick copse of trees until eventually they came out onto an open hillside. There were already dozens of camp fires flickering there.

As the Reiver took them through the camp, it became apparent to Sam that it was empty of people. He also noticed that the horses were being led to the edge of the clearing and into the trees. For whatever reason, the Forest Reivers were making themselves scarce.

When they reached the opposite end of the large clearing and re-entered the wood, he could see Reivers climbing the trees all around him. There was no doubt in his mind that they were setting a trap – he guessed the fires were nothing more than a decoy and whoever found themselves on the hilltop would quickly be surrounded and the ambush complete.

That felt reassuring, but then another thought entered his head – what if the fires attracted the Shadow? He wasn't sure that even with such numbers the Reivers could stop it. Could it be stopped by anyone? What if Oscar had no answers?

Sam knew these thoughts should have terrified him, but he could still feel the calmness of the old man gently coursing through him. He felt a little light-headed with it all.

The dark-skinned man told him and Emily to sit and then positioned himself under a nearby tree. It was obvious that he was to be their guard for the time being.

They sat cross-legged on the ground, leaning against a fallen tree, and looked at each other.

'Is it me,' said Emily, 'or are they expecting trouble? And I hate to say it, but are we the bait?'

'I think they're securing the hill and making sure it's safe. I'm not sure about being the bait – what purpose would it serve?'

'I hope you're right. The only thing they haven't done is tie our hands behind our backs, but there's still time for that.'

The fallen trunk was uncomfortable to learn against and their nostrils were thick with the smell of rotting wood. The wind was picking up and the trees on the slopes were beginning to sway.

'Are we alone now?' Emily stood up and looked around. The camp was empty and it seemed that Blarus had gone as well.

'I'm not sure.' Sam stretched his legs. 'I think most of them are in the wood. They know trouble's coming and so do I. Listen, I think we need to find this Bretta woman and tell her a little of what we know.'

'And what do you know?'

They both turned to see Bretta standing no more than ten feet away, wrapped in a cloak that seemed to have been made from the surrounding foliage. Sam guessed she'd been standing there all the time.

'We were supposed to meet Eagan Reign here tonight,' she said, 'and it's not like him to be absent from such a meeting. I see from your faces that you know him.'

'He is my cousin,' began Emily.

'Perhaps that is how you were allowed to stumble on this place.' Bretta moved towards them. 'And what trouble do you expect? If you think we are in danger then surely we have the right to know?'

Sam hesitated, wondering how much to say. He was only too aware that the sooner they were on their way the better, and the last person he wanted to see was Eagan.

'It just feels like you are expecting trouble,' he murmured. 'You have built camp fires, but you don't seem to be using them. Instead, you are hiding in the trees watching and waiting.'

Bretta turned from Sam to Emily, as if hoping for a better answer.

'I am intrigued,' she said, 'as to why Eagan would send his cousin here in his place, for I suspect this has been planned.'

'Oh no, we didn't plan anything. We just went for an evening stroll and got lost.'

'Yes, of course you did.' The Reiver woman smiled grimly. 'Now listen to me, we are here at Eagan's request and I would like to know why you are here.'

'I'm sure it won't be the first time Eagan hasn't kept an engagement,' Emily said rudely. 'And if you don't mind, we need to be finding our way back home.'

Sam cringed, but just for a second he thought he saw a flicker of a smile cross Bretta's face.

'Well, I can't let you go until the morning,' she replied. 'As you rightly say, we think there is trouble coming here tonight. My brother Jolan is meeting the heads of the Reiver families at the King's Seat and I expect him to return with news of what form this trouble takes. So it would be good to understand a little of what you know.'

She stood there watching them, whilst the wind picked up behind them and the Reiver fires continued winking through the night.

Emily sighed. It was obvious they would have to say something.

'We *were* supposed to meet Eagan here this evening,' she said, 'but we became separated in the wood.'

'Why didn't he travel with you?'

'He was on an errand of some sort and said he would catch up later.'

Sam gave Emily a hard stare. He wished she wouldn't keep lying and complicating things.

'It's worrying that he isn't here,' Bretta commented.

Then Sam jumped as she touched his arm.

'The trees,' she continued, staring into his face, 'speak of a darkness moving through the wood. It will be here within the next few hours – it seems we have arrived just in time. From what we can gather, it is seeking something or someone.'

Sam shuddered.

'I can tell by your eyes that this darkness has already touched you.' Bretta was gently holding his arm now, whilst her blue-grey eyes were searching his. 'You need to tell me what you have seen.'

'I don't think you'll like one word of what I have to say.'

'Sam!' Emily exclaimed.

'Sam,' the Reiver woman said softly, 'come and sit with me.'

She turned to Emily, whose eyes were wide with anger, or possibly fear.

'Why don't you come too, for I am sure you can tell me more about Eagan.'

Emily was just opening her mouth to reply when Blarus seemed to materialise directly in front of her. It would appear he, too, had been there all the time.

'And Blarus,' Bretta smiled, 'won't be far away either.'

With Bretta leading and Blarus bringing up the rear, they passed through a line of trees and came to a small clearing. In the middle was a pit with a small fire and several cloaks laid around it. Nearby Sam could hear the nervous calls of the horses.

'Come along, we only have a little time before we will need to part company.'

Bretta sat down and signalled for Sam and Emily to follow.

Though the fire was a small one, Sam was glad of its heat. By its flickering light he was surprised to see how young Bretta was.

'Now tell me, Sam,' she said, 'where have you been and where are you going?'

'You don't need to tell her anything.'

Emily was sitting cross-legged, staring into the fire. This time Bretta chose to ignore her.

'I have been travelling with Brennus and Drust Hood,' Sam admitted.

Bretta could not hide her surprise. 'And where are they now?' she asked, leaning forward.

'I don't know exactly. I was with them in Oxford. We travelled to Gosforth together, then separated.'

'Oxford! But why would you choose to separate? Tell me truly – I don't have much time to sift through your words.'

'Six days ago a man called Oscar visited me in Oxford—'

Sam was interrupted by voices to his left and right. The small clearing suddenly became a hive of activity. There were rangers stepping into the firelight, dressed in cloaks that seemed to be shimmering ever so slightly to blend in with the wood, and Bretta was standing and speaking to them in a thick dialect.

Even though Sam couldn't understand the words, he could sense the disquiet in the men and women now standing all around. He shot a quick glance at Emily. She, too, was watching the commotion. Then the figures disappeared back into the wood and Bretta rejoined them around the fire, looking a little ruffled.

'We know of Oscar,' she said, 'and we thought he was dead. But these are strange times. Are you sure it was him?'

'I don't know. I'd never seen him before. I can say that he brought a warning to Oxford and since then we've been pursued by a Shadow.'

Even in the little clearing, with the comfort of knowing he was surrounded by a hundred Forest Reivers, Sam wondered whether he was safe.

Bretta was watching him carefully, almost without blinking. 'And have you seen this Shadow?'

Sam thought long and hard before replying. It would always unravel just as he tried to picture it.

'I can't easily describe it,' he admitted. 'It is as much a feeling as something you see.'

'Then why do you call it a Shadow?'

'That's the nearest thing to it. But there's more to it than that.'

Again he dug down deep in his memories. He could see the gates of Magdalen, could see the bridge, and what was it that had been standing just beyond the Cherwell? What had called to him under the Fellows' House?

'I'm sorry – I just don't know what I saw.'

There was a disgusted sniff from Emily.

'So tell me about Brennus,' Bretta said kindly. 'What is he doing now?'

'He is travelling to the Dead Water, seeking answers to the nature of the Shadow.'

Bretta was shocked. 'I know of this place and so do my forefathers! It is not a place for the living.'

She pulled her forest cloak around her and stared thoughtfully into the flames. Sam and Emily were silent.

Every now and then Reivers would appear on the edge of the clearing and evaporate back into the night.

'My people are nervous,' Bretta explained. 'The wood is unsettled. My rangers have picked up a host that is moving from the north. It is clear they are coming here. We have about an hour before they arrive.'

Sam felt his stomach clench at her words. 'So what will you do?'

'We have to decide whether to make a stand or to escape east. If we stay, then it will be too dangerous for you to remain with us. If we flee, then the place we are here to defend will fall.'

'In that case, all I can tell you is that we are looking for the Garden of Druids.'

'Sam!' exclaimed Emily.

'The Garden of Druids?' repeated Bretta in astonishment. 'It is the reason we are here. A request came from my cousin Braden to travel to Birling Wood in haste.'

'Can you show us the way to the garden?' Sam was starting to feel desperate.

'I would be happier if we waited for my brother. There may be news from the King's Seat that will help you. He can't be long and I don't think it's safe travelling through the wood alone.'

'You won't get to the garden anyway,' said Emily suddenly. 'No matter how hard you walk, climb or run, it's impossible to find it without Eagan.'

'What do you mean?' Sam was flabbergasted.

'Well, if it really *is* the orchard, that is. I've been shown the way many times, but I couldn't find it back there.' Emily lowered her eyes to the ground. 'I've just put two and two together and realised I've never been there without Eagan or Jarl. I think they are the only people who can find it.'

'You knew this all along and still took us on a wild goose chase?'

'I *didn't* know it all along. I thought I *could* find it.'

Bretta listened to the bewildering conversation with interest. The girl wasn't lying – they'd scoured the wood and found no garden. She'd heard about it, of course, but no one amongst the rangers had seen it apart from Braden, and that had been when he'd been with Eagan. So was it an orchard? But they hadn't found an orchard either.

As she looked at the girl, questions rushed through her mind. Who was she really? Was she anything to do with Eagan? And the boy – she could sense something quite potent behind him. The more she looked at him, the more unsettled she became. What was she to do with them? She had to decide whether to let them go or risk them being injured if her rangers had to defend the hill.

Without warning, figures were emerging from the wood once more. They again spoke in a thick dialect, but now there was a new urgency in their gestures. Bretta was standing listening, her face solemn in the flickering firelight. Then the figures were wrapping their cloaks around them and melting back into the night.

When they were alone once more, Bretta turned to Sam, her face troubled.

'The enemy is through the place we call the Cauldron. They are moving with great speed and will be here shortly. I'm afraid it is too late for you to leave.'

'But I need to find the garden!'

The idea of being caught between the Reivers and whoever they might be fighting was one Sam wasn't willing to contemplate.

'You have no time – this hill will be surrounded.'

'Oscar is waiting for me.' The words seem to burn as he said them.

'Oscar is dead,' Bretta replied.

'No – I met him, I spoke with him. I have to find the garden.' Sam looked at Emily. 'You need to take me there.'

'I don't know where it is, Sam!'

A cawing sound resounded through the wood.

Instantly Bretta stamped out the fire, throwing the clearing into complete darkness.

'It's too late – we're being attacked!'

From across the clearing the first forms emerged, some running on two legs, others on all fours. It was a giant wave that was coming to sweep the Forest Reivers from the wood. There was a noise that struck Sam from all sides, a whooshing sound, and then there was a rain of arrows.

Sam felt the usual dread swell up in him like sickness. Amid the pandemonium, he heard Emily's voice calling for him. Then someone swung him around in the darkness and pulled him quickly into the trees. For a second he tried to twist out of the hands that held him and look for Emily, but a terrifying roar was sweeping through the wood and he felt dazed. It was unlike anything he'd ever heard before. It sounded as though a thousand wild animals were crazed and stampeding, and still it built in volume.

Blarus was darting through the wood, pulling him along with him, whilst to his left a young Reiver woman was dragging Emily. Deeper into the wood they fled, on and on until the roar receded behind them. Then Blarus and the woman turned.

'We can take you no further,' Blarus said. 'Keep heading north and eventually you'll be free of the wood.'

And with that they were fastening their cloaks and evaporating into the night.

* * * * * *

'Do you think it is the crow-men who are attacking them? I am still shaking.' Emily found Sam's hand in the darkness. 'I wish Uncle Jarl was here.'

'So do I. I'm done with all this, Emily – I'm frightened and tired, and I want it to be over.' Sam was shaking too. 'It started with Oscar and I think it has to end with Oscar.'

'Have you thought what happens if you don't find him?'

Sam didn't answer as a distant sound, shrill and penetrating, rang out through the wood.

'Let's get moving. We need to find the orchard.'

'I don't know where it is.'

'You need to find it, Emily!'

'Stop shouting – you're not helping.'

Sam let go of Emily's hand, his fear turning to burning anger. 'I don't understand why it's so difficult.'

In the darkness, tears flowed down Emily's cheeks. She was exhausted and frightened.

Sam heard her sobs, but there was a new danger coiling itself around him, a dread snaking its way through his body, coursing through his blood. Somewhere in the darkness, under the cover of battle, the Shadow was coming.

'Emily,' he gasped, 'the Shadow is here – it's searching for me.' He sank to a crouching position, his hands covering his face. 'I can't do this.'

'Get up!' Emily yelled, horrified. 'We can make it. Get up!'

She reached down and pulled him to his feet. For a brief second, they stood looking at each other. Then Sam took a deep breath and headed into the twisted trees.

* * * * * *

They moved as quickly as they could through the dense under-growth. Every now and then Sam would feel the hair on the back of his neck stiffen, goosebumps would ripple across his body and nausea would wash over him. No matter how fast they went, he could feel the Shadow's presence growing in his mind. He sensed it trying to slow him down. The forest floor became like gurgling quicksand and he could feel his feet sinking in…

'It looks as though the orchard has found us.'

Emily's voice broke through his thoughts and he turned to follow her gaze. No more than half a mile away, there was a broken wall.

Without another word, they made their way quickly towards it. Sam felt static electricity popping and cracking around him and his skin was prickling with tiny shocks.

The wall had seen better days and in places had crumbled to nothing. There were glimpses of its former splendour to the east and west, but with little effort Sam and Emily picked their way over a part of it that was now a pile of stones.

In the moonlight they could see long lines of trees separated by narrow paths. Fruit hung low and Sam couldn't help feeling a little disappointed that the orchard was nothing more than apple and pear trees after all.

Emily walked to the first line of trees.

'What now, Sam? I'm so tired.'

'I don't know. I was certain Oscar would meet us here.' Sam looked around, but all he could see was more lines of trees. 'But I don't think we can stay here long. The Reivers may be hard pressed to defend the wood.'

'Well, wake me up when we have to go.'

Emily sat down, rested her forehead on her knees and seemed to drift into sleep. Sam looked down at her, feeling guilty as he remembered how hard the last few days had been.

Not knowing what to do next, he walked back to the wall and pulled himself up onto a high point. Still all he could see was an orchard. Why had he let a letter send him on a wild goose chase?

The snap of a branch made him turn to face the dark wood. Someone was coming this way. His blood ran cold as a solitary figure staggered out of the gloom, carrying a companion fallen in battle.

Then moonlight fell on the man's face and he realised it was Jarl, his face bloodied and contorted in anguish, and in his arms was the slumped form of Eagan, ashen white, with his chest covered in blood.

'Jarl – what happened?'

Jarl didn't answer, but looked down at Eagan. Then he whispered, 'Killed by those who were meant to protect him, Sam. I didn't think it would come to this. I can't be part of this deception any longer.'

He bent his head.

'I am sorry, Jarl. I am so sorry.'

Jarl raised his head. 'We have been lied to, Sam, by the very people we would call friends – betrayed by each and every one of them.'

He stepped over the broken wall, holding Eagan close to him.

'I won't lie to you – not after tonight. They would have you believe that they are protecting you. But you are nothing more than a diversion. They have used you like they used Eagan – to distract the enemy until they could decide what to do.'

Jarl's voice had become lower and there was now anger in his words.

'I was there the night Oscar came with the Shadow to Oxford. They wanted to give it your scent. They wanted it to find you. And it did. We distracted it so you could escape from the river. Where were Brennus and Drust when you needed them? Where were they in the Fellows' House? Where were they at the gates of Magdalen?'

Sam felt his mouth go dry. Jarl had touched a nerve.

'We stopped the Shadow finding you in the reading room when they left you alone with the Way-curves. They wanted to remind it of what you looked like. I know you don't want to hear this, but it's time for you to know the truth, no matter how painful you think it is.'

Sam didn't know what to say. Had the professors been using him? Had he just been bait all along? He scrambled down off the wall and stood with his back to it, his mind whirling.

'They led the Shadow to you and let you down at every turn!' Jarl was almost raging now. 'Ask yourself, who have they really been protecting? They talk of Druids and the Fall and still they can't tell you the truth. They talk about the crow-men and don't tell you who they really are and the pain they have suffered at the hands of those Druids.'

He took a few steps forward and looked around him.

Sam couldn't speak. He leaned against the wall, staring at Eagan's pale face. How he wished he'd made things up with him before he'd left for the wood. Perhaps they could have helped each other. Now it was too late.

'Where is Emily?' Jarl asked. 'Quickly – we have little time. The enemy will be upon us.'

'Emily?'

'Yes, Sam. I seek the girl.'

Sam hesitated. He'd never heard Jarl speak of Emily in such cold tones. It reminded him of another night, not so long ago.

'She's not here,' he said quickly.

'She is our only hope, Sam.'

Jarl stepped forward again. Instinctively Sam moved sideways, inching away from him along the wall.

'We have suffered enough! Tell me where she is!'

'Who are you?' Sam whispered.

'I am here to free my people. They didn't deserve what the Druids did to them. A long time ago we fought with the people of the Mid-land and forced back the hordes of the Ruin. We were betrayed by the Druids in our hour of need – betrayed by the Faeries and men. They left most of my people behind the Fall – left them to perish! Those who remained were forced into the Underland, chased by the Forest Reivers into the deep dark places of the world.'

Jarl lowered his head.

'Who are your people?' Sam asked, amazed. Why had no one told him this side of the story? Then he froze.

'Uncle Jarl!' Emily was clambering to her feet and waving.

'Emily, come to me. Great treachery has befallen our family this night.'

'Eagan!' Emily gasped. She started to run towards them.

'*Emily!*' Sam called. 'Stay back! This is not your uncle – *stay back!*'

Confused, Emily stood still.

Sam ran to stand between her and Jarl. 'Who are you?' he repeated.

Jarl let Eagan drop with a sickening thud. He threw his arms wide, revealing claws that belonged to no human.

'I come from the Underland to free our people from the hand of the *Druidae*. I come to track down the last Druid.'

He moved with sickening speed, catching Sam off-balance, but Sam was big and strong and managed to twist out of his reach. He heard Emily's voice calling his name and a subtle light danced before his eyes, or was it in his mind? All the colours of the rainbow were swirling together in clear water. There were voices too, like the choir of Magdalen.

Silently, he called to the light. It flowed round him and he saw the creature go crashing to the ground.

It spun quickly back around and something had changed. It was no longer standing like a man, but was hunched over, watching him and baring its teeth.

Emily screamed, but Sam barely heard it. In his mind's eye the voices were washing through him, climbing ever higher until he could see them as filaments of flowing colour.

The creature charged, running on all fours, but an unseen force knocked it clean off its feet. When it hauled itself back up, Jarl's face was now mixed with grey feathers and snarling jaws.

'Let the girl go!' Jarl's voice rang out through the quiet night.

Again the creature tried to charge Sam, but the voices and threads of vibrant colour were still strengthening, and without knowing how or why, he brought the flow to bear on the creature, flinging it back as if it were made of straw.

When it got to its feet again, it no longer resembled Jarl, but had long grey feathers protruding from its face, a snapping mouth that looked half-jaw and half-beak, and glittering eyes that oddly reminded Sam of the grey heron on the banks of the Coquet. It was a hideous and grotesque representation of nature and he knew it was no better than the crow-men. It raised long thin arms, threw back its head and started baying.

Sam knew it was calling to its brethren and if he stayed a moment longer he would have the horde who had attacked his home swarming through the orchard. Anger exploded in his head and then raced down through his body. He swept his arms up through the night and the air became a fizzing, galvanising flow, crackling and snapping, flowering through the darkness – and then a deafening silence brought everything to a stop as the creature dropped to the ground, unmoving and silent.

The voices, colour and electricity left Sam as quickly as they had come. The quiet night rushed in to fill the void and Sam and Emily were left standing like statues, breathless and immobile, whilst in the distance the sounds of fighting rang out through Birling Wood.

Then Emily ran to Eagan and bent down beside him.

'What have they done?' she cried.

She touched his face, but there was no response.

'Is he alive?' Sam asked.

'I don't know. We have to get help.'

Together they lifted Eagan. With Sam holding his body and Emily holding his legs, they moved off through the long lines of trees.

* * * * * *

Bretta was standing on the edge of the clearing, watching the Reivers' whistling arrows thumping into the frenzied mass of terror that was spilling out of the dark trees. The horde came a second time, and again they were met by a wall of arrows that stopped them in their stride.

Bretta was readying herself for the moment when the arrows were spent and the rangers would come down on the horde on horseback. Her hope was that they would drive them from the clearing and back into the wood. She wasn't sure how their fortunes would hold up once the arrows were gone and the advantage from the cavalry had faded. But if necessary, her rangers would break up into smaller fighting units and would fall back through the wood, fighting hand to hand with their short swords.

The crow-men were unnaturally quick, even though it looked as if they were having difficulty standing. Bretta quickly realised they weren't fighting with weapons, but with claw-like bones protruding from strange twisted limbs. The noise that issued from their cruel beaks made her almost nauseous. She was hoping that Jolan would arrive soon from the King's Seat. She would need his experience to repel these hordes from the Underland.

The girl and boy flashed through her thoughts. They'd given her only half the story. She'd heard of Oscar, of course – every self-respecting Reiver knew of him and of the journey of his fellowship to lands that were now part of Reiver folklore. But as far as she could tell, he'd died several years ago.

Her thoughts came back to the crow-men. More of them had reached the clearing now, as the shower of arrows was lighter.

She'd come across these creatures once before. She'd trailed several through the Blindburn only days earlier. They had been different from the ones she was now facing in the wood, though. They had been dog-like, though her brother had said they'd reminded him of wolves.

Bretta shivered. Then she noticed that Blarus and Erin were now standing beside her and she drew strength from them.

'Sam and the girl, have they gone?'

'Yes,' they said almost together.

'Then let us do what must be done.'

And with that, Blarus was moving quickly to her right, whilst Erin, wrapped in her ranger cloak, was disappearing to her left.

The wood was catching the edge of the storm and the wind was beginning to strengthen. The last of the Reivers' arrows sank into their targets and the archers quickly descended from their hiding places in the tallest and thickest trees.

They formed a tight line behind Bretta, whilst the Reiver lancers came galloping out of the trees on both sides of the dark host assembling in the clearing. Their spears did savage work and soon they were pushing the crow-men back to its southerly edge.

Bretta was signalling to Reivers armed with short swords to move in behind the horses and the long spears. The Forest Reivers were made for fighting. Few were taller than six foot, but most were thick-set and powerful. Bretta felt certain they could drive these beasts from the wood.

There was a new roar as several hundred Forest Reivers began charging through the clearing, nimbly avoiding the camp fires that had done their job in confusing the enemy. Those on horses were now pulling up their spears and retreating, making way for those on foot, who would sweep the enemy from the hill.

Bretta reached the first crow-men bodies. Some had been killed by arrows, others by the sharp thrusts of Reiver spears. Gazing at the hideous beasts, she could feel the reek of poison tightening its noose around her throat. The Reivers who had been wounded were now feeling its sting. Weapons were falling from fingers that would no longer do their bidding.

Without the force of arrow and spear, Bretta felt there was a subtle but noticeable turn in the battle. It was becoming clear that the crow-men were not fearful of dying and this was having a profound effect on the Reivers. On each side Bretta noticed that some had stopped fighting and others were watching in horror as those around them were dropping to the ground in agony. Some were beginning to tend to those who had been wounded.

With a sinking heart, she knew that she'd called off the cavalry too soon. She'd underestimated the numbers of crow-men still hiding in the wood. Endless waves of crazed animals had been available to replace the fallen.

'Bretta, we cannot keep this hilltop!' Blarus called, as he turned and struck down one of the crow-men only inches from her face.

The noise of battle was drowning her senses. The whole line of defenders was waiting for her every command. It was as if she had woken in the middle of a nightmare only to find it real.

She watched in horror as another swarm of misshapen forms descended from the trees, clambered over their dead and launched themselves forward. She knew they would not stop until each and every one of the Reivers was dead.

Once more she sent the cavalry sweeping through the hilltop to meet the horde. But some of the horses could bear the terror no longer and were rearing up, hurling their brave riders into the seething mass. Bretta looked down, unable to bear the sight. When she raised her head, the Forest Reivers were dragging the wounded back.

Someone was shouting, 'Retreat!' A hysterical voice in the night, it echoed in her head until she realised it was her own.

The Reivers began slowly moving back through the fires, whose embers were sparking back into life as the wind was whistling across the clearing. Horses were also returning, many without riders, others with two.

Every ranger from Kielder in the south to Dun-Rig in the north had travelled to this place. There had been perhaps three hundred in number and now a quarter lay dead or wounded.

All around Bretta the wounded were being put on horses and taken from the battle. She barked orders to the rangers as they led them away into the murky trees. She hadn't counted on paying such a heavy price. It would seem the whole of the Underland was here in Birling Wood.

She wiped the sweat from her eyes and stretched her arms. They felt like lead. She knew they would have to give the wounded time to get away. Beyond this, she could not think. She felt herself shaking from the shock that was settling across her body. She was praying that Jolan would arrive soon. She couldn't face this a moment longer.

The horde began to move slowly forward, their wretched voices amplified by the wind. They stretched a mile from end to end, their numbers swelling as more joined them from the wood. The arrows had taken hundreds down, a hundred more had fallen on their spears, and her brave foot soldiers had slaughtered a hundred more, and yet it felt as though they had made no mark on their numbers.

The twisting mass of strange limbs and feathered snouts had reached the first fires and were extinguishing them one by one. When they reached the last, smothering its flames by their sheer numbers, the clearing was thrown into absolute darkness.

The Forest Reivers prepared for the final onslaught. Without archers and cavalry, they could not hope to last long. Bretta could feel her people's fear. Her own was thick around her throat. She did not wait for the attack, but called her people back into the wood.

Moving as quickly as their legs would carry them, the remaining Forest Reivers melted into the wood. Soon they could hear the horde crashing through the trees behind them, their calls echoing their frustration at losing sight of the fleeing Reivers.

Bretta urged the Reivers on. If they were caught here, they could not counter such numbers. The wood was now alive with her people weaving through the dense foliage, making sure they kept together, not wanting to leave anyone behind.

The crow-men's cries were becoming muffled. They were beginning to fall behind. The Reivers were now catching up with the wounded stragglers who had succumbed to the poison. Many were drooping over their mounts, almost unconscious. Quickly, the Reivers mounted the horses and spurred them forward.

Bretta knew they could not outrun the horde indefinitely, not with so many wounded. Where could they go? Alnmouth?

As she moved through the darkness, she wondered what else was happening. Why hadn't Eagan kept his appointment with them? Had he really sent the girl she had met? And what about the boy? Why was the mysterious Shadow searching for him? Perhaps after speaking to Braden, Jolan would have some answers. But would she ever see her brother again?

They came out of the tangled wood to find a broken wall ahead of them. Beyond it, they could see long lines of trees.

'The orchard!' Bretta exclaimed.

She wondered whether Sam and the girl had found it after all, but there was no time to think about them. The first lines of trees were already full of horses and wounded. Several healers were attending to them and further Reivers were pouring out of the wood on all sides. She called to them to help the wounded over the wall.

'This is it,' she thought, 'a last chance to repel the horde.'

The horses were rounded up and taken deep into the orchard, along with the Reivers who were succumbing to the poison. Where the wall had crumbled into piles of stone, the sturdiest rangers were set to stand guard with their jagged short spears.

But even as she arranged her forces, doubt was creeping through Bretta. Should they stay here or make for Alnmouth?

Then faint noises from the wood stopped any thoughts of escape. The crow-men were coming.

In the darkness Bretta could sense her people's fear. There were two hundred of the Forest Reivers' finest there, but they faced an enemy several thousand strong. And the angry calls of the crow-men were rising.

Suddenly the dark edge of the wood came alive. From east to west, a jeering ocean of feathered bodies and loathsome beaks was crowing in glee at catching the Forest Reivers with nowhere to go.

Bretta felt Blarus touch her shoulder.

'You will be needed to protect the wounded,' he said calmly. 'You must go to them.'

She shook her head.

'Bretta, please, we can ill afford to lose our leader. Go to the rear.'

Bretta shook her head again. 'You ask too much, Blarus. I cannot leave my people.'

As she spoke, it seemed that the hideous cawing was lessening. It died away until the entire hillside was silent. It was strange to be in the middle of such calm when there had been such tumult only minutes before. The quiet was almost as unsettling as the sea of noise. Bretta gripped the handle of her sword until her knuckles hurt, stopping only when the pain lessened the dread in her heart. What were the crow-men waiting for?

Then there was a ripple amongst them. It seemed they were parting to make a passage through their ranks. A figure was stepping through.

A murmur came from the Forest Reivers, but they held their ground. Bretta felt dazzled. She could not make out what they had seen, yet she knew something was out there, surveying the ranks of her people, looking for any weaknesses.

The woman's voice took her by surprise. It was the most beguiling music she had ever heard.

'Why do you fight my people?'

The question was equally unexpected.

'Who amongst you is your leader? Show yourself.'

Bretta found herself stepping through the broken wall.

'Bretta,' began Blarus, but his voice gurgled into silence as an icy grip tightened around his throat.

'Who are you, child?' came the voice, soft and seductive.

'Bretta Raeshaw.'

'Raeshaw…' repeated the voice thoughtfully. 'Now, Bretta Raeshaw, I seek a girl who can bring to an end my people's suffering.'

Bretta still couldn't focus on the figure before her, but she could feel it in her head, moving amongst her thoughts, searching for any memories of the girl. She tried to banish it by making her mind blank.

'*Where is the girl?*' This time the voice was threatening. The figure moved a step closer.

Bretta tried to raise her sword arm, but it would not move.

'No, no, I am not your enemy.' The voice was gentler now, almost falling to a murmur.

'There is magic at work,' thought Bretta.

'No magic, only the truth,' came the soft voice in her head.

Bretta relaxed, beguiled by the voice. The truth … yes … Sam and Emily's faces and their conversation about the orchard and the Garden of Druids flooded through her mind.

Then came an icy snigger.

'Know that there is a great darkness coming for them. It is already in the wood. It steals the dead and wages war on the living.'

The words ran a long claw down the inside of Bretta's mind, making her stagger backwards. The voice no longer sounded human. In front of her, giant wings were unfolding and taking to the air.

The black edge of the wood appeared to be breaking up. Bretta found herself crouching down as a seething black mass took off from the trees. The silence was shattered by the flapping of wings and the shrill calls of several thousand crows flying over the heads of the Forest Reivers.

It was long minutes before the last stragglers disappeared over the dark horizon.

* * * * * *

They stepped through the corpses of the crow-men with their swords drawn, half expecting to see the bodies start to twitch.

'There are Forest Reivers among the dead,' said Braden, as he looked across the clearing.

'Bretta would not have left the fallen if the rest of our people were not in danger,' said Jolan anxiously.

'We should press on and seek our revenge,' added Dwarrow, gripping his sword handle more firmly.

Jolan was crouching down, looking at the ground. 'Yes, we must relieve the rest of our people,' he continued. 'By these tracks, they have moved into the wood, with crow-men after them. But how do we know the crow dead won't spring to life behind us?'

'We don't,' said Braden grimly. 'But we must get back to our people. I'm afraid we can't wait here for Ged to return from his scouting trip. Our people are clearly hard pressed. We have to warn them what is coming from the King's Seat.'

The companions left the hill with heavy hearts and followed the tracks through the murky wood.

* * * * * *

It was Blarus who saw the men emerge from the wood. He instantly recognised Jolan, Braden and Dwarrow, but could not put a name to the fourth man. All along the wall, the battle-weary Forest Reivers let out cheers as they saw their leaders and scrambled back over the wall to greet them.

Bretta was with the healers and the wounded down by the trees. For a second as she saw the long line of defenders beginning to disappear over the wall she thought they must be under attack, but then she heard the cheers beginning to roll through the night. In an instant she was up and running.

'Jolan!' She felt her feet leave the ground as her big brother swept her up in his arms. 'Are you okay?'

Then she saw Braden Bow.

'Braden, it's been—' She stopped, suddenly unable to go on, remembering the stench of the poison.

'I know, Bretta,' he said quickly. 'Don't think about it now. This is Jarl Reign, a friend of my family.'

Bretta extended her hand. 'You are Eagan's father? I am pleased to meet you.'

'Yes,' said Jarl with a brief smile. 'Have you seen him?'

'No, but before we were attacked we came across two teenagers on their way to the orchard. A tall red-headed boy and a dark-haired girl. She said she was Eagan's cousin.'

'Yes. My niece, Emily. Where are they now?'

'We were attacked so quickly and by such numbers that Blarus and Erin had to leave them at the edge of the wood.'

'We must find them. They cannot stand alone.'

'We have found some tracks which could be theirs, but they vanish some distance into the orchard. It looks as though they met a third person and there was a skirmish.'

Panic begin to cross Jarl's lined face. 'Tracks can't just vanish. These are dark tidings. Are you sure my son wasn't with them?'

'Yes. There were only the two of them when we met them.'

'Bretta,' Braden broke in, 'listen, we can't stay here. We were attacked at the King's Seat. We can't be sure they won't come here next. Whilst we have time, gather the wounded and let us make for Bamburgh.'

'Bamburgh!' Jolan and Dwarrow said together.

'I can't leave Emily and Sam!' Jarl cried.

'You aren't leaving them,' Braden said calmly. 'They aren't here. And you've seen what we face. Come with us, Jarl. You can't stay here alone.'

'I was sent here by Brennus. I must find them – the Hoods have sacrificed enough.'

'My people have paid a heavy price too.' Dwarrow kept his eyes on the ground as he spoke. 'Surely nothing more can be expected of us. Let us go to Bamburgh.'

Jarl drew a deep breath. 'All I ask is that you show me where those tracks vanish. Then you're right, no one could expect more.'

* * * * * *

Ged Broadflow took a sip of water. He was listening to the eerie silence of the wood. He was dressed in hunting leathers, with long knives strapped to his thigh and his long sword across his back. He had slipped through the twisting roots and knotted branches soundless and unseen.

He was a loner, happy to volunteer for this scouting mission. He spent winter with the Forest Reivers, spring with the Marcher Lords of Bamburgh and summer travelling the wild coastal routes of his people. He had even ventured into the Underlands, the warren of tunnels that extended deep beneath the Cheviot Hills. And he had never been scared, not until today. Now he wanted to know how the dead could rise.

There was something else, too. He followed the ways of the weapon masters of old. He could use a bow better than any other Reiver.

And yet the people who had helped them at the King's Seat had been able to use a bow like no one he had ever seen before. Who were they? Where had they come from? And why had they helped them? These were the thoughts running through his mind.

Crouching against a tree trunk, he looked back down the way they had come. He wanted to know whether they were being followed. If they were, then their trail could easily be found. Already the hair on the back of his neck was warning him that something was approaching. Then he felt an icy blade touch his throat.

'Calm.' It was a woman's voice. By the way she spoke, the word was alien to her. Then came another word, whispered into his ear, 'Shadow.'

Instantly he felt it sweeping through the wood – a feeling, a foreboding that made him want to run – but the knife was pressed against his windpipe. If he moved, he would be dead. An icy chill passed through his body, freezing his thoughts as a slender hand was pressed over his mouth.

They stayed locked together in the darkness until he felt the knife and the hand release their grip. He turned to find a woman standing watching him. Silvery-white hair flowed down her back and her eyes were grey and clear. He had never seen anyone like her before, but now he noticed that there were others, men and women, just on the edge of his vision.

'Come quickly.'

It was clear she wanted him to live.

As he stood, he heard empty wails echoing through the dark wood – the unforgettable cries of the dead crow-men. It was enough to terrorise the hardiest of souls.

The woman and her ghostly companions didn't linger a second longer. They moved through the tangled wood with such speed that Ged found it almost impossible to keep up. There were figures moving on all sides of him now. Every now and then they would stop and, in perfect synchrony, fire white-feathered arrows back the way they had come. But no matter how hard they ran, the dead were gaining on them.

Sweat poured from Ged's body and once or twice he reached for his long knives as a howl broke nearby, but the strange company still sent their arrows cutting through the darkness and still they ran.

How strange it was, Ged thought, that their quivers seemed to have a never-ending supply of arrows. But it was also beginning to become clear that the arrows were having no effect. The cries of the dead were now coming from all directions.

Eventually the woman and her strange fellowship came to a clearing in the wood. Ged could tell a ferocious battle had taken place there and yet there were only the bodies of Forest Reivers lying still. Poison hung in the air and it was clear the crow-men had been here, but someone had removed their bodies.

As Ged stood there, apprehension washed through him. The woman was talking to her people in a language that he could not identify. She was signalling to him to follow, but as he crossed the clearing he wondered whether they were already too late.

* * * * * *

Jarl could see by the marks on the ground that there had been three people in the orchard. He could also tell there had been a fight of sorts. Someone had been injured, as he could see where they had fallen. Several grey feathers were lying there that he could not place. But that was all. Nothing was making sense. Blarus had been right – it seemed Sam and Emily had disappeared into thin air.

The wounded Reivers were already making their way down through the orchard. Jarl walked the short distance to the wall and joined Braden, who was standing there, staring at the black rim of Birling Wood.

'I've never seen tracks disappear entirely,' Jarl confessed. 'I just don't know what has happened.'

Braden seemed not to hear him.

'What is it?' Jarl asked quickly.

Braden was staring into the depths of the wood. 'I've never in all my days known a day like this,' he sighed. 'I never thought I would see the dead rise again.'

Jarl remembered the crow-men jerking back to life and shivered. 'Where are they now?' he muttered.

'Out there somewhere. We have to move on from here. Are you ready?'

Jarl nodded.

'Where are the others?' Braden looked round.

Bretta and Jolan, followed closely by Dwarrow, were climbing the small slope to join them.

Braden turned back to the forest. 'There's something in the wood. I can feel it.'

Jarl thought he felt it too – a niggle, an apprehension that was trickling through his mind.

The Forest Reivers on the wall were falling silent. A hush descended, broken only by the scrape and clink of weapons being drawn. All eyes were on the black unmoving edge of Birling Wood.

A freezing wind started to blow, a sudden penetrating rawness that took them all by surprise.

'What menace is this?' growled Braden as he, too, drew his sword.

The freezing wind was building. Heavy branches were beginning to tremble, leaves were raining down. Without warning, a rattling black mist hit the wall's eastern corner, shattering both flesh and stone. Wails filled the air as the Shadow brought its terror down on the Forest Reivers.

And then it was gone as quickly as it had come and a giant flicker of light lit up the night, showing a scene of devastation, before thunder rolled across the night sky.

Braden was running towards the injured when he heard the cawing of the dead crow-men. He turned to see them stumbling out of the wood, hundreds of blazing eyes filling the night with their hatred. They had already spotted the gaping hole in the wall and were heading towards it. Only dazed and wounded Forest Reivers stood between them and the orchard.

Jarl could hear Bretta, Jolan and Dwarrow rallying the stunned defenders. In his mind, everything was slowing down. How had it come to this – Brennus and Drust lost, Sam, Emily and his own son vanished into thin air? How could they have failed so utterly? All their sacrifices had come to nothing. The Shadow had still found the Garden of Druids. In fact, they had led it to the Garden of Druids.

Chaos broke out across the wall as the dead came to claim the living. The two sides came together in a devastating collision. The sheer ferocity of the heads of the Reiver clans, supported this time by the fighting prowess of their rangers, threw down the crow-men, pushing them from the breach.

Braden knew they could not let the crow-men into the orchard. At the very least they had to let the wounded get away. On he fought, as the snapping beaks and the empty eyes of the dead tried to take his people down.

Jarl was tired, his body burned with fatigue, and yet he fought for his son Eagan and his niece Emily and the person they had all been fighting for: Sam.

Bretta was scared beyond her wits. There was an unnatural strength to these crow-men that she had not seen in the others. She struck them with heavy blows, but she could not kill them. But she was angry too, angry about all the good Reivers who had fallen in the wood and all the wounded who would never recover. She fought for them.

Jolan fought to protect his people and his only sister, bearing down on the grasping claws like a crazed animal himself.

Dwarrow was leading a charge, pushing through the ranks of crow-men and sweeping them aside as if they were made of straw. But a poisonous wound made him stagger. It was quickly followed by a second and third. He dropped to his knees and sank beneath the sea of feathered arms.

*　*　*　*　*　*

Ahead he could hear battle cries, whilst behind the wails of the dead crow-men showed they were still gaining. By now he was drenched in sweat. He had never run so hard in his life. This ghostly company had almost worn him out.

He had counted no more than two dozen of them, although it was difficult to know their precise numbers, as they had fanned out over some distance. But they had now come together in a tighter formation. He knew they were preparing for battle and yet he could sense no fear about them.

On a signal from their leader, they were moving out of the wood. Ged followed them out from the cover of the trees and reeled. A group of Forest Reivers was making a stand atop a crumbling wall. He almost gasped in horror at the numbers of crow-men before them. But once more a hand covered his mouth.

As she removed it, the woman looked around and gave a brief nod. Silently, the ghostly company drew short swords that glimmered white in the night.

A terrifying force, impossibly quick, they came down upon the dark horde of the dead. Ged would never forget how they danced through them with their weapons shining like beacons of light in the blackness.

*　*　*　*　*　*

Bretta was praying with all her might when she saw the lights spinning in the darkness. She knew she couldn't hold on for much longer. She'd taken a wound to the arm and could already feel the poison snaking through her body. But then the lights were flitting from place to place and the horde's attack was diminishing as the crow-men turned to face the new threat. Perhaps they would be saved after all.

Braden had seen the ghostly company before and had the scar to prove it. He was mesmerised as the dark mass realised it was caught between two foes and began twisting round to defend itself.

To Jarl's mind, the ghostly company were angels answering the prayers of the desperate defenders, a shining force that was beginning to turn the tide.

But just as hope was returning, a roar burst from the wood and seconds later the enraged horde from the King's Seat poured onto the battlefield, snarling and shrieking their hatred for those who had evaded them.

* * * * * *

The roar shook Ged to his boots. He was bending over the crumpled forms of Blarus and Dwarrow, who were lying where they had fallen. He stood and looked around him. As far as the eye could see, dead crow-men were bounding towards them on all fours like crazed dogs. They would be caught between thousands of these wild creatures with their grasping claws and frothing maws.

The woman was standing next to him. He met her grey eyes and for the first time saw what he took to be fear. At long last, their luck had run out.

Then she leaned towards him and shouted, 'Our time is not yet!'

There was no chance of a reply. Without another word, Ged followed the shimmering lights of the woman and her company of strangers as they turned to meet the blind hatred of those from the King's Seat.

They were hugely outnumbered, but Ged was beginning to see something remarkable unfolding: the company were beheading the crow-men and whatever force had filled them with life was leaving them. He was the best fighter amongst the Forest Reivers and yet those before him were moving amongst the enemy with a deftness that he had thought impossible for a human. But the more he looked at them, the less human they looked. They were like nothing he had ever seen.

* * * * * *

Jarl watched in horror as the grey company was quickly surrounded by a black sea of feathered and twisted bodies. He looked along the length of the wall and knew the Forest Reivers could not survive another onslaught. He could hear Braden rallying his people for one last defence, whilst Jolan fired the last of his arrows into the horde. He watched as the tall blond-haired man slowly put his bow down and went to stand by Bretta, who was learning against the crumbling wall, pale and clutching her arm.

Then there came a sudden flash of light that turned night into day. A tortuous wail broke from the orchard and some of the Reivers fell to their knees, wondering what new terror had come for them. Then it was gone as quickly as it had come.

Stunned, the Reivers watched as the crow-men simply fell where they stood, whilst a dark mist rose from their still bodies and drifted into the darkness.

The entire field of battle changed in an instant. Those on the walls stood motionless, unable to accept the battle was over. They looked down at the grey company, who were standing in a circle, back to back. Then they were breaking out and running through the mounds of unmoving dead, heading towards the breach.

Jarl and Braden stepped over the broken wall and went to meet them. They were surprised to see Ged amongst their number, his short sword still in his hand.

The night was filled with a heavy silence and there was sadness in the air. Some of the Forest Reivers were beginning to tend to the wounded, but others were standing still, transfixed by the unearthly company.

A woman came out of the ghostly ranks, her silver hair shining brightly in the night. She looked first at Braden and then at Jarl, her eyes delving deeply into their hearts.

'We have come to seek your help.'

Her words took Jarl by surprise. It seemed as if these strange people had come to help them.

'What help do you need?' he answered.

'We seek the help of the *Druidae*.'

THE GARDEN OF DRUIDS

Eagan was heavy and the going was slow. Every now and then Sam would lean against a tree, mindful that they didn't want to be caught in the open.

Around them, soft moonlight flowed through leafless trees and glinted off icy trunks. Frost was thick across the orchard floor and Sam could feel the bite of a chill wind. His breath left his mouth in a swirling maelstrom, curling like smoke rings into the icy night, and he could feel himself beginning to shiver. He turned to see Emily looking back the way they had come.

'It's so cold. How has autumn turned to winter?' she asked through chattering teeth.

'I don't know.' Sam watched his words spiral and drift up through the open canopy. 'Where are we? I can't feel the Shadow anymore, or hear the battle.'

They paused for a moment, laid Eagan down and looked through the orchard. Where the fruit had been, there were now only bare branches. It was eerily quiet and in the peculiar half-light of the moon it felt for a moment as if time itself had been captured in the silence.

They looked at each other, their faces pinched and cold.

'What's happening? My compass is of no use at all.'

Emily watched the needle stubbornly pointing north no matter which way she turned.

She wheeled round. 'Look, there's a river.'

Sam stared at it, mesmerised. He had an eerie feeling that he knew where they were.

'Emily, this way.'

When they rounded the corner and he saw the bridge, he knew for certain. He stopped, his back and arms aching with the effort of carrying Eagan.

'You're not going to believe me, but you must.' He turned so that Emily could see his face. 'This is the wall round the Fellows' Garden in Magdalen. Where I met Oscar for the first time. Where it all began.'

Emily looked at him, her eyes wide. 'How…?'

'I don't know.'

Whether it had been there all the time Sam could never quite recall, but there was the thick round oak door leading into the Fellows' Garden, with the emblem of Cherwell College clear to see. It reminded him of the solid round doors in the old school house and on the seventh floor of the bookshop. Surely he had even seen these doors in his own home?

He was surprised to find himself calm. There was no apprehension, only the knowledge, somehow comforting, that things were not always what they seemed. He reached into his pocket and found the key he had brought all the way from Oxford. Without hesitation, he placed it in the keyhole, turned it gently and heard the lock click back.

* * * * * *

Sam pulled the heavy door open and he and Emily, still carrying Eagan, stepped into a place of absolute stillness. At first Sam couldn't tell whether it was the Fellows' Garden or some other place. The moonlight was gone, replaced by a serene darkness. But it wasn't just the calmness of the place that stole over them, but also its awareness. It was alive with electricity, with consciousness.

As they moved forward, the darkness lifted and Sam saw they were without doubt either in the Fellows' Garden or an exact replica. Fluttering around him in the half-light was the electricity he had felt at the Eagle and Child and in the reading room looking at the tapestry. He shook his head. It was difficult to focus, but the further they went into the garden, the softer the beat of the hummingbirds' wings became and the firmer the ground beneath their feet.

He took them up a slight incline and through the circle of ancient trees until they were standing in front of the central pond, ringed by the wooden benches.

'I don't recognise any of this,' said Emily, looking around her.

'This is where I met Oscar,' Sam told her. 'He was sitting on that bench, on a night like this. It feels as though I've come full circle. Or am I meant to wake and find this has been nothing more than a nightmare?'

'I don't know, Sam. I don't even know where we are. I'm not sure we're anywhere.'

Sam knew what she meant. When he looked back the way they'd come, there was a wall of darkness like the tapestry before it had burst with light and colour.

'You don't need to be anywhere to understand that this is some-where,' said a voice behind them.

Even before Sam turned, he knew who it was.

'What place is this?' asked Oscar.

'It's the Fellows' Garden in Oxford. We met there almost seven days ago. You brought a message to me.'

'Did I? The last time I visited Oxford was in 1960 something or other, I thought, but, as I say, only places matter in this place.'

This wasn't supposed to happen, thought Sam. He had come here convinced that Oscar would have all the answers and yet he seemed a little befuddled, to say the least.

'Who is this man you are carrying? Let me see his face.'

'Eagan Reign,' said Emily, faintly.

'Lay him in the waters quickly.'

Sam's arms were burning with the effort, but he walked heavy-legged to the edge of the pond. He would not let Eagan fall. He stepped into the cold waters and kneeled down, still holding Eagan, who seemed to grow heavier with every second.

'Culluhin.'

The hair on Sam's neck prickled as the night moved behind Oscar and Emily and the shadowy figure came into focus. He was tall and dressed in what Sam could only guess was armour, for no light revealed it. He could have come straight out of Arthurian legend. He looked strangely out of place, towering above Oscar and Emily.

Then Sam noticed something shimmering from his head to the ground. It could have been a staff, but it seemed to shift and every now and then a hint of light would cascade down its length. It reminded him a little of Professor Whitehart's cards.

'Sam, you must leave Eagan to our friend,' called Oscar. 'Already part of him is travelling to a place only Culluhin has the skill and strength to find. He may bring him back. Quickly now, for I am guessing we don't have much time.'

Sam could only watch as the giant man calmly entered the water and took Eagan from him.

Emily reached out a hand and helped Sam to the bank. When he turned back, he saw Culluhin holding Eagan with his left arm whilst in his right he held a staff made of light that glowed like molten rock. He was speaking, but Sam couldn't catch the words. He would later describe his voice as like a falling mountain. There was a purity in it that moved him to tears. When he turned to Emily, she was also crying.

Then the light danced with the water and gently caressed both Eagan and Culluhin until there was nothing to be seen but fizzing water. The droplets fell back into the pond and the figures were gone.

Oscar looked from Sam to Emily. 'There is no other way, for the poison of the Grim-were flows through him. Now, whilst we have some time, come along, both of you – tell me why you have brought me here.'

They sat together on a bench. Sam was dazed. Hadn't Oscar brought *him* here and not the other way round?

Sitting beside him, he quickly noticed some differences between this Oscar and the Oscar he'd met in the real Fellows' Garden, though he was no longer certain that that had been any more real than this. But this Oscar had two perfectly good hands and his face and clothes looked unruffled, whilst the Oscar he had met before had definitely looked as though he'd been in a fight. That one had had answers, but this one was looking for them.

'So tell me,' he repeated, 'why you have called me to this place.'

Sam took a deep breath. 'You brought a message to me that day in Oxford. You asked me to deliver it to Brennus and Drust Hood. You gave me two letters. You said the Circle was broken and a Shadow was moving through the Otherland, that the Dead Water was lost and the Fall was dying. You asked the professors to seek the help of the Three.'

A look of profound disbelief crossed Oscar's face. 'That is a message that was delivered to me a long time ago! If you're certain that it was me who delivered it, then we have very little time. You've done well to reach me, for no doubt the Shadow will have come through the Fall. Tell me quickly all that has happened since we met. Come now, speak – you look as confused as I did all those years ago!'

Sam opened his mouth, but then came a noise that stopped him in his tracks, a low thrum that seemed to break across all their thoughts. They watched as a thousand tiny ripples skittered across the surface of the pond.

'Ah. It would appear that you have led the Shadow to me.' Oscar said the words quietly, almost to himself.

The heavy thrum cam again. This time made their vision jump. It seemed to be getting louder, perhaps closer.

Oscar resumed, speaking quickly, 'Today is not the day for a history lesson, but to offer you a little of what I know is a start. Two thousand years ago the borderland became the scene of a war between two peoples from the Otherland, a collection of lands entangled through the Dead Water. The Faeries and Grim people fought a war that raged for many years. At the time they did not realise it, but the magic they used against each other fractured their lands and let a great darkness into both their worlds. We named it the Ruin, but we never truly understood its nature or its reason for existing. Perhaps we never will.

'A terrible war was waged to keep the Ruin from passing from the Otherland to the Mid-land, but it was a war that could not be won against such an enemy. The Faeries and the Grim people came together, seeking help from the Druids, who dwelt in the Mid-land. It was they who led a fellowship into the Darkhart.

'The Druids called upon a magic only they could speak with – the First Light, the flow from the beginning of time. As they fought the Ruin, they sacrificed themselves and were trapped in the Darkhart. Trapped with them was the most powerful of the Dagda's daughters, Brigit. Together they created a circle, the Circle of Druidae, and Brigit became the Druid-Fall, or simply the Fall, the barrier that holds back the Ruin.'

Sam felt a shudder pass through the ground beneath his feet and the moonlight flickered as if something had passed through it. Oscar chose to ignore it.

'The Druids thought that their magic would be eternal, but we know now the Druid-Fall can only exist whilst they do. Now their

Circle is broken, and the Fall endangered. She is dying, but she can be reborn.'

He let his words sink in, his eyes settling on Emily.

'Who were the Druids?' Sam asked.

'No one knows where they came from, only that they chose to dwell in the Mid-land and could speak to the flow.'

'And they sacrificed themselves?' Sam didn't like the sound of this.

'Most, but not all. Some came back. And since then, they have had helpers in the Mid-land, the Keepers of the Druids, men who study their lore and preserve their bloodline. The Shadow has been sent to eliminate this bloodline. If it succeeds, then when the time comes again to complete the Circle, as it will, there will be no one left to do so.'

'So, does—?' Sam was interrupted by a haunting wail that echoed through the mist. It was a sound to break a man's courage.

'Even now,' said Oscar, 'the Shadow seeks a way in. Come along, follow me.'

He rose to his feet and stretched before offering them a hand each. Sam found it warm to the touch and felt a tingling as their hands met.

No sooner had they stepped away from the pond than they were enveloped in a strange half-light. Static electricity seemed to crackle both inside and outside Sam's head. Emily felt it as an invisible spider's web that was impossible to brush off.

Just ahead, the landscape unravelled as it had done in the tapestry. They could no longer tell whether they were walking forward or whether the ground beneath their feet was coming to meet them. There was a dizzying stillness that in places covered them in a suffo-cating mist. But every now and then Oscar would squeeze their hands and his voice would pull them back from the emptiness of their thoughts.

They were no longer walking in the Fellows' Garden – it had fallen away to reveal a tree-lined path that formed an avenue through the strange grey twilight. Every now and then it seemed to Sam that the trees and avenue would jump and flicker. Whether the place was Addison's Walk, he could not tell. A river meandered beside them, but he couldn't see where the waters started, or where they were going.

Then Oscar came to a stop and in the twilight they could see a circle of stone statues.

'I've seen this place before.'

This time it was Oscar's turn to look surprised. 'It is the Circle of Druidae, Sam, though only a reflection of it.'

'The circle – like the emblem of Cherwell College,' said Sam.

'And the symbol on the reading-room door,' finished Emily. 'And on the key to it.' At last she'd remembered where she'd seen it.

'But what has this got to do with me?' Sam's voice cracked – perhaps he already knew the answer.

'You must know by now, Sam,' Oscar said quietly. 'The Shadow is trying to extinguish the bloodline of the *Druidae*. It is not just the last few days that have been preparing you for this journey, but a lifetime. But I think you already know this.'

In the strange shifting twilight, Sam and Emily's eyes met. They were both coming to their own conclusions.

'I did not think I would face the Shadow again,' Oscar continued. 'This time I will be ready. It is only a Shadow in this world and it can only hurt the living. I will be its equal.'

Just then they heard the deep thrum as if something huge was breaking the surface of the sea and drawing its first breath.

'The Shadow is searching for you,' Oscar said. 'When it arrives, I will trap it here.'

With the landscape shifting around him, he looked out into the darkness.

'Let it come – we are ready.'

Sam wasn't sure who he was talking to, then he realised Culluhin's brooding presence was back. Or was he? Was the shadowy figure there or were his eyes playing tricks? Where was Eagan? But more importantly, what was going to happen?

'Is it wise to let the Shadow in?' he whispered.

'Let me be free to deliver the message that starts the wheel turning,' Oscar said calmly. 'It is time we fought back against the darkness. It begins.'

Sam could feel panic rising. He was about to face it all over again, and even with Oscar beside him, he didn't know whether it would be enough.

He suddenly felt Emily's hand in his. When he looked at her, she was white with fear. 'I don't like this,' she managed to say through gritted teeth.

Oscar was calling in an unknown language and Sam heard other voices rising in the mist, too, the voices of the Druids coming together in a powerful resonance.

The landscape was changing again and he wheeled round to see what he thought were the gates of Magdalen rising behind him. In front of him was a bridge, and beyond it a movement, a darkness, a horror that could be felt but not seen. Yet again Sam could feel it reaching out to strip him of his senses. It was moving, rising up before him, black and shapeless.

Tears slipped down his cheeks and he was unable to stop himself from sinking first to one knee and then a second, but a hand stopped him from sinking further. When he looked up, he found Emily's tear-stained face pleading with him not to fall.

Oscar was already on the bridge when a giant wave of black fire came convulsing towards him, bursting down to crush the life out of him. But Oscar's voice rose high above the chaos and his hands appeared to catch the wave in mid-air. It shattered into a million twisting sparks, and a terrifying wail burst out of him as they tore through his flesh.

Sam tried to call out to him, but his throat was blocked, as if with broken glass. And out on the edge of his awareness, formless and soundless, something was moving again. He could feel its malignancy, he could feel its anger rising like a black tide against Oscar.

The black burning mist came again, a hissing fire that was meant to kill. Oscar's arms were charred and his face blackened, but he was facing it once again.

When the attack came, it was ferocious. Sam and Emily were nearly knocked off their feet. They held on to each other, as the wind howled round them. But Oscar would not be moved. His voice rose again, his charred, withered hands shielded him from the onslaught, and this time he threw it back, stepping into the black burning wind, his screams tortured and terrifying.

Sam watched helplessly as the black swirling tempest rose above Oscar once more. His clothes were whipping around him, his face contorted with pain. Then above the storm he heard Oscar's voice, strong and commanding and full of anger. He was challenging the Shadow to show itself fully, mocking it with a courage that Sam knew he would never see again. Light was pouring from every inch of him, driving back the dark hissing wind and the burning air.

Then the tempest caught him and threw him down in the middle of the bridge. It rushed forward and Sam knew it was coming for him.

In that second, he heard Emily screaming his name. He held out a hand as the black fire erupted all around them. But he could hear the Magdalen choir resonating through his being. He could see the light in his mind. He could see it streaming from his left hand. He threw down the black fire and it was gone.

He stood there, dazed. Then he raised his eyes to the bridge.

Oscar's shredded form, head bent, hands raised skyward, was standing there, directly in front of a vast monstrosity that was contorting itself into a towering Shadow.

'Sam!' came a rasping voice. It was Culluhin. 'Our trap is sprung. Run. Don't look back.'

With that, he turned away and joined Oscar.

A second later their sacrifice became apparent as with outstretched arms they became flaming brands holding the Shadow in a fiery embrace.

The tempest split apart, hitting Sam with the force of an explosion. For a moment he could neither hear nor see.

When the light faded from his eyes, Oscar and Culluhin were gone. He was looking down a long field of trees, and even in the darkness he could see they were heavy with fruit.

* * * * * *

'Did you see Oscar?'

When Sam closed his eyes, he could still see Oscar silhouetted against the roiling night. He sat in the orchard, stunned, bewildered and unable to speak. He was beginning to shake. His body was on fire and it was all he could to hold back a wave of sickness.

'Was Oscar in the garden?'

When the second question came, he realised the voice asking it wasn't Emily's. He sat up and turned to find Eagan leaning over her, trying to wake her.

'You're alive! I thought you were dead.'

'I hope not, for my sake,' said Eagan with a smile, stroking Emily's hair.

Sam felt that he was waking from a nightmare.

'There was a creature that brought you to the garden,' he explained. 'At first I thought it was your father, but then it turned into something else.'

'It was a Grim-were from the Underland.' Eagan was now stroking Emily's face. 'I want to know why the garden revealed itself to you, Sam. Don't get me wrong – it's probably what saved your life. You can tell me how you survived the Grim-were, too, but for now we need to get out of the wood. Come on, Emily.'

Suddenly she sat bolt upright. 'Eagan! I thought you were dead!'

She grabbed hold of him, taking everyone by surprise.

'Oscar's bodyguard took you into the pond and there was light and water and you were gone!' She was almost sobbing.

'I'm okay.' Eagan hugged her back, laughing. 'It's all right – you don't need to prove you care.'

'And then Sam saved Oscar!'

'I could be wrong,' Sam said thoughtfully, 'but I think Oscar lured the Shadow to the orchard. I think it's been an elaborate trap.'

'*That* wasn't the orchard,' Emily corrected him. '*This* is the orchard. That place was right out of a nightmare. However did you stand up to the Shadow in Oxford? Look what it did to poor Oscar. I can't bear to think about his arms!'

She lowered her head onto Eagan's shoulder.

Sam was already thinking ahead. 'You're right, Eagan, I don't think we can stay here. Whatever the Forest Reivers were fighting sounded almost as bad as the Shadow. I suggest we make for Alnmouth and try and get a message to Professor Stuckley.'

He walked back up the short slope and found the wall. From it, he looked back over the orchard. What had Culluhin said? 'Our trap is sprung.' Had that been their plan all along? Had Brennus, Drust, Jarl, Eagan and Oscar been working together to bring the Shadow to the orchard?

There was no easy way of knowing, but it now seemed clear that Oscar had brought the Shadow to Oxford. And yet wasn't it he himself who had brought the Shadow to an unsuspecting Oscar?

What about Oscar's message about the broken Circle of Druidae? Would making it whole again keep the Ruin back?

And what of the creature that had portrayed itself as Professor Whitehart and Jarl? Why was it seeking Emily? What part did she have to play in this?

'It's time to go.' Eagan's words cut across his jumbled thoughts. He had helped Emily to her feet and they were waiting for him.

* * * * * *

They set off as the first light of dawn began to throw a red haze across the eastern sky.

Sam could still see Oscar's fiery silhouette in his mind. He wondered whether he had made it back to the beginning and delivered his message to the innocent boy he'd been only seven days ago.

He looked across at Eagan. His carefree attitude had gone and in its place was a look of grim resolve. Beside him, Emily was stumbling with weariness. Looking at her haunted face, Sam was nearly overcome with guilt.

And yet at that moment a single burning thought pierced the mist that had been hiding the truth from him. He now understood why the Shadow had let him live. He had, unknowingly, led it to the last Druid.

Dear Reader,

Thank you for reading my book. I really hope that you enjoyed reading it as much as I enjoyed writing it. If you can help spread the word about it, you will be helping me to make a difference in the world through the G L Hall Foundation, which works with charities to improve the lives of children and young adults. Thank you.

The idea for the foundation was planted when I read David Hamilton's book *The Five Side-Effects of Kindness*. I have come to realise just how powerful acts of kindness can be. I grew up on the Holme Wood estate in Bradford in the 1970s and also have seen how detrimental poverty and deprivation can be.

When I was seven, my primary school teacher, Mrs Flather, gave me a copy of C.S. Lewis's *Prince Caspian* and that started a love affair with literature that has lasted to this day. I hope *The Last Druid* will do something similar for you. It is my attempt to bring together my love of books, my love of business and my desire to give something back. I hope it will make a big difference to a number of charities doing exceptional things for children and young adults.

All royalties from *The Last Druid* will go to G L Hall Foundation. We are already working with several charities and looking to partner others in the future.

I would love to connect with you and share more about *The Last Druid* books at:

www.thelastdruid.co.uk
https://www.facebook.com/glenlhallauthor/
https://www.twitter.com/glen_l_hall
With kindest wishes,
Glen

ABOUT THE AUTHOR

My love affair with books started with my primary school teacher, who gave me a copy of Prince Caspian when I was seven, leading thirty years later to the publication of The Last Druid and a continued love affair of fantasy. From the moment I was captivated by C.S. Lewis's chronicles of Narnia, I devoured the whole seven books and could have cried when I came to 'The Last Battle' and realised it was the final book. You can imagine my joy when by pure chance I came across an old copy of 'The Hobbit' in my middle school's rickety school library. That one act of kindness from my primary school teacher led me to read English at the University of Leeds.

I have come to realise just how powerful acts of kindness can be and what affect they can have on an individual. I wanted therefore to combine my passion for business with my passion for all things literary. The Last Druid is a five year project that attempts to give something of me back to all those children who are at risk of never having a family or the fortune of a loving childhood that every child deserves.

All royalties from The Last Druid will go to G L Hall foundation.

Lightning Source UK Ltd.
Milton Keynes UK
UKOW01n1004310317
298008UK00001B/1/P